Windmaster Golem

The Windmaster Novels

By Helen B. Henderson

Print ISBN
Amazon Print 9780228615002
LSI Print 9780228615019
B&N Print 9780228615330

BWL Publishing Inc.

Books we love to write ...
Authors around the world.

http://bwlpublishing.ca

I0676436

Dedication

Gratitude to the Nova Scotian pixie who helped romance take its rightful place alongside adventure, to the wandering sailor for her friendship and support in all things writing and to Sandra for her sharp eyes.

Lastly my husband, Tom, for his patience and support over the years.

Chapter One

Tendrils of fog clutched at Brodie's ankles. The thick haze not only dampened the sound of the surf crashing against the cliff, it hid the trail along the cliff edge. Not even the light from the gibbous moon showed anything other than shadows.

For several breaths he stood and marked his location on a mental map of the trail. Switchbacks and a sharp drop-off marked the downhill slope to the village. A tug pulled the long sword from the scabbard hanging on his back. "Good thing I have TânOer with me," he told the night. He kept the weapon in his cottage in the main village unless being used in a lesson. "The short sword I usually carry while on the Isle of Mages is too short to be useful as a pointer." The memory of why he had the enspelled long sword with him flickered into being. That afternoon he had shown the folly of hubris to a pair of second-season students and spent the rest of the day at the forge.

One final breath to center himself and he dragged the tip along the ground in a long arc in front of him. Step by step, he listened for the scratch of steel on dirt or the swish as the blade slid into the grass alongside the trail. Boulders filled the space from the grassy verge to the cliff's edge, so a scrape on rock told he was no longer on the path. Every snick of steel on stone dropped him to the ground. On hands and knees he explored the area until he determined if it was a single rock or a pile of them marking a sharp turn of the path to warn the unwary to slow down.

His fingers didn't meet more rocks, just open air.

"Too close for comfort," he growled. Crawling to the right he found dirt. Once again he checked his mental map. "The bench is not too far ahead. Just a hundred steps."

The slow exploration of the invisible world around him resumed.

Foot by foot, he probed and listened. The sword scraped on stone, and again when he moved it a foot higher. A screech, dampened by the fog, was quickly snatched away. Three more times he tested the rock face until the blade hit open air. Mental calculations revealed the stone was a head taller than his own considerable height. Only two people on the island were taller, the archmage and Murdo, the former mercenary who was now the head cook for both the mages and non-talented who lived on the island that was home to the school of magic and the council of wizards.

"I'm at the bench," Brodie whispered. "Safe, at least for now." The path grew steeper from there. It was dangerous even in daylight, now with the dew-slicked grass, near impossible to navigate blind. TânOer sheathed, he sat down with the weapon across his lap. No sooner had he stopped moving than his skin crawled from the cold. Only where his hand lay on the hilt of the sword did the chill fail to penetrate and the fingers remain warm.

The fog seemed to come alive. Icy fingers slid around his neck … and squeezed. More hands gripped his arm and trapped the sword in its sheath.

"No," he moaned. "Magic is controlling this fog." Yet again, he cursed his lack of talent. *I may not be able to break the spell, but I can reach Denai. If she can't help, she can at least contact her parents.*

She will be a good one, hope said. She used TânOer this afternoon in practice and both metal and mage should retain their sense of link.

His hands scrabbled for purchase. *I have to reach the metal.* He forced his fingers to inch down the leather grip. Cold steel greeted his questing fingers. *Denai … help … trapped … fog.*

As it did with the sound of the crashing surf just a few lengths away, the fog snatched away the mental call. The ethereal noose around his neck tightened. Blackness narrowed his vision.

Fear added power to his call. His thought turned from a cast net to a silver thread tied to a dagger. A silent prayer to his ancestors to guide his aim and he threw the message towards the sleeping village below. Denai ... help ... trapped ... fog flew along the lifeline. This time the impression of a sleepy "Ummm," and the flick of fingers greeted his attempt.

The fog vanished and with it the stranglehold on his neck loosened. Overhead, the twin moons shone brightly. Their light clearly showed the path in front and behind.

Evaluation of the two routes took only heartbeats. His workshop at the forge might only be a lean-to, but the archmage had laid protective spells around the entire area and the iron itself would dampen the effects of an attack. Downhill was steep and potentially full of roots that could trip and send him over the edge. Brodie's feet flew along the trail back towards the clifftop and his forge.

* * *

Boredom added to Relliq's dark mood. He blew on knuckles bloodied once again from scraping the edge of the bowl as he ground herbs for poultices. The bag Ysbail had left to be ready for her return was still three-quarters full. "I'm not a healer," he snarled. "Smashing herbs into small pieces isn't magic. It's just woman's work."

But Ysbail was not only the healer of Montrat, she was also his teacher. At least for the moment, he thought. Soon the student will surpass the master. Sighing, he dropped another clump of the dried leaves into the bowl and picked up the heavy stone grinder. The cool stone rubbed against skin not yet callused. Only three turns later, sharp pain meant another blister raised and broken.

"Enough is enough," he hissed. Swift movements dumped the clumps of herbs back into the bag and half-filled a bowl with water. The liquid cooled the sting in his hands. A slight movement of his fingers swirled the drops of blood that oozed from his knuckles into an intricate design. The rune for fog appeared, then the one for entrapment.

Snatching his spellbook from the shelf, he quickly flipped through the pages looking for instructions on how to pair the two runes. "There must be something that will work," he muttered. "Even if the fog only affects the mind, confuses the will, it will be a useful tool. But how to direct it?"

His search of the book revealed no answer, still, the lure of the envisioned magic called him. Careful so as not to disrupt the symbols, he cast the spell and peered deep into the bowl to watch the result.

The image of a rolling surf changed to a narrow, rock-lined path. Recognition dawned. *The Isle of Mages?*

What if the archmage finds out? fear wondered.

It doesn't matter, Relliq countered. One day, and not too far away, I will be in charge. His plan settled, he threw more magic into the spell. A man appeared. Tall and wide-shouldered, he strode with confidence along at steep trail. Gray ropes snatched at his legs. The air around the figure thickened and within a heartbeat became an impenetrable haze.

Now the liquid in the bowl once again showed its true nature. As he had just moments before, Relliq searched his memory for the means to use and control the spell. A pairing came to mind. "Night be dark, light be gone, mist turn into a living fog," he hissed.

What had been a haze thickened and pulsed in a rhythm that mirrored a heartbeat.

Relliq's lips parted. He leaned closer to the bowl. The shadowed man fell, rose to his feet, shambled a few paces, fell again, then on hands and feet crawled through the swirling mass. Movement ceased when the figure placed his back against a sheer rock face.

The liquid in the bowl shimmered, then exploded. Sparks flew around the room, landing on the table, the floor, and in Relliq's hair. Slaps put out the embers that burned his skin and clothes. Remnants of the shattered spell danced along the bowl's rim as glowing sprites. After a frenetic dance, they merged and flared into a solid flame. A shriek at the pain in his hands and Relliq threw the bowl against the wall. Fire flowed down the wall where the blood droplets touched the stone.

His hastily whispered dispersion spell touched the flames which flickered into nothingness to cast the room into darkness. A single moonbeam pierced the gloom and moved across the room to pin the doorway in a spectral glow.

Expletives not consistent with the discipline of the Way filled the small space. "Who broke my spell? The archmage is out and about on the mainland and no one else is powerful enough. Not even that woman he calls his mate. There is no one else at the Council Isle smart enough to recognize my spell, let alone destroy it."

No answer to the question appeared and reality interceded. His gaze lingered on the broken bowl. The shards no longer glowed, but a master wizard could still pull information from them. All evidence of the spell had to be destroyed. Wrapping a cloth around his hand, Relliq gathered up the pieces and set them on the hearth. Several blows with the brick used to prop open the door in summer crushed the shards into pebbles intermixed in a fine powder. Sweeps with the cloth pushed the remnants into the back of the hearth. A kick and the powder mingled with the pile of gray ash.

Another general dispersion spell and satisfied he had done all that he could to cover his tracks, Relliq lay down in bed. However sleep remained elusive. A single thought kept pulling him back to awareness. *Who broke my spell?*

* * *

Warmth on his face woke Brodie. A leonine stretch to his full height removed more of the night's chill from his skin—and his soul. Picking up his sword where it lay across the open space in the wall that led to the forge, he hung it on the hook on the wall. Other hooks held finished blades awaiting their hilts. Competing thoughts fought for control. One said to tell the archmage about the fog attack.

9

Another voice hissed to talk to Lady Ellspeth. She is as powerful a mage as Lord Dal.

And the archmage is not at the school, reality countered. He is out and about seeking candidates for the next recognition ceremony.

Use the signal bowl in the council chambers, the urge to contact the archmage added. Or have Denai reach out to her parents.

The light chatter of children's voices preceded their owner's appearance.

Denai will be busy with her lessons came from the part of Brodie that didn't want to reach out to Denai. Of late, she had been making special efforts to be near him. As he had done so often for the fast few sevenday, Brodie wondered how to handle the fifteen-turn-old's crush.

Sooner or later, I'll have to speak to the archmage and his wife about it.

If they don't already know, fear hissed.

Denai's appearance at the trailhead ended the racing thoughts. Behind her, a half-dozen children, ranging in age from ten to fourteen, followed in single file. Her older sister, Elendl, brought up the rear of the line. Even though only older by a few heartbeats, she often emphasized the "older" aspect of the twin's relationship.

A nod to the girls and Brodie returned his attention to the blades laid out on the workbench. Several pumps from the bellow and the coals glowed a deep red. Picking up an iron blade, he examined the edge for imperfections. The recognition ceremony would soon take place and he wanted to finish the blade for Denai. Instinct told him she would answer the call and need a journeyman's blade to serve as a focus of her powers.

"And this will be hers," he muttered. "I may not have a wizard's magic, but I can make sure that the tool she uses for the rest of her life is special." Satisfied nothing more needed to be done, he selected another formed-strip of iron. Although nothing irregular could be seen, one spot bothered him and he placed the future blade into the heart of the coals. Watching the metal shift color from black to red to white when the desired malleability was achieved helped calm his mind.

Strong swings of the hammer worked the hot metal, narrowing the edge. The metal's glow changed color. Thrusting the hot metal into the oil, he snatched a rag from the workbench and sauntered over to the wall and leaned against the cool stones. Memory of other stones, those chilled by the fog, surfaced.

No one on the Isle, no one who studies the Way, would without provocation use their powers against one who had none. So who attacked me?

Chapter Two

Morning brought with it a stop to the endless rounds of wake and worry before dropping back into a restless sleep. *If no one has raised an alarm by now, they won't,* Relliq thought. Pleasure at his success rippled through his body. A smile twitched his lips. *Ysbail is clueless as to my true abilities.*

Besides the instructors at the Isle of Mages, there is the archmage and his lady. What if they come searching for answers? worry interjected.

The reminder of his situation as an apprentice to a healer darkened the joy. "Montrat is so far from the school of wizards that the so-called instructors won't even begin to look here," Relliq hissed to the walls.

It will make no difference, arrogance growled in answer to the contrary thought. *The dispersal spell was perfect. No evidence of the fog casting remains.*

One aspect remained unanswered and refused to be quieted. *The one called Brodie is a mere servant, a blacksmith who works with his hands. He is a non-tal, has no magic. He didn't break the spell. Someone cleared the fog and allowed him to escape.*

"But who?" bounced off the walls, unanswered. Anger at his failure raised his pulse. His magic surged out of control. Across the room, tinder laid out on the hearth for the night's fire burst into flames. Surprise at the strength of his power shocked Relliq. The fire in the hearth flickered into nothingness. Grasping control of the spell, he encouraged the glowing coals to relight.

For a candlemark he sat and pondered the dancing flames. Contrasting thoughts danced with each spark that flared up the chimney. Ysbail always preached keeping emotions under control, he mused. *The ease by which I brought fire to cold wood proves she is wrong. Anger boosted my abilities.*

Now just learn how to control them, reality added.

A snatch pulled a bowl from the shelf. He had bartered a love potion for the bowl from a caravan passing through town. "Which will have an unexpected surprise attached to it," Relliq laughed. "The wielder of the potion may find achieving his desire is not the pleasure he expected."

The sound of his voice returned Relliq's focus to why he wanted the bowl. Untouched by food or drink, it was perfect for casting a spell. A splash of water to form a mirror and to consecrate the vessel and he whispered an incantation.

"Nothing happened," he snarled. *There is no anger, no surge of pleasure or lust,* he realized. Once again he called forth the rage that he could not control the living fog.

"Vision near, vision far,
Show me a caster of power."

The water in the bowl shimmered. A solid wall of stone replaced the reflection of the room around him. Relliq leaned in closer. What had appeared as the mortar between stones now revealed itself as the outline of a door. The perspective shifted to the other side of the wall and the slender figure whose arm raised as if to knock on the hidden door.

At first he thought his spell had centered on the man from the night before. "No," he hissed. "It's not the smith. The image isn't the chamber room of the wizards' council. It's not any place I've seen in my scrying stone." A ray of sunlight penetrated the gloom of what he realized had to be a narrow alley. Braids of brown hair formed a crown in which crystal pins danced.

"A woman," Relliq breathed. "Look up. I need to see your face."

As if in reply to the command, the woman looked skyward.

* * *

Cold enveloped Kia. Her hand stopped in mid-knock. Although she knew no one was in sight, she still looked over her shoulder and scanned the street. Use of the postern door was restricted to senior members of the temple. I will not betray Brantly's trust in me, she thought. Neither Brantly my brother, nor Brantly the Oracle of Givneh.

Ghostly fingers caressed her hair. The touch slid down her arm, not a lover's touch, but that of an icy wind. The feeling of a presence was so strong she put her back against the wall. What heat the stones retained from the noon-day sun did nothing to warm her skin—or soul.

No one is there, reality encouraged.

No one you can see, caution answered.

For long moments she stood watching the street. Finally, the bags of vegetables she had purchased at the market grew heavy. "This is ridiculous," she growled. "There is no one there." *This is just a case of nerves.*

A toss of her head cleared an errant strand of hair from her face. A whispered incantation to cloak herself from the prying eyes of villagers and she knocked.

The hidden door slid open to reveal the same young soldier who was on duty when she left earlier that morning. "Greetings, mistress." However, instead of the usual wave, he brushed past her and scanned the street.

He feels it too. Her unease growing stronger, Kia stepped over the threshold into the darkness of the building. Hurry up and close the door, she silently urged. Then she sent a prayer winging skyward that the sanctuary of the temple would stop whoever, or whatever, spied on her.

As the door closed, the image of a silver cord being squeezed filled her mind. With a snick, the lock bar slid into place. With the door secured, the eerie contact vanished.

I have to speak to Brantly. As the Oracle he can explain what happened.

You already know the answer, fear retorted. Someone used magic to track you.

But who? And why?

* * *

"Tell me your name," Relliq cooed. "I must know your name."

In response, a sense of determination, then a clear rejection of the command came through the silver cord connecting him to the woman in the water. The image shifted. Even at the distance, Relliq could feel her gathering magic into a protective cloak.

Despite his demand for her to stay, the water returned to its natural state. Not even a ripple noted the passing of the ethereal connection. "No," he yelled. "I will have you." His mind searched through the spells and incantations he knew. A quick search of the room and he realized he didn't have the necessary materials for a spell. The image of the place of torment, the healer's workroom, filled his mind. Containers of herbs lined the shelves and withies hung from pegs. "Ysbail's shelves are full. She won't miss a few things.

His feet took control and a heartbeat later he raced through the empty streets to the healer's office. He barely slowed as he barrelled over the threshold and didn't slow until he reached the back room. Rummaging through the wooden box in which she kept small items needed for the casting of magic, he palmed a spool of thread. A twist removed the cap from a finger-length wooden tube and he slid a needle out. "I just need one more thing." A moment to center his thoughts and he cast his senses outward until he slipped into the Cyrcle of One. His hand hovered over the rolls of tubes containing maps of the known world.

"Powers that be, work through my hand,
Show me the place so I can command."

15

Where before the shaft of light coming through the window lit a small dot on the floor, now the beam slid across the stones and up the bookcase. It lingered at one spot until a tube glowed.

"That is the map I need." Relliq crowed. A thought darkened the joy. "I can't leave anything that might raise Ysbail's suspicion." Shifting the map containers to hide the one he planned to take took several tries before he was satisfied with the result. A whispered dispersal spell cleared the lingering magic. Again and again, he repeated it until no remnant, no errant sparkle remained. Silent steps took him to the door, where after a glance at the empty street, he strode out, closing the heavy panel behind him.

Before he crossed the courtyard, legs that would normally be strong felt weak, unable to bear weight. A darkened alley between buildings beckoned and he staggered in and collapsed against a wall where the cool stones eased the burn in his muscles. Although his hand still shook where it held the rolled-up map, he was soon able to stand. Questions swirled in his head. *What caused the unexpected tiredness?*

No answer revealed itself during the cautious slide from shadow to shadow back to his quarters. Closing the door behind him, he watched the spider web of red lines appear in the doorway. Collapsing on the bed, he gazed at the spell shimmer. Its rhythmic pulse lured him to a half-sleep and eased the turmoil in his mind. Only one possibility for his exhaustion surged forward—the use of magic. The spell to locate the map and the dispersal rituals used more energy than he had expected. "I'll have to rest before the next phase," he muttered. Satisfaction with having achieved at least part of his plan accompanied him into sleep.

Voices in the street outside his door tugged Relliq from the lethargy of exhaustion. Evaluating the sounds and activity he determined it was nothing more than tradesmen returning home from their shops. It must be later than I thought, he mused. The ache of muscles when he stood confirmed the candlemarks that had passed since the visit to the healer's office. After a quick meal of cold meat left over from the previous night and a slab of buttered bread, he lay back down and pulled a cover over his bare arms.

Morning came and its glow on the back of his eyelids woke Relliq. This time the stretch didn't come with aches or tiredness. The need to check the healer's office to see if she had returned from her out-of-town trip pulled him out of bed. He dressed against the morning's chill and headed across the village. The smell of freshly-baked bread detoured him and he bought a sweet roll and a cup of fruit juice to break his fast. Rejuvenated, he rehearsed the next phase of the search. *Now to find that woman.*

Confirmation that the village healer had not returned added to his energy and he retraced his steps back to his quarters. Two steps over the threshold and his plans changed. He remembered one of his lessons. The incantation to locate the unknown woman required a stronger magic than he had ever used before. The more powerful the spell, the more it penetrated the surroundings. No matter how many dispersion spells were summoned, residuals of the workings remained behind. "That is why there are sites considered special and avoided by the non-tals," he muttered to the walls.

One by one he evaluated the sites closest to Montrat. The nearest one was over three days ride. Even the memory of his one visit to the trillion stones called forth the sense of serenity—and power.

"But the stones are too far away for what I need," Relliq growled. No matter how much he despised the desert, there was a protected spot out amongst the dunes where the sands formed a circle and the winds never blew. Half a candlemark later he had stuffed the items needed for the ritual into a backpack, saddled a horse, and headed out past the wall that surrounded the town.

Sweat rolled down his back and soaked his shirt from the heat of the sun directly overhead before he reached the spot where the healer ritually cleansed the vessels she used. Deft movements spread out the map onto the ground and weighed it down with rocks pulled from the edge of the firepit. The thread wrapped around his little finger, he let the needle swing free over the map.

His eyes closed, he sought the quiet of the Cyrcle of One. If the woman had actually cut his spell and the failure wasn't a result of some outside influence, he would be able to find her in the Cyrcle. The bobbin swung in wide circles. Each repetition tightened the arc, spiraling in on a specific spot.

The farther it moved towards the representation of the western edge of the desert, the more Relliq tried to force the pointer to the east. *All those who study the Way, who can use power are on the Isle of Mages. Why is the pointer in the opposite direction?*

Frustration flooded his frame. Pain accompanied the shock of the ejection from the ethereal plane. All energy fled the spell. The needle hung lifeless.

Relliq cursed. "I've lost the link."

A deep breath to re-center his energy and he suspended the needle over the middle of the map. "I have the way of it now. This time it will work," he chortled.

"Thread of silver, cord of gold,
Show me now the place foretold."

The back of his eyelids became his scrying surface. A steep road leading up to the plateau didn't provide the location. "I need more." In response, the view shifted to one of golden gates aglow in the setting sun.

"Thread of silver, cord of gold,
Tell me the name of the place foretold."

The needle hung for a few moments. A power beyond Relliq's own took control and the needle swung wildly. The string snapped taut.

"I will not lose again." He opened his eyelid a slit. The needle stood straight up. Its tip centered the mark—Givneh.

A review of what he knew of the area yielded few details. Residents of the high desert plateau had little interaction with those in the lands beyond the sands. One by one he brought forth the images from the scrying. He focused on the symbols on the golden gates, the mark of the Oracle. *His followers are non-tals who donate their last copper to the religious leader,* Relliq thought. *Supposedly for giving to others more needy.*

It is more likely, greed hissed, *that the Oracle pockets three coppers for every one he gives away.*

The tracker cord ended at the temple wall, reality interjected. *No non-tal can do that. There must be someone there who can enter the Cyrcle of One, someone who has powers.* Rumors he had heard about the temple being a site of magic refused to be denied. He cast out a searching spell to locate the mysterious woman. As it had the time before, it stopped at the temple wall.

"Those who live there may be non-tals, but the building itself must have runes of protection around it," Relliq growled, "I can't magically penetrate the temple so I will need to physically go there." He fought down a groan at the time and energy the trip across the desert would require. "Until then, since I have the location, maybe I can find out a name." A deep breath to center his magic and layer by layer he filled his mind with the image of the unknown woman.

"In the Cyrcle of One,
Connected by a cord of gold,
Tell me the name of the person foretold."

A wind came up, tore the words from his lips and carried them away. Relliq threw more power into the spell and felt the search travel farther along the Cyrcle of One than he had ever gone. Just as he was about to give up, silver letters marched across his closed eyelids.

The cord connecting him to the Cyrcle of One exploded into fragments that flickered into nothingness. A thousand tiny cuts accompanied his return to his body forcing air from his lungs in a hoarse gasp.

Memory of a face turned skyward warmed his body and overrode the pain. *At least I now have a name. Kiansel.* It rolled off the tip of his tongue. *And she is in Givneh.*

Chapter Three

"The Oracle is back. He has returned." The excited voices of the kitchen workers penetrated Kia's swirling thoughts. The temple had been a place of refuge for her since the false oracle Bashim was deposed and the archmage and her father had selected her older brother, Brantly, to take over the white robe and teach the true path. As she had for the past sevenday, she fingered the amulet she wore around her neck. The circle's metal retained the heat of her skin and the mark of the Oracle worked in the silver comforted her soul. Once again, she quashed the urge to seek out her brother. While the runes laid on the temple walls cut off the initial contact with the unknown observer, the continued watching, no she amended, call it what it is, spying, had grown stronger. And the ethereal touch? Not even crossing her arms across her chest removed the bumps raised by the icy fingers. *I'm not even safe in my quarters. Only the back corner of the library provides a safe haven.*

"I can wait," she whispered, "Brantly will need time to get caught up since his walkabout the country." *But not too long.*

Less than a candlemark later an acolyte approached the desk where Kia sat studying an ancient tome. His brown robe blended against the background of the leather-bound books until his figure disappeared, leaving only the globe of the boy's face visible. "Mistress, the Oracle requests the honor of your presence at dinner tonight after the evening service."

Rapid calculations meant she had two candlemarks before the gathering. Just enough time to change. "Please convey my thanks and that I will be happy to join him. In the garden or his quarters?"

As if her question had taken him unaware, the youth paused. "He didn't say. Should I ask?"

"No, he will be meeting with his senior teachers and preparing for tonight's service. There is no need to disturb him. But you can check with the kitchen staff to see where the food will be taken and let me know."

"Very well, mistress." A bow and the acolyte left, leaving behind a sense of hope.

The rest of the afternoon passed quickly. The youth returned to say the meal would be delivered to the gazebo in the garden before racing out to join his class for the evening lesson. Slow steps took her through corridors full of people heading towards the large room where the Oracle would lead the service. Despite the chaos of the outer halls, those adjacent to the audience chamber were pools of quiet solitude. The only noises were the soft shuffle of sandals on stone as a person here or there slipped into their assigned position in line.

A deep breath to center herself and Kia checked the small group of six students that were her personal responsibility. The evenly matched number of boys and girls stood in attentive silence. When those ahead of her moved into the hall, she followed. Her group merged into an even longer line that snaked back and forth to form neat rows until they filled the cavernous audience room and not a single person remained in the hallway.

Once in their assigned space, she signaled her group and in a synchronised motion they sank onto the cushions that served as seating. Every sconce held an oil lantern. Their bright light transformed what had been black featureless walls into life-like murals. Here, one showed the bountiful harvest owed to those who worked hard. In another, pilgrims followed a white-robed Oracle up a gold path to paradise.

Her attention shifted to the front of the hall where a dozen gray-robed acolytes entered from a side door and climbed the three steps to the stage. Their bare feet softly slapped on the stone floor as they shuffled into position. Their faces danced as amorphous shapes above the lighter color of their clothing. An elder stepped forward and lifted his hands in command. On the downstroke, the group launched into a hymn hailing the virtues of service to others. A second leader in a purple robe moved to the center of the stage and read some passages extolling kindness, charity, and love. A choir of a dozen singers ranging in age from thirteen to sixty replaced him. The tenor's voice rose above the others in a tune that Kia had sung since childhood.

Her pulse beat in silent rhythm with the melody. Deeper and deeper she fell into a trance caused by the hypnotic rhythms. A shipfish diving towards the depths, she slid farther into the cottony warmth of the Cyrcle of One until all remnants of the observer disappeared.

Gasps for air accompanied the shock of being pulled from the ethereal plane. Kia hugged herself at the memory of an alluring voice. Its words froze her soul. "Come to me, little wizardling. I am your master."

* * *

The nighttime sky greeted Kia as she stepped through a narrow door into a verdant courtyard. The delicate scent of night-blooming flowers filled the air. Only two steps from the wall, the sense of being watched grew. Not even the natural serenity of the garden relieved her unease. *My brother will know what to do.* Holding onto that thought she headed deep into the maze. At each branch, she heard her father's soft voice in her head. The multiple interpretations were a standing joke between them as she was growing up. "But, it wasn't until I returned home and attended Brantly's ordination in the garden that I understood the truth of the saying. 'You can never be lost if you follow the right way.'"

The path among the tall hedges wound back and forth onto itself until it reached an open gazebo in the center. Her older brother rose from one of the cushioned benches and beckoned. Smiling, Kia climbed the two low steps to join him. His hug chased away the earlier chill.

"Welcome back, Brantly," she said. "Did you have a good journey?"

"Very good. The trading went well. A handful of new pilgrims will be joining us after their planting is done and will be staying until harvest time."

After settling Kia on a bench, he moved a small table from the corner and set it in front of their seat. With a flourish, he removed the covers from a pair of steaming plates. A low stand in the corner held crystal goblets, a pitcher of water, and a stoppered bottle of wine. He gestured to the bottle and at a shake of her head filled a glass with water.

Small talk of happenings at the temple and the state of the family occupied the rest of the dinner. As a youth of ten turns bowed and took away the dishes, Kia gathered her nerve. *Now is the time to broach the subject of the watcher. Brantly will not censure.*

"Kiansel, I sense something wrong."

The encouragement in his voice and eyes broke through the barriers she had built around herself. In terse words, she told him about the watcher. How the unseen observer now followed her everywhere except the lower room of the library where the most ancient volumes were stored. "He even breached my meditation during tonight's service." Her fears slipped out in a rush. "I believe he is using magic."

"He?"

With that one word came the realization her stalker was male.

"Kia, I want you to close your eyes." Warmth from her brother's hands wrapped around hers helped chase away the chill from her fingers—and her soul. "Remember the touch. It won't hurt you, won't feel cold. Look beyond the veil to see the watcher." His voice hardened into a command that had to be obeyed. "Describe him."

A handsome face with dark curls falling over a forehead gave way to piercing brown eyes.

After the recitation, the look on her brother's face chased away the earlier fear that he wouldn't believe her. More frightening was that he looked worried. His hands still holding hers, she felt the gathering of magic. Not the slow building of a glacier, but the flare of a fire into life.

"Follow me, Kia. We will find this one who upsets you so." Her brother's voice guided her deeper into the Cyrcle of One than she had ever gone before. Down and down she followed the purple cord that was Brantly's essence. It paused at a solid wall then went through.

Her spirit hit the obstacle and bounced back. No matter how hard she tried to follow the cord into the darkness beyond, she couldn't enter the void. Frustration rose. The ethereal plane collapsed around her and she jumped back to the real world. She didn't know how much time had passed in the netherworld, but the night air now held a crispness that was not there before.

Brantly stood. Low words crossed his lips as he paced the confined space of the gazebo. Three circuits and he snatched up two crystal goblets from the side table, splashed wine into them and handed one to Kia. "I'm sorry, Kia, to put you through that."

His compassionate words startled her. *I'm the one who failed.* "Brother, I couldn't enter the blackness. Couldn't follow the cord."

His light touch on her shoulder held more sympathy and understanding than she thought possible. "You didn't fail me, nor yourself. A little more training might have helped, but I don't think it would have made a difference. I am sure now that your unseen visitor is, if not a mage, then one whose powers are emerging. I was right with you in the Cyrcle of One and couldn't break through the protective block he used to cloak himself."

He took a sip of wine then gestured at the untouched glass in her hand. "I'll contact the archmage to see what he and his lady say, and in the meantime we will also investigate." This time when he nodded at the glass, Kia took a sip. The sweet liquid helped clear her mind and chase away the malaise of the failed search.

Memory of the couple as they presided over Brantly's ordination surfaced. The tall Lord Dal with the dark curls. Muscular as the mercenary he once was, his frame implied not just physical strength, but a restrained power. And the archmage's lady, Ellspeth, with her long silver hair braided into a glittering crown atop her head. Although the archmage could tuck his wife's head beneath his chin when they stood, she radiated the same level of magical ability.

"Please, Brantly, don't. I wouldn't want to interrupt their teachings."

The smile he turned on her held a reassuring warmth. "There will be no untoward interruption. The archmage and I talk frequently."

Kia felt the strength of the Oracle in her brother's gaze. Unlike the other times she had seen him in his official role, for the first time she saw him in the full splendor of this position. He seemed a pillar of lambent energy. Before she could react, he was once again the brother of her childhood.

"There is more, little sister, that upsets you than just the unseen watcher. Is it the use of magic?"

"No, I've seen you and father do too much to be afraid. Both Lord Dal and Lady Ellspeth were very kind to me."

His smile brightened and Kia's soul warmed in response until the other worry slipped out. "The last time the archmage summoned those with power to the council fire I heard him do so." She dropped her gaze to her hands. "No, it is not magic, as such that makes me uneasy." In hesitant words, she told him about the faint call that broke into her dreams the night before the spying began. "I don't think it came from my watcher. I had the impression of a living fog attacking a man, felt the plea for help but before I could respond, he was cut off." Her voice quavered. "It had to be magic, and being worked by someone stronger than me."

"So, my little sister, what bothered you about the contact?"

"I don't know if the person survived. There was the feeling they did, but I didn't feel anything in the Cyrcle of

One. And no one in the temple or the city knows of such a place as I described."

"Have you had any other requests for help, or other messages?"

Kia searched her memory for any dreams that might have been more. "No. If there was they've been overwhelmed by the watcher."

"I will mention the caller to Dal as well. Or maybe Lady Ellspeth. I think, Kia, that the site you mentioned is the cliff trail on the Isle of Mages. They might also be able to set your mind at ease as to who the man was and his fate.

"Now, dear, it has been a long day—and night—for both of us. I'm off to my quarters and on the morrow I will contact Dal and Ellspeth." His hug held more brotherly love than given to most members of the temple. *But he is my brother.* She returned the embrace holding tighter when a ghostly echo called her name.

* * *

The full moon overhead cast an eerie glow on the road, illuminating some holes and hiding others. "Come on, you nag," Relliq growled. A kick in the gelding's flank brought the animal's head up, but did little to increase its speed. "The faster you get to the barn, the sooner you'll get your grain."

At this encouragement, the animal quickened its pace.

Relliq left unsaid that the sooner they reached town and his quarters, the sooner he could see Kiansel. "This will be the night," he vowed. Every night for the past sevenday, he had gone on a spectral visit to her, but each time his magic was stopped at the temple wall. Each failed attempt only added to his vow to possess her. *With her powers combined with mine, nothing will stand in my way. Tonight is the night. Temple runes or not, with the full moon to boost my powers, I will see her.*

Alone in his quarters, he set out the bowl and carefully dribbled water in it to create a thin layer on the bottom. Research had shown that less water made for a better mirror. A deep breath and he gathered his magic. The water in the bowl shimmered and the room's reflection vanished, replaced by long, brown curls hanging free. Pearl combs held waves of hair away from a face, but it was turned away from him.

Moonlight came through the window and framed the bowl. The feeling of power grew.

"Yes," Relliq breathed. "Now, Kiansel, you will be mine."

* * *

Loud pounding on the door pulled Relliq from a deep sleep. Aching muscles and a stiff back proclaimed he had fallen asleep at the table. The bowl lay on its side and the water from the scrying had spilled over the table. Curses bounced off the walls. He had forgotten the penalty for the use of a powerful incantation was a toll of his energy.

I will have to be more careful, he vowed. It wouldn't do for Ysbail to learn of my true abilities before I am ready.

"Master Relliq … master." The thump of fists pounding on wood echoed in the room and Relliq realized what had awakened him in the first place. Staggering to the door, he slid the plank out of the lockbar and opened the door to see one of the village boys standing there, his fist raised to knock again.

"Wha d'ya want." Anger added to a deep exhaustion put a sharpness in his tone.

The youth ducked as if expecting a blow. "Sorry, master. Mistress Ysbail requests you attend her in her office."

"Tell her as soon as I break my fast I'll be there."

"She said she wants you there immediately."

Relliq raised his hand and swung at the boy who backpedaled out of reach, turned, and sped away in the direction of the healer's office.

Fear urged immediate obedience.

After you clean up here, caution advised. A dispersal spell won't take long or use much magic.

28

Putting actions to thought, he raced around the room. The last of the cleansing spell sparkled into nothingness. A final glance around the room and he slipped out. Hurrying through the village, he ducked through back alleys and only slowed his breakneck speed when he reached the garden behind the healer's office.

A deep breath to slow his racing pulse and he knocked. At her light, "Enter," he pushed open the door. Ysbail sat at her desk, a journal open in front of her. Brown hair heralded the appearance of a woman about forty-five turns. A few wispy strands of gray peppered her curls.

I'll have to be careful, Relliq thought. Ysbail may only be a healer, but she is of the House of Cszabo, as is Ellspeth, the archmage's lady.

"Relliq, where are the herbs I asked you to prepare before I left? I have need of them. I used almost all my stock treating those stricken with fever at Gelligaer."

Thinking fast, Relliq gestured at the cabinet in the back of the room. "They aren't there?" Without giving Ysbail a chance to object, he flung open the doors and peered at the shelves. "I put the bags on the second shelf."

"Well, they aren't there now. Are they?" Ysbail pulled a bulging bag from beneath her desk. "Apprentice Relliq, I need these herbs prepared and ready for use by morning. A caravan will be coming through late tomorrow afternoon. They sent word ahead that the healer's supplies are low and several people are sick."

"But, Mistress Ysbail, it takes time to get that much into appropriate form. Why can't I have Gwers help?"

"Because you were supposed to have things ready before my return."

The woman's stern gaze reminded Relliq that he needed to stay on her good side. *At least for now.*

"Gwers will be washing the potion bottles."

I can't stay here, Relliq thought. Ysbail will find the bags of herbs I didn't finish. An idea came to mind. "Mistress, may I take the bags to my quarters. Then I won't be in your way." He held his breath for a seven count as the healer remained silent.

29

"Very well. You may work in your quarters. Just be sure to purify the room before you start and seal the door, window, and hearth."

Hiding his pleasure beneath lowered eyes, he grabbed the bag the healer thrust at him. Shielding his actions from his mistress, he pulled an empty one from the cabinet as well as several bowls and the tools needed to cut and crush the herbs. A glance over his shoulder to make sure Ysbail was not paying attention and he pulled out the bags of herbs he had left undone while he scried the temple—and Kiansel.

I need Ysbail in a good mood if she's going to give me permission to visit Givneh. He smiled as he crossed the courtyard. *If I can't get these other herbs ready in time, they can be added to the compost pile in the garden.*

Pleased with his plans, he headed to the village's pub. *A chilled mug and a meal will provide energy for the night's work. After all Ysbail would not deny me food and drink.*

Chapter Four

Although there had been no further strange apparitions, Brodie kept a sharp watch of his surroundings. Not even walking along the beach looking for elements to incorporate into journeyman daggers failed to loosen his attention. The soft swish of waves reminded him of another time the sound had been a warning—the night of the fog attack.

A glint of light on a seashell trapped in the seaweed that formed the high tide line caught his interest. Three steps and he bent down to brush away the refuse. The more he cleared away the more the shell glowed. Resting it in the palm of his hand, he examined the silver and gold whirls in the pink shell. The shape and markings reminded him of how Denai described the Cyrcle of One.

"This is perfect," he breathed. "Now I can finish Denai's journeyman dagger." The blade had been done since the last full moon, but he hadn't found a suitable element to serve as the future mage's focus. Precious or semi-precious jewels or polished stones served most mages, but, he thought, Denai needs something special. Ellspeth and Dal's second-born is young for a journeyman, but exhibited power from her first words. "Forcing her parents to bind her powers until she learned restraint. Which she did at the age of six."

Memories of how both Denai and her older sister learned discipline raised a smile. Older by at least a few moments, he mused. "It is surprising how a few rounds with a wooden staff against a trained master will give a student a new perspective." Secretly he was pleased that although the girls' parents were capable of delivering the lesson, they had chosen him to wield the opposing staff while Murdo counselled and guided their moves. *Now, with the exception of their parents, Denai and Elendl are the most powerful of the mages in the world.* And he admitted, the two girls felt like his own kin. *Even if I am a non-tal.*

A moan interrupted his reflections. He listened for it to repeat. *There.*

Splashing through the surf, he raced towards the sound. "No. Leave me alone. Help." Loud yells and the sound of flesh on flesh rose over that of wave against stone.

Long strides wove him around piles of rocks that had fallen from the cliff face and he saw what the reason for the yells–an older boy bent over a younger one. While Brodie watched, the larger figure raised an arm and struck the smaller one.

"You ... stop."

His head down, the attacker raced away. "Damn," Brodie snarled. He couldn't see the boy's face. By the time he reached the spot, the youth had rounded a curve on the narrow trail up the cliff and vanished into the woods. From there he could slip unseen into the village or farther down the beach.

Unable to catch his prey, Brodie stopped alongside the crying boy lying on the sand. "Easy, Jago, you're safe now."

The boy looked up. His eyes red from pain and unshed tears.

"Who attacked you?"

Silence greeted the question. Again, Brodie silently cursed. *Jago is too scared to talk. He's probably been bullied for a while. And since the attack took place just outside the village, the other boy is someone he knows.*

"Don't worry about it, Jago." Brodie said, reassurance in his tone. "I'll walk you home."

As he escorted the boy back to the stone cottage he shared with his parents and younger sister, Brodie hoped Jago would open up, but by the time they reached the cottage, the youth still hadn't said a word. Once safely inside his room and a healer fussing over the bruises, Brodie explained in terse words what had happened then added one last reassurance. "I'll discuss the issue with Lord Dal at the earliest opportunity."

The promise lingered in his mind and instead of heading back to his forge he changed direction to take him to the council chamber tower. Dal would be there this time of day.

The open door encouraged Brodie and instead of climbing the steps to the council chamber he went to the archmage's private office. His light knock was answered by a cheerful, "Come on in, Brodie."

A wave sent him to the chair alongside the desk. "Now, Brodie, what brings our resident weaponsmith to my door? It isn't a problem with the journeyman daggers is it?"

"No, Dal, the daggers for the next crop of mages is well in hand. In fact, I just found the element that I'm pretty sure Denai will choose as hers." He looked out the window. "Do you think she'll answer the next summons?"

The archmage's look told Brodie that Dal had similar thoughts. Whether as the archmage and responsible for all wielders of magic or as Denai's father, Brodie couldn't tell.

"They are a little young to be a journeyman, and have many turns of study ahead of them," Dal admitted. "But, yes. I believe both Denai and Elendl will step forward at the next bonfire."

"Then it's a good thing I found the element. I think the shell will fit perfectly and blend with Denai's inclination for the sea."

Brodie felt Dal's gaze pierce his scuffed clothing, to scan him down to his soul. "That is not why you came by." The archmage's tone was more statement than question.

In terse words, Brodie explained the attack on Jago. "I couldn't see his face, but I think I know who it was."

"I'm not surprised," Dal said at the end of the recitation. "Although no one in the dormitory has said anything, I've heard rumors about a pair of boys who came from Barris' home village of Montrat. That Fwlïaid and Gurrod have bullied some of the younger students." His gaze turned thoughtful. "They've been at the school for three seasons, but it has only been recently that the rumors started."

The archmage's smile reminded Brodie of their common experiences dealing with second-turn students at the mercenary school. "They're about the right age," Brodie laughed. "They will have learned enough skills to believe they know it all; but are not mature enough to realize there is always someone bigger and faster."

"And stronger," Dal added. "I'll reach out to Ysbail to see what if anything she's heard about Fwlïaid and Gurrod, and ask how her new pupil is coming along. I understand Relliq wasn't too happy when the boys' parents decided to move here and bring his 'assistants' with them."

Images of a pair of tow-headed boys, with ruddy complexions came into Brodie's mind. "Fwlïaid and Gurrod are in Denai's and Elendl's classes. They'll let us know if they do anything untoward," he said. "And I'll keep an eye on the boys to make sure they stop bullying Jago and anyone else they might be using their size and age against." He saw his shrug mirrored in Dal's smile. "If need be either myself or Murdo will spar with them."

"Our former sergeant-at-arms is good at helping a recalcitrant youth learn discipline," Dal agreed. "Even if he blunts the lesson by dressing their bruises with liniment and baking them a special treat."

Before Brodie could censor the words, "Can fog attack?" slipped out.

The concern in the archmage's gaze chilled. "What kind of attack?"

At Dal's encouragement he told him about the tripping and attempted strangulation. "I might only be a non-tal, but it felt like a magical attack."

Dal's nod of agreement encouraged Brodie to bring up a part of the event that had been bothering him. "I think Denai broke the spell." The urge to pace was strong, but he bridled it and remained seated. "I don't have the ability for mindspeech. I thought she heard me because she had used TânOer in practice earlier that day. And there was the touch of another mage. But no one from the island."

34

"Well, I can't speak to why Denai heard your cry for help," Dal said. "But I'm sure we will find out. We always do." His tone brightened. "I can help you with the other question. You spent a season at the Temple of Givneh and met Brantly. Well, his younger sister Kiansel heard your summons, but Denai apparently rescued you before Kia did." Dal's hand was warm where it lay on Brodie's shoulder and he felt his friend's compassion and strength. "Brantly will be glad to hear you survived. Kiansel was worried that she had failed to save someone."

A few more moments to coordinate the details of the watch on Fwlïaid and Gurrod and Brodie headed to the open-air oven where Murdo liked to create his sweet concoctions. *The big mercenary should have a freshly-baked batch of cookies ready and I'll take some to Jago. Maybe that will loosen his tongue.*

Everything settled that could be, he retreated to his forge with a haunting thought as his shadow. *How did Kiansel know I was in trouble?*

Maybe I should visit Givneh and meet her.

* * *

Each blow took more energy as the metal resisted being marked. Brodie watched the metal change color. "It's cooling too fast." He didn't dare work any faster and risk making a mistake. A review of the sheet of paper bearing the marks, and he repositioned the chisel for another strike. He had been awakened each night for the past sevenday by the same image of glowing runes. Finally, he accepted the dream as an unconscious message from one of the mages— or future mages—on the island and started engraving the symbols. Satisfied with the current mark, he placed the blade in the hot coals.

Movement on the trail pulled his attention away from plans to go to Givneh. Dark curls announced the archmage's arrival. His wave of greeting and determined steps told Brodie that the other man had not come to visit. He'd lived with the mages long enough that he knew why

35

Dal had come. He was going to send out the summons to invite those with power to come to the Council Isle.

The other man walked a short distance to the far side of the grassy field to where a ring of white stone obelisks had been raised. The five outer ones were as tall as a man, while the center spire twice as tall as the others, held court. An outer circle of white pebbles, a handspan wide and three or four fingers high, gleamed as a halo around the rocks. Brodie knew the archmage and his lady had raised the stones soon after they had re-established the school of wizards.

Dal raised his hands in summons.

A welcoming, then the urge to travel, to go somewhere, overwhelmed Brodie.

But where?

Images of the Rainbow Bridge and the council tower were followed by the dock where Ellspeth's ship, *Windmaster,* usually bobbed.

Dal bent his head for several more moments, then waved a goodbye and headed back towards the village.

Brodie watched the archmage disappear down the trail and wondered at the power of the summoning. He had never felt it before in all his seasons at the isle. *It must be because Dal was so close and my submersion in the fog the other night. I am not a mage.*

A hint of the responses unexpectedly whispered at the edge of his senses. One, with a male signature was cold and calculating. But it was the second, warm and female, that he focused on. *Kia?* The urge to visit Givneh and meet the Oracle's sister in person grew stronger.

* * *

The intrusions had grown worse, especially after dark until even the deepest recesses of the archives failed to provide refuge. The whispers of, "Come to me," prevented sleep. Kia knew if she drifted off into too sound a slumber she would not be able to resist the command. Finally, the bright sun lured her outside the walls of the temple.

For the first time in days, she didn't feel the unseen presence. She wandered the garden, not paying any particular attention to where her steps took her until a bench in a small cove near the heart of the maze beckoned. The growing warmth from the sun overhead took away the stone's chill except where she leaned her head against it.

A teasing at her senses pulled her from her dozing state. It came with a desire, no she corrected, a need to go somewhere. Unlike the other times, she felt no worry, no fear. If anything, this was the call to visit an old friend. Curiosity overcame caution. Rather than fight, she closed her eyes and allowed the heat of the sun to take her down into the Cyrcle of One. An image formed in her mind. A bridge more sensed than seen shimmered against the sky to be replaced by a round stone tower. The final picture was more striking and alluring. Five tall stones circled an even larger spire. A low wall of white pebbles surrounded the taller rocks.

"The Isle," Kia breathed. "This is a summoning...a call to be a mage."

She stayed enjoying the comfort of the ethereal plane until the sun started its descent. Chilled air pulled the warmth from her skin. Retreating to within the walls of the temple, she sought out her brother.

"Well, Kiansel, what causes your pensive look?"

The encouragement in his gaze and the light touch of his hand on her arm brought forth a spurt of words. "The summoning is getting harder to resist." She waited to see if he understood.

Sorrow danced in his eyes even as a smile twitched his lips. "I always knew you were not meant for the temple."

"I didn't mean..." Kia couldn't finish the sentence. The guilt of the betrayal of her family, of the temple, of Brantly, washed over her. She lowered her head and closed her eyes so that she couldn't see the pain in her brother's face.

A finger tilted her head up. "Kia, sister, you should know by now that there is nothing untoward about the archmage. You've met Dal and his lady enough times to know that."

"But, my family belongs to the temple. You, our father, our grand-dam many times removed, and every generation between have served the temple." Even speaking the words added to her sense of treachery. *How could Brantly ever forgive me? Let alone allow me to study the Way.*

"Yes, I am the current Oracle of Givneh, and many of our family have worn the robe of a servant of the temple. But, Kia, there have been some who walked other paths. The sadness in his face lightened. "In many ways life here and on the Isle of Mages is not dissimilar. Studying the teachings of the Oracle and mastering the Way is more of a difference in type and ability than right and wrong."

His soft tones helped calm Kia's whirling thoughts. "So you would not refuse if I asked permission to go to the isle."

"I will admit we will miss you," Brantly answered. "But in answer to your question, I will contact Dal tonight to make your travel arrangements. After all, it wouldn't do for you to miss the ceremony because you stayed here an extra sevenday or didn't catch the winds to Aigeal." His eyes unfocused and when his attention returned, his expression no longer showed a hint of regret. "The archmage sends his greetings and that you would be most welcome. But there is one more thing."

Even as he said it, Kia knew what her brother referenced. She had to talk to the one man who could demand she stay at the temple—their father. "I planned on going home to speak to him tomorrow."

"Don't wait, Kiansel. This is too important. I'll arrange for Lehrer to take your classes. If you're going to the Council Isle, he had better get used to a new role."

Where the thought of leaving her students had worried her, a sense of calm replaced it. *Lehrer is well ready to take over the teachings.*

Brantly's voice broke into her reflections. "Go this afternoon. Take one of my special horses." He paused and added. "Spend the night with the family and tomorrow as well. When you return, I will have more details for your journey. And Kia, know that you will always have a place here."

The benison from the kiss he gently placed on her forehead removed the last of her reservations. *Even if I can't be a real mage, I can use what I learn from the archmage to help Brantly and those the temple serves.*

* * *

A stray beam of moonlight speared through the thickening clouds. Relliq watched them join together in dark ranks until no sign remained of the moon—or its power. Curses he was careful to keep silent twitched at his lips. Something in the temple walls blocked magic so he needed the extra power of the conjoined full moons to breach them. Even then, he had to reach out to her at night when she was asleep and her barriers were down.

I haven't been able to see Kia for two nights. And now the impending storms threaten another sleepless night with neither rest nor vision. Still, he gathered his magic and cast a line westward towards Givneh. "Come to me," he whispered. "My darling Kia, come to me."

The ethereal link wavered and shifted. When it settled, the tone was different. No longer did the vision hold Kia's image. A sense of welcoming flowed along the link. By the time the images ended and Relliq's consciousness returned to his body, he knew who sent out the call—the archmage. And that the message was an invitation to join him.

Maybe I should go to the Isle of Mages, Relliq thought. There must be things I can learn about magic there. A dream formed. *And a means to make Kia mine. Willingly or not, I will have her.*

Chapter Five

Assembling his face into the appropriate expression of obedience, Relliq entered the healer's office. Ysbail looked up from the notes she was writing. Even upside down her neat script was easy to read. He caught his name and the words obstinate, uncooperative, and can't recommend.

Control, he said in a private mantra. Ysbail might only be a healer but she has gotten too good of late at reading strong emotions. "Mistress, a moment please?"

The healer's nonchalant shift of her hand to cover her notes came with a soft, "Go on, Relliq."

All the carefully rehearsed words froze without voice. "I'm going to the Isle of Mages," blurted out.

Ysbail's lips tightened. "You have not yet finished your training here. Your assignment at Montrat is for at least another two seasons. Maybe then I'll discuss your attending the School of Mages with the archmage."

"But mistress, I have done everything you asked." Relliq held up his hands. "Even literally wore my fingers to the bone preparing the bags of herbs you requested."

"Yes, Relliq, those bags of herbs that mysteriously were nowhere to be found have reappeared. However, I still need help compounding the potions for the upcoming cold season or we will lose people here and in the neighboring villages."

"Use Gwers," Relliq growled. He bit off, "He's your special student anyway."

Ysbail's cool gaze fueled the fire building in Relliq's soul. The longer she sat and looked at him, the more tenuous his control became. "I heard the summoning last night. The archmage sent out a welcome to all with powers." He raised his chin. "I'm going to the Council Isle and you can't stop me. You're only a healer." In one final flare he added, "You have no power over me."

* * *

The smooth gait of her brother's private mount gave Kiansel too much time to think. Although Brantly the Oracle as well as Brantly her brother had given approval for her to go study at the Isle of Mages, she still worried about her father's reaction. The warm hug and greeting did nothing to dispel the unease.

He had no sooner turned the horse loose in the pasture with a request to return in the morning, than her father led her to the rocking chair on the porch. "Sit easy, Kia. Your brother mindspoke me so I know why you're here … I approve. Now tell me about the summoning."

The words rushed out about the desire to go somewhere and the images that followed. "I've felt this before from time to time." At his raised eyebrow she added, "It began two cold seasons ago, the one where the snow drifts blocked in the town."

Her father smiled. "I remember. Storm after storm rolled through, each pushing the snow higher and higher. The horses had a good time. All they had to do to get grazing was to walk a few steps to where the snow had blown clear." He nodded for her to continue.

"The desire grew stronger and this morning it was so strong I almost started walking before I realized what I was doing." She paused, afraid to put a voice to the fear in her heart.

"Kiansel, my daughter, you have the blessing of both myself and the Oracle." The hand he laid on hers warmed and comforted. "Although my own are meager, more suited for the land, talent runs in our family. Wait here. There is something I want to show you."

While she sat and watched the stallion roll in the grass, Kia let the serenity of her homestead seep into her soul.

The clang of a door closing behind her ended the reverie. Her father came around and sat down on the stairs in front of her. A small wooden box was in his hands.

"I remember that," Kia said. "It was on the top shelf in your office for many turns." Her voice faltered. "Until the time of the false oracle." She saw the pain of her banishment and of the death of a brother reflected in her father's gaze and lifted a hand to his cheek. "Sorry."

Sorrow deepened the creases in her father's tanned face. He had always said, "It wasn't the turns but the miles that aged." However, before the false oracle she hadn't remembered him looking so old … and tired.

A shake of his head, as if banishing a bad memory and he smiled. "Kia, your mother and I knew you would be a mage from the moment of your birth. That's why we sent you to study at the temple."

Kia's gaze went to the small plot beyond the garden and the white stones that marked her mother's grave.

"Your mother would be proud you want to study at the Council Isle." Her father's voice dropped to a whisper. "She was a mage herself and studied there for four seasons before returning home to be with the family." Once again, shadows darkened his face. "It was a good thing too, although she regretted it for many turns. If she had stayed she would have been killed by Bashim along with the rest of those who practiced the Way."

He opened the box and pulled out a pendant. "This was my great-dam's." Sunlight glinted off the metal. Kia swore the markings on it glowed with an energy of their own.

"It bears the mark of the Oracle," Kia said when he placed it in her hand, the metal still warm from his touch. "I can't take this when I will be studying the Way."

Her father flipped it over. What had appeared as a glow now could be seen as runes for protection, love, strength, and wisdom. His finger traced each one, lingering on "love." "There is magic in this token from both my lineage and your mother's. This is your heritage. You don't need to deny the temple to study the Way of magic, nor give up your powers to be worthy of the Oracle."

42

His words lingered behind when he went inside.

I can be a mage, Kia thought. And it will not be a betrayal to either my family or the temple. Her soul soared with the hawks hunting above.

Sunset brought with it more than an orange glow in the sky. A soft hum came from the kitchen where her father prepared the evening meal. Its tone sounded similar to the one that haunted her nights.

In her mind, an unseen speaker whispered, "Come to me, Kiansel. Come to me, my little wizardling."

* * *

Curiosity as to the reason for the archmage's call quickened Brodie's steps. Denai hadn't specified why her father wanted to see him, just that Dal wanted Brodie in the council chamber as soon as he could get there.

Whether it was to avoid unspoken questions or another reason, no sooner had Brodie entered the room than Dal shifted into what he called the archmage's briefing face. "There have been several responses to the summoning. I know time is short, however, I need you to provide security for them as they travel from their homes to the Isle. Tairneach will provide mounts."

A smile twitched Brodie's lips. He remembered his first ride on a fàlaire. Like most boys—and men—something in the powerful legs and barrel chest of the magical equines resonated at an instinctive level. And Tairneach was the head stallion of the herd of fàlaire that resided in the valley beyond the Isle of Mages. Like the others of his kind, Tairneach had chosen a rider to be his own and no one besides Dal could ride him without either Dal's or Taer's permission. From time to time, with the head stallion's approval, Brodie had ridden one of the fàlaire as he journeyed around the country on tasks for the archmage.

Dal gestured to the large table in the middle of the council room and pulled out a map. His finger tapped the plateau of Givneh, then traced a route through the Mtwan

43

Mountains. "My mother wants to come for a visit. So besides stopping in Givneh, I need you to swing by my family clanhold. I'd like you to escort her through the vale to the Isle."

Givneh? Where Kia lives? Maybe I'll get a chance to meet her?

The possibility of meeting the mystery woman almost obscured the rest of Dal's sentence. With a wrench he returned his attention back to his friend. "Brantly has sent word that Kia wants to answer the summoning." With it the archmage sent a mental image of Kia.

The picture triggered another realization. *It was Kia's mental touch I felt at Dal's summoning.*

Dal handed over a small notebook. "Besides Kia and my mother there will be six girls and four boys in your party. Their names, as well as information on their families, are within. The girls range in age from twelve to fourteen and the boys are the same."

Brodie fought back a groan. "So I'm to be the big, bad mercenary escort to ease the father's fears about bandits and footpads, while Kia is the matron protecting the girls' virtue?"

"Someone has to do it," Dal laughed. "And don't forget that my mother will be traveling along with you. She has a long ear and a knack for catching mischief before it gets too far."

Calculations as to when the twin moons, Shartle and Neba, would be full did nothing to ease Brodie's rising worries. There wasn't much time to make the trip to Givneh and back in time for the council bonfire. "When do you want me to leave?"

"Can you be ready the day after tomorrow? Taer should have returned with your mounts by then."

"I guess I will have to be," Brodie acknowledged.

Something about the archmage's stance ranged along Brodie's nerves. "There is more isn't there?"

The flash of surprise in Dal's eyes was quickly suppressed and he ran his fingers through his dark curls.

"I'd rather not put this on you, but I need an assessment of someone."

To allow the other man to gather his thoughts, Brodie waited. He had done this service before for the archmage and his lady.

"Relliq is supposedly a healer, but Barris' mother says he's hiding his true abilities." Dal's shrug conveyed frustration and more, a hint of anger. "Ellspeth or I would do an evaluation, but whenever we try to speak to him he's never there."

"But I'm not a mage." Even as he said them Brodie had to fight the disappointment the words brought forward.

Dal's sympathetic look didn't salve the emotions but heightened them. "I need your assessment of him as a man, not as a mage."

Tension radiated off the other man. Brodie wondered what other task the archmage had in mind. Whatever it was, it boded no good.

"Brodie, I'm also sending you not just for your mercenary background, but also because of TânOer. The Oracle has confided to me that he thinks someone is stalking Kia—by magic." His voice deepened. "We haven't been able to track down who is doing it,"

Brodie felt his own anger that someone would abuse their power.

A power I don't have and never will.

Now the archmage's intent became clear. The possibility of refusing the task flickered in Brodie's mind before he quashed it. "I'm to be her bodyguard."

What if her pursuer is a mage? worry asked.

Dal's voice broke into Brodie's thoughts and he realized he had voiced the concern. "Your sword is enspelled enough against someone of journeyman level," the archmage said in reassurance. "Brantly and Kia's father, Forsom, will make sure that Kia can utilize TânOer's abilities before you leave the temple."

"Because I can't," Brodie growled. *I'm a non-tal. How am I to protect her?*

* * *

Preparations for the trip made and supplies packed, Brodie paced the invisible bridge that linked the Isle of Mages to the mainland. *If Taer promised some of the fàlaire as mounts, then we will have them.*

He repeated the statement as a mantra. Time was short to accomplish his task and he didn't want to let the archmage and Ellspeth down. The pair have done so much for me, he thought. Unbidden the memory of his first meeting with Dal rose. "I was an unbearded youth," Brodie whispered. "And Dal saved my life. I owe him." He fought down a darker thought. *What would have happened if I had stayed to defend Ruaridh?* Only one answer was possible. *I would have been killed. I was no match for the archmage. Either as a man or as a soldier.*

The thoughts occupied him until the thunder of heavy hoof falls rolled across the grass. Beneath Brodie's feet, the ground vibrated providing more evidence that members of the fàlaire herd were fast approaching.

A dozen large horses appeared from the tall grass. Their long manes shimmered in the early dawn. Only these weren't ordinary horses, Brodie knew. They were larger than any he had ever seen before he came to the wizard's isle, including the draft animals used by boat builders to pull felled trees down from the hills. The lead horse, a dark gray stallion raced forward. The white specks of its dappled flanks flickered in the sunlight. Not moving, Brodie waited. The animal checked its headlong rush in a hail of dirt and snapping teeth.

The dust from the fàlaires' arrival settled. "All right, Wirake. I'm happy to see you too." Brodie pulled a green fruit from his pocket and offered it to the stallion who gently lipped it from his hand. The fruit disappeared in a loud crunch.

A nudge knocked Brodie back into the pile of supplies and saddles. Before he could regain his feet, a wet nose tried to reach into his pocket. "Go away, Wirake." Slaps and a push and the animal retreated a step, although it

46

flicked its ears in a clear command. Well, give me another treat.

Laughing, Brodie snatched up a bag and handed out a fruit to each of the waiting fàlaire. "Well, if you're all satisfied, can we get ready to go?"

Wirake stomped his foot in what Brodie interpreted as a snarky, Well, if we have to.

With the speed of one used to packing for fast exits, Brodie soon had the pack saddles in place and the supplies tied down. One last tug of the strap to tighten the girth on Wirake's saddle and he stepped into the stirrup.

The stallion looked over his shoulder. His ears flicked in the command, Hold on. Beneath his legs, Brodie felt the animal's muscles tense. A neighed command and Wirake leaped forward. No sooner had his hooves touched the ground than he shifted into a ground-eating gallop.

One journey started, Brodie thought. But where will it end?

With Kia, hope whispered.

* * *

Her back against one of the columns that surrounded the courtyard, Kia watched the line of pilgrims snake through the golden doors on their way into the temple. None of them matched the description Brantly provided of her escort. The urge to pace kept trying to take control of her feet. Time was short to get to the wizard's isle and Brodie still hadn't appeared. Once again, she exerted her will and remained where she was.

Something drew her attention to a figure leaning against a pillar at the back of the courtyard. He was surrounded by pilgrims, but his clothing and attitude set him apart. In fact, Kia noted, he appeared to be patiently waiting for the pilgrims, allowing them into the temple first.

The last of the pilgrims entered the doors and Kia hurried after them. The senior cleric on duty tolerated no tardiness and once he shut the doors allowed no one in.

And, Kia thought, that includes me. I'd have to walk around the entire building to use the postern door.

"Excuse me, miss. I have a message for the Oracle. Could you please escort me to him?"

Startlement at the voice near her ear halted her mid-step. The speaker was the man from the shadows. Yet she felt no fear, only a curiosity as to who he was. He stepped closer, bringing his face into the light. Warmth that nothing to do with the sun crept up Kia's back, heating her neck. *This is my escort.* She scanned him with a new eye, noting his easy stance and the hilt of the sword peeking above his shoulder.

He held out his hand. "My name is Brodie." A smile lightened his previous expression. "And you are, Kiansel. In the name of the Archmage, Lord Dal, and his lady, the mage Ellspeth, you are welcome to attend the council fire on the Isle of Mages."

As soon as her fingers touched his, a shock raced up her arm. *It will be an interesting trip.*

Brodie was speaking, yet the words made little sense. Kia cast her mind back a few seconds to see what he had said. "The archmage sent horses for you and the rest of those traveling to the school." A pause and he appeared to be carefully choosing his next words. "They are a special breed that roams the vale just beyond the isle. Is there a stable I can leave them at while I meet with the Oracle?"

"There is a place where the Oracle keeps the horses he uses as his private mounts," Kia answered after a moment. "We can take your animals there until other arrangements are made."

"Then, let us get them there. They should be getting a bit antsy by now. I've been gone longer than I promised." Brodie slipped the bag from his shoulder and pulled out a small, round green fruit. "Here, this will serve as an introduction. You'll know who to give it to."

His ambiguous tone gave no indication as to the hidden meaning, but his laugh lightened her mood even more. For some reason she trusted him so she followed him through the public part of the temple and out into the city. Rounding a corner, he let out a short, piercing whistle.

The rumble of thunder had Kia searching the sky. However, no storm clouds darkened the horizon. The sound changed into a drumroll. Again without any obvious source. *What kind of magic is this?*

As if he read her mind, Brodie laughed. "No magic. Just Wirake showing off."

Just then a large gray stallion came into view. Behind him followed more horses in paired columns of twos and the cause of the rhythmic clap became obvious. The animals pranced in a high parade step. Their hooves struck the stones so perfectly synchronized the sound rolled back from the lead animal through the two columns. They stopped and the big gray flicked his ears at Brodie.

Kia laughed at the obvious command of, Introduce me.

"Kiansel, this is Wirake, son of Tairneach, head stallion of the herd of the vale. Wirake, this is Kiansel, a special guest of Dal and Ellspeth. She'll be travelling with us."

The stallion stretched out one leg and when it bent nose to knee his shimmering mane cascaded down, a curtain of stars. When he rose, Wirake nickered and flicked its ears towards Brodie.

"I understand that order," Kia said with a laugh at the animal's antics. "Now he wants a treat."

"And he shall get one," Brodie answered. "If he behaves himself."

His response was Wirake's nudge to the shoulder the bag hung from. A swish of his tail said, I always behave myself.

One of the green fruits appeared in Brodie's hand. The horse looked at Brodie's hair—then the fruit, as if pondering his decision whether to pull the one or eat the other. His teeth snapped and the fruit disappeared.

A gray mare with a white blaze on her forehead trotted over to Kia and performed the same knee bow. The long red tail fell over the spotted rump like the feather in a courtier's hat. Remembering the fruit in her pocket, Kia offered it to the horse. "Nice to meet you, my dear. I gather we'll be sharing the road together."

Although his demeanor didn't change, the scan Brodie gave the surrounding street sent a chill down her spine. An unbidden thought rose. *Does he know about my stalker? Is that why he wears a sword?*

With a soft, "apologies," Brodie lifted her into Wirake's saddle and climbed up behind her. "Just tell Wirake where the stable is." His arms went around her and he picked up the reins.

The cold left from the memory of the unknown man vanished where their arms touched. The previous warmth rose, this time even stronger. *I think I need to learn more about my escort.*

Chapter Six

Kia wandered from hall to hall. No matter how much she sought inner calm, her whirling thoughts pulled her down into the maelstrom. The meeting between Brodie and the families of two of the boys traveling with them had gone well. In fact, Brodie seemed to be a natural diplomat. From the first handshake, the boys who sometimes could be pranksters acted more mature than she had ever seen them to. And the parents' anxieties were salved by the time they left.

Could it be magic, she wondered? She answered her own question. *I sensed no magic, no activity in the Cyrcle of One.* The reality added a sad layer to her excitement. *Brodie is a non-tal.*

But, her heart countered, nothing says that a non-tal and a mage can't be together.

For that she had no reply.

Her internal clock finally indicated it was time for dinner with her brother—and Brodie. Once again, she wondered at her reaction to him. They had only shared a fleeting touch, yet her entire being vibrated and she yearned for more.

At least, she mused, I will see him at dinner. Maybe I can gain more insight. Even if my father and brother will be there.

Dinner went by too quickly. After hugs from her father and brother, Kia headed back to her room. Her last image of the night was the three men huddled over a large map, reviewing the route to the hold of Clan Daimh. Her father's farewell echoed in her ears. "Trust Brodie. He is a good man."

But he can't help with anything magic, she wanted to say. He's a non-tal. And the one who haunts my dreams has to be using magic. She grasped onto the hope that her brother was right, that the archmage would be able to end the spying.

Unable to sleep, and everything packed for the morrow's leaving, she mentally practiced the incantation her brother gave her to contact the archmage.

"I can't sink into the Cyrcle of One to do it." She felt the amulet's metal cool against her skin, felt the power pulsing through it. Grasping the energy, she formed a connection between it and Brodie's sword. A breath and she cast out a line.

Yes?

The touch was feminine, but the contact was supposed to go to Dal. Surprise weakened the link until the unknown receiver strengthened the magical cord between them.

Sorry to interrupt, mistress, Kia stammered. *I was trying to reach the archmage.*

Light laughter rippled through the ether. *Don't worry, Kia. My mate is busy and asked me to take your call. What can I do for you?*

Unused to mindspeech, Kia blurted out the truth with both words and mind. "I was practicing what the Oracle taught me."

Your voice is strong and clear and I would say you have mastered it.

As if the other woman sensed Kia's uncertainty, she added, *There is no problem, my dear. There has been no interruption. In fact, I was hoping you'd reach out so I could add my welcome to that of my mate's. Contact either of us anytime.*

The warmth of family washed over her and the link vanished.

As the linkage broke, another presence lingered, one neither friendly nor welcoming. Despite the newness of the skill, Kia threw up her mental barriers against the malignant wraith.

* * *

Carefully, Relliq arranged the spoon, bowl, and a cup of water freshly drawn from the well in a triangle on the white cloth. A pair of six-inch blades formed a cross in the center of elements. He scooped up a tablespoon of ash from the hearth and spread it in the bottom of the bowl. With a finger, he smoothed the white powder. "Careful," he muttered. A dip of two fingers into the glass and when they lifted water hung from them. A flick and two droplets splattered in the ash, each leaving behind a small circle.

"No way Ysbail will interfere with my plans. She is just a healer. Her powers are nowhere as strong as mine." Instead of using the power of the moon, he used the rising sun to boost his abilities. Spoonful by spoonful he dribbled water into the bowl until a thin film covered the ash. A finger swirled the water and powder together. As he had each night since the last full moon, he cast his senses toward Givneh. A purple cord leapt from the bowl to the fireplace and disappeared skyward up the chimney.

The water shimmered. Golden gates, aglow with the rising sun, appeared in the impromptu mirror. His finger touched the water, blending the ash and water into a new pattern. The cord shifted and with it the vision changed.

"Yes," Relliq hissed. A herd of horses, their manes streaming out behind, raced through the early morning fog. For a second, he considered turning the gray mass into a living thing. A moment's consideration and he dismissed the idea. He had never consciously sent the fog and the horses made a big target. "If only they weren't moving so fast," he cursed. Even in the vision, he could tell their gallop covered the ground at a high speed. The horses left the fog behind and broke into a sun-lit trail. Light glinted off water. "I recognize that spot," Relliq said to the walls. "They are leaving Aigeal." He wondered how the group that had just left the temple could have already crossed Botunn Loghes. Those horses were making better time than any he had ever seen.

Desire parted his lips. Dreams of the herd he could create with the mare Kia was riding and the stallion that led the group quickened his breath. "And what an heir Kia will provide me."

The features of the rider of the lead horse came into view. "No!" It was the same man who escaped the fog. *The one who broke my spell.*

But he is a non-tal, argued anger. Someone else saved him.

There is no one else, reality countered. Except Kia.

Rage at the possibility that she had feelings for the man surged through Relliq.

Storm clouds filled the horizon. Rank upon rank stood ready to march down the valley. "What an opportunity," he hissed.

"Winds strengthen, be mine to control.
Rain blind and wind blow,
That one over the edge must go."

At the command, the clouds shifted. Relliq watched the wind strip the leaves from the branches. Soon sheets of rain pelted the string of horses. But the intended target of the assault remained in the saddle. "Fall off," he commanded. However, the man just dropped the reins and held tighter to the stallion's neck. "Winds knock him off his horse and throw him into the abyss."

Brown hair whipping in the gale pulled him back to his senses. Hastily, he added a restriction to put Kia in a bubble of safety.

Pleasure at the ease of the casting added to the energy that coursed through Relliq's frame. *My powers are growing.* He ignored the fact that with each incantation, the time to recover lengthened. Still, he held onto the ethereal cord and watched, waiting for the storm to remove his competition. Instead of the rider plummeting to the valley floor, he disappeared into a dark slit in the mountain. One by one the horses followed.

"Come on," he urged the bowl when the image blurred. *"Power of earth add to that of sky. Show me what I wish to see, the dream of mine."*

A spark of light appeared in the darkness. It didn't grow to fill the bowl, just enough to show Kia's features reflected in the dancing flames of a fire. He watched the other riders climb down. Their slender frames foretold their youthful ages, as did the first signs of awakening powers. "I will have a new crop of apprentices," Relliq crowed.

Red lines shimmered in the air. More joined them in a ritual sealing. The threads wove together into a solid dome that spread downward until it touched Relliq's cord. A flash of light and the connection exploded. Not just in the ethereal plane but in his hand. Yelping, he dumped the remaining water in the mug on his hand to put out the flame. When he looked in the bowl for his tracker spell, there was no sign … only darkness. *The smith is no mage, no match for me. Yet this is the second time he's broken my spell.*

"I will find out how he does it." He added a second vow. "And take the ability for my own."

* * *

Arms and legs moved in a slow sequence of well-practiced moves. Each strengthened the coordination of hand and eye. His muscles sufficiently warmed up, Brodie pulled the short sword from its sheath and repeated the routine. Then he added the moves to coordinate the sheath as a block while the hand with the sword stabbed and slashed. Faster and faster he moved, the blocks harder and stronger. A final spin and he sheathed the short sword and pulled TânOer from its scabbard. The weapon slid from the well-oiled leather with a sibilant hiss.

Two-handed figure eights gave way to one-handed ones. A final series of blocks and Brodie, sweat running down his face and darkening his shirt stopped his furious moves. One clean rag wiped his face and another removed

55

the moisture from the sword's hilt. Careful of the sharp edge, he wiped the blade.

"Brodie?"

He spun at the soft word. Kia stood a few feet away. "I saw your practice. Would you mind giving me a lesson with the short sword?" Her face communicated an unresolved conflict. "No reflection on your ability as a bodyguard, but it seems prudent to have at least basic skills with a weapon." Now a smile tweaked her lips. "My brother said that using magic is well and good, but sometimes steel is needed. I figure if he doesn't object to being able to use a sword, then the archmage shouldn't."

"I don't know about your brother, but Dal has insured both his wife and daughters are skilled with whatever weapon fits them, whether it be bow, staff, or sword." Brodie said. "Since your brother doesn't object to your learning, then no reason I should." He glanced at the sky. "There's enough time for a lesson before I take over guard duty. For this first one, to get the feel of both the long sword and short, hold TânOer. By the time we get to the isle you should know your preference." His smile countered the reality of a weapon in her hand. "And then I'll make you the perfect weapon, whether wood, steel, or iron."

He lay the blade on his arm and offered it hilt first to her. "Lady Kiansel, may I present TânOer."

The moment her fingers touched the hilt, Kia smiled. "The sword, it hums."

"TânOer is not your usual blade," Brodie explained. "Magic was imbued in its steel during the creation. Then Dal and Ellspeth linked their powers in its final blessing." He shrugged. "I had planned on giving it to Denai, but she prefers wood and her sister Elendl is like her mother who prefers the short sword. Dal said he already had a special long sword, so TânOer is mine, at least for now." He left unsaid the final conversation with the archmage who said to keep TânOer close. That although telling the future was not his specialty, he knew that someday Brodie would need the power that resided within the sword.

Kia stood waiting, her fingers lightly touching the hilt. For a heartbeat, a dulcet note sounded from the blade.

Pleasure filled Brodie's frame. The sword accepted Kia. Otherwise the hum would have been a warning, not a welcome. "Like the fàlaire stallion who chooses his rider, the sword chooses who can wield it. Except for the archmage and Lady Ellspeth no one can use TânOer without my permission to do so." He leaned forward. "You heard the chord. I think he likes you."

Brodie left unsaid. *And so do I.*

Each night between the evening meal and moonrise, the lessons continued. Brodie looked forward to the time with Kia, even though they weren't alone. The prospective students watched and when they also expressed an interest, Brodie had them gather branches. This time it wasn't for the fire, but to create wooden swords.

"I want a real blade," the oldest of the boys said. "I can't fight with wood."

"Just because they are wood, doesn't mean they can't do damage," Brodie cautioned. "Come, it is time for your lesson. You can use my short sword and I'll use your wooden one."

The youth's expression told he recognized there was something wrong with the deal, but accepted it anyway. No sooner did he take the sword than he attacked in a flurry of wild swings. Brodie took a step back, then another, leading the boy off balance. A swat on his opponent's bottom with the flat side of the wooden practice sword sent the boy sprawling.

"See?"

"Not fair," the boy groused. "Didn't hurt."

The posture rubbed Brodie. Normally, he smiled at the second-turn student mindset. *I'm not in the mood and this one isn't skilled enough for the "I know everything" attitude.* Extending a hand, he grabbed the youth's wrist and pulled him to his feet. He fought to keep the smile off his face when the boy hissed in pain. "The bruise will fade in a day or two. Until then I suggest using an extra blanket as a cushion." His tone softened. "Would you like another lesson?"

The youth shook his head and backed away to join the line of those watching.

* * *

The early morning mist shrouded the valley and penetrated Brodie's fleece-lined, elk-skin coat. He glanced at the frost-covered pile of furs, barely recognizable as Kia's sleeping body. A neat circle of small humps on the other side of the fire showed the future mages' locations. Beyond were the larger mounds of the fàlaire. When he turned back to his examination of the forest below the cliff, the gray veil had lifted. Brodie searched the granite wall opposite his position for some indication of Clan Daimh's village. But the native stone of the clan's cottages created a natural camouflage against the steep rock face and the dwellings remained hidden. The morning's cloud-filled sky obscured any sign of chimney smoke. Only by sighting along the sentinel rocks at the head of the trail could he determine the outline of the large building that served as dormitory and gathering place.

So lost in his reflection, he failed to notice Kia and the others had risen, until the smell of caffa and toasted sweet bread brought a rumble from the pit of his stomach.

"Will we reach the clanhold today?"

Brodie stiffened at the voice close to his ear, despite the softness of Kia's tone. "We'll be there in a candlemark. We made good time and I figure we can let the fàlaire rest until tomorrow morning."

Breakfast completed and everyone back in the saddle, he gave the traditional trader command, "Roll out."

As if eager for the shelter of a warm barn and a bait of grain, the fàlaire surpassed their previous speed. Landmarks passed in a blur and well before the estimated candlemark they pulled up in front of the large double doors of the main hall of Clan Daimh. The doors swung open and a woman stood on the threshold. Her gray hair

58

hung over her shoulders, unrestrained by knots of rank. Although her appearance was that of someone well past seven decades, she radiated the strength of someone turns younger. "Welcome to Clan Daimh. Our fare is modest but filling. You are welcome to share it."

Brodie smiled in recognition of the speaker and quickly dropped to the ground. Hurried steps carried him to Kia's side. A kick freed her feet from the stirrups. After a swing to bring her leg over the pommel, she slid into his waiting arms, but pulled away as soon as her feet hit the ground. Together they turned to face the speaker who had been joined by more clansmen including four groups which appeared to be families. The rest of my charges, Brodie guessed.

He turned to the waiting woman. "Chieftain Eilidh, this is Kiansel, daughter of Forsom and sister of the current Oracle of Givneh."

"Hallooo." The call rolled down the valley.

Brodie's hand grabbed at the hilt of his sword only to have the motion stop even as it began. "It's a friend," he said in a low aside to Kia. "I'm sorry, Eilidh, I didn't know Barris was joining us."

The older woman smiled. "The archmage sent word the other day. I was going to tell you once everyone was settled." She waved at the watching students. "You might as well get down and untie your packs. That way you'll be ready to go into the hall when Barris gets here."

Loud hoof falls announced the new arrival as he rounded the last of the rock cairns that flanked the path to the clanhold. Foam lathered the horse's neck and sides and flew from its mane. Mud caked its legs. Its rider didn't look in much better shape. His clothes appeared soaked from an unplanned river crossing. Brodie remembered the last creek they forded and how quickly the water was rising. *We barely made it across and Barris must have tried it candlemarks later.*

The horse stopped and hung its head between splayed legs. Its rider swung down and immediately loosened the girth strap. A bow acknowledged Kiansel and the waiting clanswoman.

Brodie felt a surge of heat at the attention the mage paid Kia. Then breathed a prayer of thanks that the jealousy vanished as quickly as it came. *Barris is a friend—and a mage. If Kia chooses him, I have to be happy for both of them.*

"Sorry, Mistress Eilidh," Barris said. "It took me longer to get here than I expected." He shook his head and water flew from the reddish-blond curls. "I didn't want to miss Brodie so I couldn't wait out the storm in the traveler's cave shelter." Now a wry smile raised a lip. "Your winter storms are so strong I don't think anyone other than your son could have turned it aside."

"Well, you're here now, Barris." The clanswoman looked at the sky. "We all better get inside or we'll look like you." She gestured towards the massive wooden doors of the hall. "Time enough for introductions before the fire." Several youths stepped forward, desire on their faces. "Go ahead, boys. You may take the horses into the stable. Rub them down and give them a bait of grain." She called out a name. "Be sure to walk Barris' mount to cool him down."

Barris, a smile on his face, extended a hand to Brodie. "Good to see you again, old friend. I'm glad you haven't left yet. The archmage didn't know when you would head out to the Council Isle and I wanted to be sure to catch you. I'll be accompanying you at least as far as Montrat."

"Not if you stay out here talking," Eilidh interrupted.

Hefting his valise, Brodie nodded at Barris' unencumbered hands. "Most of my material is still in my room here at the clanhold. I had planned on spending a few sevenday, but Dal wants me back at the school for the recognition ceremony." His shrug conveyed no information. Yet Brodie caught the other man's quick glance at Kia.

Better get it over with, Brodie thought. "Kiansel, this ruffian that looks like a drenched rat is Barris." He dropped his voice to a conspiratorial whisper. "Don't let his appearance fool you. He's the archmage's first apprentice—and a good friend."

Barris bowed to Kia with a "Greetings, my fair lady," and when he rose, proffered his arm. "Shall we go in?"

Heat burned along Brodie's collar and this time it was harder to push down. *It is going to be a long trip.*

Curiosity added its own note. *Why has Barris been recalled? What trouble does Dal expect? And does it concern Kia?*

Chapter Seven

The first rays of the dawning greeted Relliq. He spent the entire night searching in the scrying bowl for Kia. No matter how much he called upon the power of the full moon, her image had refused to appear for two days. Even the chicken blood he had snitched from the butcher didn't help. The instructions in the book hidden in Ysbail's office didn't specify what type of creature's blood the spell required. Again, he cursed the cryptic notes that failed to provide the information he needed.

"It is not my fault I can't locate Kia," he hissed at the walls. "It is as if she is within a circle of impenetrable runes that shield her from me." Yet he knew that she was not that trained a mage to accomplish the task. The image of a man shimmered into being. "The smith is a non-tal," Relliq said, referring to his intended victim by his occupation rather than name. "Someone else is helping Kiansel." *But who? If the archmage is keeping her from me, he will be the first to feel my wrath.*

Four more aborted tries yielded no better results. A quick look at the street outside showed the town not yet rising. No smoke wafted from the chimney of the baker's oven. No children chased chickens from their coop so they could gather the eggs. Now would be a good time to search Ysbail's office, he decided. She is still three days ride away. "And I have the spell to shield me," he chortled. "The healer never expected me to find that, let alone use it."

Stuffing a few things into a leather satchel to hold whatever treasures he found, he wrapped himself in an actual cloak as protection against the early morning's chill.

A muttered incantation to avoid detection from both human and animals, including the dogs that freely roamed the town, and he headed across the village.

A check of the stable and the paddock beyond showed no sign of the blue roan mare Ysbail customarily rode. As he suspected, the healer had not yet returned and was still at an outlying village where several children had come down with a fever and red spots all over their bodies. The youngest of them had just celebrated his ninth birthday a season earlier.

Ysbail wanted me to accompany her, to search for the cave the children had been exploring. "As if I have nothing better to do than trek through the desert looking for holes in a rock," he growled. "Then she said it was 'well within my powers'. As if I care if it was good training in tracking down causes of a disease. I don't plan on caring for sniffling babies or crippled oldsters for the rest of my days."

Loud barks from behind pulled Relliq from his reverie. He realized inattention had weakened the spell, enabling a dog to sense unusual movement. The incantation only blocked vision, enabling the dog to track him by his voice.

Relliq waited until the animal closed, then kicked. The blow missed what he now saw was a puppy, only sending dirt into its face. "Go away, you noisy whelp. Or you will get a kick in the ribs." Whether it was the threat or the dirt, the puppy gave a half-growl and turned to chase an errant chicken.

The rest of the walk to the healer's office was uneventful. Working the latchkey, he pushed open the door. "Mistress?" he called out softly. No response meant as he had suspected that Ysbail had not yet returned. Practiced moves replaced the rope and peg through the hole so it appeared the office was still secure.

Quick steps took him through the public area of the office and into the backroom where the healer mixed her potions and created the poultices of her trade. Ignoring the cabinets and boxes he had already searched, he headed straight for the bookshelves and removed a small, wooden box that served as a bookend. A twist removed the lid. Crystals and polished stones caught the light and winked at him. "These will do nicely to embellish the hilt of my master's knife," he chuckled. "I will leave her the box." With that, he removed a velvet bag from his pack and dumped the crystals and stones inside.

A scan of the stack of messages on her desk revealed little news he had not already discovered. The crumpled corner of a sheet of paper stuck out from beneath a ledger piqued Relliq's curiosity. *Why would Ysbail feel the need to hide this?*

Silently he read the note. Make arrangements for quarters suitable for head of Clan Daimh, two escorts and a party of 10 mixed boys and girls. "Now I know why I can't track Kia," Relliq cursed. "The archmage is of Clan Daimh and he must have given his mother a protective token." *Not only is Kiansel among them, she is coming to me.* Warmth at the welcome he would give her at Montrat and during the journey to the Isle of Mages dampened his collar. Lists of items he would need for the trip—and for the spells to implement his plans for Kia—quickly filled a sheet of paper.

At the mention of his target, the pouch containing the crystals glowed, pulling his attention from his travel plans. A tug opened the bag to reveal the stones inside. One crystal's colors shifted through the rainbow. Deft movements wrapped a string around it. The stone swung to the end of its tether and pulled Relliq towards the map case. His pointer dropped onto the second shelf down and he opened the indicated drawer to expose the map. Holding the string between two fingers, he suspended it over the sketch.

"Stone of power, map to earth.
Show me the location of the one of worth."

The stone wavered over the map, gently swinging back and forth. As the swings grew wider, he shifted his hand until the thread spun in a tight circle. The magical pointer whirled a final time, then dropped onto the map and stood upright. Relliq leaned in close. The spot marked a divergence in the mountain trail. One of the passes would bring the caravan to Montrat. The other took it on the opposite side of the dunes.

"Come to me." His whisper held the authority of a command.

The crystal dimmed but when he focused more power into it a figure appeared.

Relliq's heart raced expecting to see Kia. Instead, the image of an old, gray-haired woman imbued the heart of the stone. The note pertaining to quarters told him her identity—Eilidh, Chieftain of Clan Daimh. Her arm swung in the direction of the other pass.

"No," he yelled. "Come to me." Even as he watched, she turned her horse's head to the more westerly of the trails—the one that would bypass Montrat. *If they won't come to me, I will go to them.*

Noises from outside announced the first of the tradesmen heading to the center of town to fire up the ovens to bake the bread and cook the meats for the day's customers. Relliq's mental calculation showed he had two candlemarks before the merchants opened for business and he could gather what he needed for the trail. "I might as well look at a few more of the books to kill the time."

One by one, he pulled the aged, leather-wrapped tomes from the shelves. Some were just ledgers of daily activities or lists of who had what ailment and the treatment recommended. The ones Relliq lingered over contained detailed instructions of what incantations could be worked under what kind of moon. From these he jotted down notes in his own journal for later research.

He reached for a book and found his hand forced towards another. Whispered words of a reveal spell from his notebook showed not the empty spot of the shelf he originally saw, but a thick volume. None of the other books were so protected and curiosity overrode caution. It took several tries, but he managed to break the magic seal that prevented the book from being read.

Again he repeated the incantation. This time when a flick of his finger lifted the cover, tight lettering scrolled across the first page. Deciphered it said Book 138-74 and the date of the first full moon of the turn. Realization that it was an official journal and so important it had to be protected against casual access increased Relliq's interest. Fast scans through the entries ended at what appeared to be an evaluation. His finger stopped at, "No further training should be provided. Recommend his powers be bound at soonest opportunity."

Red obscured his vision. His hands shook. "How dare she, a mere healer, pass judgement on me!" A tug tore the page out of the ledger. Only after ripping it into tiny shreds did the rage recede at all. "I'll show her. Bind my powers? She will be the one grovelling at my feet for my blessing." Tightened lips helped add to his control. "Which I may or may not give her."

Coherent thought returned as the fury left.

Kia is not coming to Montrat, coming to you, reality warned.

Desire answered the negative thought. Then go to her.

The sound of paper crinkling pulled Relliq's attention to his hands. He had picked up the list without even realizing it. Carefully smoothing the wrinkles out of the sheet, he folded it and slipped it into his pocket. Soon he had his supplies organized. An internal debate warred whether to leave the door open to Ysbail's office or to leave no sign of his visit. Putting everything back into its place, he tried one of the new spells found in the healer's notebook. After the sparks dissipated, there was no evidence that he had ever entered the office. Quick steps took him to the door. No running child or waiting oldster darkened the threshold. Deft movements wrapped the rope of the latchkey around the lockbar. A tug and it slipped into its place without a sound.

I'll stop by the baker and break my fast, he thought. Then arrange for the supplies for the trip. The noonday sun cast squat shadows of the people hurrying along. With the shortened candlemarks of daylight, there wouldn't be enough time to leave today. Instead, he decided to leave first thing in the morning. *And still be gone before Ysbail knows I've left.*

What about the village? conscience asked. What if someone gets sick? Gets the spotted fever?

Not my concern, pride answered. Let a healer deal with it. I'm a mage.

* * *

Kia swayed in rhythm to the mare's movements. She had learned to keep her gaze focused on a point just beyond the animal's head. At the speed they were moving, the woods to the side of the trail blurred into a mass of green. Despite the fàlaires' fast gallop, even the youngest of the party was now able to handle the pace.

Brodie called a halt at mid-day for a quick meal and to allow the fàlaire a breather. "The girls and I will be over there," Kia said, pointing to a sun-warmed rock.

A smile on their faces, Brodie and Barris bowed. "As you wish, m'lady. Your meal will be ready in a few moments."

The very unlady-like snort that came from Eilidh's direction told of her amusement.

Early mornings and hard riding took their toll and Kia allowed the warmth and serenity to lull her into a half sleep.

"Come to me, little wizardling." The alluring call repeated. Rising to her feet, Kia headed towards the woods. Her skirt swished through the tall grass. Its sound echoed the summons.

"Kia, no!"

Brodie's yell from behind her penetrated the meditative state. Still she continued on, unable to resist the order to go to the woods.

Cries of "Kiansel, come back" fought with the other summons. Something grabbed at her, prevented her from her destination. Kicks and slaps failed to remove the impediment. "Let me go."

Cold steel pressed against her skin. In a flash, the thrall that held her vanished. "Where am I?"

"You're safe now." She turned at Brodie's voice to stare into his tortured eyes.

Eilidh arrived leaning heavily on Barris' arm. "Are you all right, my dear?" Anger and fear colored her tone.

A shake of her head cleared out the remaining cobwebs and Kia looked around at the worried faces. "I'm not sure. Someone or something called me. I think it was my stalker." Her shoulders shook within Brodie's embrace. "I don't know if it is because we are closer now than when I was at the temple, or if I am just extra tired from the road." A gasp escaped. "I couldn't resist."

"Well, you are safe now, Kiansel," the clanswoman reassured. "When we stop for the evening, Barris will place double wards around the camp." She looked at Brodie. "I suggest Kia sleep with TânOer tonight."

Kia held up her hands to ward off the sheath Brodie held out. "I can't take TânOer, Brodie. It has chosen you."

Brodie's smile warmed and reinforced the offer, even though Kia knew his attachment to the blade and the sacrifice Eilidh had ordered. "TânOer likes you, Kia. I don't need it tonight. My short sword is sufficient for sentry duty."

Eilidh looked at the boys and girls standing in a line with the horses. "If you're well enough to ride, Kiansel, I think we should leave now." Her eyes unfocused, then just as quickly their intelligence returned. "When we stop for the night, I'll ask Barris to work with you so you can use TânOer to boost your powers if need be."

Kia pushed away. She staggered a step, then recovered her balance. Barris took her arm and headed with her towards the horses.

"Walk with me, Brodie." The anxious edge in the clanswoman's voice told Brodie she knew something.

"Eilidh, did Dal tell you about Kia's stalker?"

"No, but that explains the dark miasma I see around Kiansel."

Brodie tried to see what Eilidh did, but all he saw was Kia talking softly with Barris as they walked. "Don't worry about the shadow around her." Eilidh's reassurance failed to lessen Brodie's swirling thoughts. "Kiansel is young and strong enough to bear it for the few days until we reach the isle. And Dal and Ellspeth will clear it off once we get there."

Gray hair swirled with the shake of Eilidh's head. "I'll apologize to Barris later, but I'm taking us on a shortcut through the mountains. I know that he wanted to spend a meal with his mother but Dal messaged that Ysbail is out on a healing mission."

Brodie hoped his silence would encourage the elder clanswoman to say more. For a long moment, she watched the retreating Kia and Barris. "The portents say avoid the town. Although they gave no clue as to why." The stare she pinned on Kia sent a chill up his spine. Her voice took on a tone of command and a hardness Brodie had never heard before. "We're going to use a trail that doesn't go near Montrat."

Despite her age, Eilidh set the pace. The day passed in bursts of speed and short breaks to allow the slowly recovering Kia additional time to rest. Every time Brodie looked back, the clanswoman rode alongside Kia. For the last section of the trail, Barris took over the scouting position while Brodie brought up the rear. No sooner had they stopped for the night and the boys gathered wood for the fire, than Eilidh ordered the fàlaire brought in close and no one to go beyond the marker showing where Barris paced out the protective runes.

A sense of gathering magic came over the area. Brodie watched Barris spin in a circle in front of the fire. No matter how hard he looked, he couldn't see the runes. Yet, he knew Barris formed a protective dome around the camp.

I wish I could do that, he thought. Then ruthlessly suppressed it. No sense dwelling on what can't be. Sparks from the flintstone in his hand set the kindling on fire. A whoosh and the cookfire blossomed into flame. All during the meal he kept one eye on the woods and the other on

Kia. *I won't be caught unaware again.* Across the campfire, he noticed Barris doing the same.

The meal over, he paced the markers set by Barris. From time to time he looked over his shoulder to the fire where the mage worked with Kia as she practiced the incantation to access the power of TânOer. He smiled at how a word from Eilidh clarified the instructions or provided support when the task seemed too hard to do. Unlike the other times when a wave of jealousy rose at the interaction between the two, this time Brodie was happy that Kia had found a friend.

The lesson ended when Eilidh declared Kia had done enough for the day. With TânOer at her side, Kia curled up beside the fire.

"I'm going to strengthen the runes around the camp one more time," Barris said at Brodie's shoulder. "Then I'll take the first watch."

I guess I better take advantage of Barris' offer, Brodie thought, and get some sleep. The urge to move far and fast sapped strength from both man and beast. Beyond the fire, Barris paced the camp. Instead of returning to his bedroll near the boys, he stopped next to Kia facing outward.

Unable to watch, Brodie joined the boys in the sleeping furs. One's eyelids parted at his approach. "Go back to sleep," he whispered. "It's not your time to stand the watch." After the youth's lids closed, Brodie wrapped his bedroll around his shoulders and lay down facing the night. Despite his plan to stay awake, sleep overcame him. Whispers of, "Come to me, little wizardling," haunted his dreams.

Chapter Eight

Relliq's horse balked at the solid wall of thorn bushes. "No ... no ... no," he yelled. Something beckoned him, something that refused to allow a delay. He had to keep moving forward. A kick in the recalcitrant animal's flanks failed to make the horse move. Even more stubborn than normal, the animal refused to go forward despite repeated commands.

Climbing down, Relliq tugged on the reins. The animal braced its legs and no matter how hard Relliq pulled he couldn't break the deadlock. Tying off the reins on a tree, he followed the invisible beacon. Two steps from the thorn bushes the flicker of purple runes came from within the dense groups of leaves. Poisonous thorns or not, he had to answer the siren call of magic. He reached out, weaving his hand through the finger-length thorns trying to find a way to clear away through the obstruction. Finally, he closed his eyes and muttered an incantation to show him the way.

A soft whisper and the impenetrable wall vanished to reveal a narrow deer trail. Four wagon lengths up the trail, light glinted off a small spot where bare wood showed through the leaves. One of the tree trunks bore the blaze mark used by woodcutters to mark the way home. "Yes," Relliq said. Quick steps took him back to the horse and moments later he urged it ahead. This time, it didn't fight the bit and moved on.

Dusk came and it became harder to see either the blaze marks or the even less frequent mage runes forcing him to once again leave the saddle and lead the horse. Each time he measured his length in the dirt, Relliq cursed the archmage and his ancestors. His vow to take over the rule of the Council Isle hardened.

A stumble forced him to grab an overhanging branch. He looked to see what tripped him, but instead saw a steep drop and at its bottom—rushing water. His pulse raced. Two more steps and he would have slid into the rapids and been swept down river. "Not again," came out in a growl. He had already lost half the day backtracking when the wagon trail ended at an unfordable river. And now the latest deer trail had done the same. Options on how to find the hidden trails through the forest to the isle came to mind. The map he had studied at Montrat didn't show the hazards placed there by the wizards. And to make matters worse, he kept losing the locator cord that was supposed to lead him to the invisible bridge.

"I can't ask for help from the archmage," Relliq told the wind. It seemed to laugh at him. The wizard would discover that Ysbail had not given permission to leave. It was bad enough the plan to take an extra horse from the Montrat stable failed. None of the horses except his would cross the boundary of the pasture. Even then he had to leap the fence. Long days in the saddle, short nights under the stars and cold meals made for rough travel.

I have to catch the caravan before they pass through the vale. That is the only way I'll reach the Isle of Mages. Yet again, he cursed the clanswoman for not stopping at Montrat.

The struggle through the forest continued the rest of the day. When he stopped in a small clearing to water the horse, he decided to give the animal a longer rest. "And my bottom, too," he muttered to the bird watching from an overhead branch. Full dark in the mountains came quick this time of year and he could do nothing until moonrise. After a meal of cold meat and bread that had been squashed into crumbs from the rigors of travel, he watched the sunset. Well-practiced movements placed hobbles around the horse's front legs and a twist tied the reins around his wrist as a warning if something spooked the animal. His preparations done, Relliq sat down against a tree with the intention to just stay a candlemark. His eyes closed and he slipped into the cottony warmth of a deep sleep.

Evening's chill and the horse's sudden jerk of the reins pulled him to full awareness.

The rest that should have refreshed him and the horse had done little for either. The gelding no longer stood with its head hanging down but had collapsed onto the ground. Relliq's initial instinct to kick the animal to its feet vanished with the realization the horse couldn't go any further. "I can't ride him into the ground," he groused. "The only replacement is my own two feet. And, I'd never catch up with Kia and her party."

Maybe Kia isn't having any better luck, he prayed. After all, their group is being led by an old woman and a non-tal. Gloating at their perceived misfortune, he pulled out the scrying crystal. It dropped on the map at a spot well ahead of where Relliq expected the group to be. I can't believe how fast their horses are moving, he thought. But at least the crystal will allow me to follow them. Holding the map before the teapot-sized fire, he located Kia's position. A finger traced from his target back to his own location. Excitement coursed through his veins. Not far from where he was, there was a bridge over the river—and a trail that would shave candlemarks off his travels.

Morning came and with it a repeat of the previous day. The horse kept fighting the bit. Relliq rubbed a shoulder still sore from being pulled when the animal had tried to take off the night before. Frequent dismounts to lead the horse through the rough terrain only added to the discomfort. Shoes wet from splashing through rivulets and ankles swollen from tripping over tree roots added to the ardours of the trip. And each time he fell, he lost a hold of his tracking spell.

Sunlight ahead indicated an open space just beyond the next clump of trees. Good, Relliq thought. I can finally make some time. A wagon-length within the treeline the horse balked again, tossing Relliq to the ground. Tendrils of grass wrapped around his legs. Others snatched at his hands. Curses slipped from his lips. He had tripped yet another of the wizards' defenses. Four swings of his sword freed him enough he could scramble to his knees. No sooner did he regain his feet than the grass yanked him back and he measured his length in the dirt. "Enough of this," he growled.

"By the power of the earth and sky,
Grass turn brown, wither and die,
Let me pass, I command,
For those of power rule this land."

A firm grasp on both his locator spell and one against the attacking tendrils, he gathered up the reins and hesitantly took a step out of the safety of the trees. At the far end of the meadow, a column of smoke rose skyward.

Relliq's pulse quickened. The crystal showed a line of horses pulling away. The dissipating smoke obscured the faces of the riders. "No," he muttered. "Not smoke. Magic is blocking my sight." He swung into the saddle, suppressing a gasp at the pain. A kick to the horse's flanks got it moving, then he whipped the reins from one side to the other. The horse squealed and broke into a gallop.

"Faster, faster," Relliq yelled.

At the far end of the meadow, the small dots rapidly grew smaller and smaller. *The caravan.* They didn't appear to be moving quickly, yet no matter how fast his horse galloped, he did not close on the ones they chased.

"I will not be denied," Relliq cried. In response to the sting of the reins, the horse staggered into a faster pace. Foam flew from its neck. Its breath came in laboured gasps. The distance to the other horses finally shortened enough to reveal sunlight dancing in brown curls on a rider in the midst of the group.

"Yes," Relliq crowed. "There is my prize." His strident "Move, you bag of bones," was accompanied by more use of the reins as a whip until his arms hurt.

"Wait up," he yelled to the retreating forms. No response answered his cry. Gathering a nugget of magic in his hand, he threw it at the group ahead of him. The flare rose to the clouds, then arced back as a cascade of sparks. But it achieved his desired effect, those he pursued stopped.

Using the extra time, he allowed the horse to pause and draw deep gulps of air down its throat. Finally, it moved forward at his urging.

All during the ride to the caravan, he fought the fear that they would move on. Breaths held too long came in gushes. They weren't just waiting, he realized. They were preparing to meet him. What appeared to be groups of boys and girls formed a line. Two men and an older woman had pulled their horses between him and the youths.

* * *

Lust… frustration… anger.

The emotions rolled over Brodie, a massive wave that threatened to submerge him. Closing his eyes, he whispered a prayer to his ancestors asking for strength. As quickly as they had come, the rage and frustration vanished. What they left behind was not much easier to withstand—the sense of unrestrained desire. Deep breaths returned a measure of control.

Scans of those riding ahead of him showed nothing untoward. No one appeared visibly upset. So who was the source of the mental disturbance? Brodie shifted his gaze to Kiansel. He didn't know how, but one fact was irrefutable. Kia was the target.

The stallion tensed beneath Brodie. Its ears swiveled. Fighting the reins, the animal spun on his haunches to face their backtrack. Even before Wirake nickered the warning, Brodie knew the approaching rider was the source of the emotions.

Brodie's piercing whistle stopped the caravan. His hand gesture sent Kia to wait with the students. Barris moved into position at Brodie's right while Eilidh moved her mount to the left. A fast scan evaluated their potential as a fighter. The clan chieftain's hand rested lightly on the hilt of her sword. Dal's mother may have a few turns under her belt, Brodie thought. But he'd felt her strength. Barris might be young, but his magic had already been battle-tested.

The approaching figure raced through the tall grass on a path that would intercept the caravan.

A sharp pain rippled down Brodie's arm, forcing his attention from the intruder as he looked for a wound. However, no blade stabbed or magic rope entangled his arm. One by one, he forced the fingers of his clenched fist open. Quick shakes to loosen his hand and he grasped TânOer's hilt. Despite the thick sheath that protected the blade, he felt the power within the steel waiting to be summoned. *Even if I can't use magic,* Brodie thought, *Barris can tap the sword's inherent magic. And, even as mere steel, TânOer is a considerable weapon.*

The sword hummed an encouraging note.

Still something about the approaching rider set off a warning and Brodie found himself pulling the sword a finger-length out of the scabbard and shoving it back in. A glance at Barris showed the mage was having the same reaction. *Barris is the most easy-going person I've ever met,* Brodie thought. Yet his friend was clenching and unclenching his fists.

Wirake shifted beneath Brodie. The change, although slight, signalled the stallion's readiness to do whatever Brodie ordered. The fàlaire Barris rode pranced in place as if ready to charge.

Brodie's thoughts raced. *Fàlaire won't attack a person unless provoked or in protection of a member of their herd. And since Wirake is herd leader here, he is the one Barris' mount is reacting to. But why?* Once again, Kia came to mind. *Is Wirake protecting her because Dal ordered it? Or for me?*

A foam-covered horse staggered up. As soon as it stopped, the animal hung its head down. Its rider glared at it before turning the glower on Brodie. The man's arrogance was almost palpable.

Ancestors beyond the veil, please give me strength.

First impressions aren't always accurate, Brodie thought. *Except when they are.* Hiding his distaste of

76

someone who would mistreat an animal, he greeted the newcomer. "Well met, traveler. You don't see many in these parts."

"I am Relliq, special envoy to the Archmage and bring him an important message from Ysbail, healer mage of Montrat."

At the mention of Barris' mother, Brodie tried to send the other man a message. He had communicated with the mage before, but only when Barris had established the link through the Cyrcle of One. *I have to try. I don't dare send a signal and alert Relliq.* With no other options, he took a breath. *Barris, don't betray your true identity.*

A faint, "Agreed," from both Eilidh and Barris returned along the ethereal link.

Relliq scowled. "I will accompany you." A hard tug brought his horse's head up. The following kick had the animal staggering forward. The direction took him to a single target—towards Kia.

Resisting the urge to smash the smirk from Relliq's face, Brodie kneed the stallion which shifted position to block the other man's way.

* * *

Sweat ran down Relliq's back. The need to possess Kia was stronger in person than when he viewed her in the scrying bowl. He glared at the horse that now kept him from his target. All the earlier frustration he had felt on the trail rushed back. *How dare a non-tal, and a smith at that, refuse me?*

That one serves as bodyguard. It is his duty to protect Kiansel, reality urged.

But I will have her, Relliq vowed. No one will stop me.

A strange look crossed the face of the elderly woman he had identified as the archmage's mother.

Panic raced along Relliq's nerves. *It feels as if she is reading my thoughts. But how? She is a non-tal.*

She is also the archmage's mother, reality corrected. She might not be a full-fledged mage, but that doesn't mean she doesn't have some limited latent ability. After all, where did the archmage get his powers?

"So, you have a message for my son," she said. Her tone implied she expected a response—and the truth.

An internal debate as to whether to answer truthfully or not lasted less than a heartbeat. *They will find out I have powers soon enough, so I might as well admit it.* "I also journey to the Isle of Mages for the recognition ceremony."

If any signals passed between the three in front of him, Relliq couldn't tell. However, the one blocking his way relaxed. "Then I guess you had better join us." The other man glanced at the sun. "However, it is getting late. I want to make an early morning start for the final push to the isle, so we'll make camp." He gestured at Relliq's mount. "And to be honest, Relliq, your horse looks like it needs a rest, as well as food and drink. The grass here is thick and rich for good for grazing and there is a spring just inside the woods so the horses can be watered."

* * *

Relliq alternated his attention between the two men and the campfire where the archmage's mother directed Kia and the female students in preparing a meal. While he had pegged Brodie's position in the caravan, something about Barris tickled at Relliq's senses. And a troubling thought kept surfacing. *What if Brodie is more than a bodyguard? What is he to Kia?*

The urge to grab Kia and drag her into the woods ravaged Relliq's frame. It made it hard to maintain his distance. No, reality cautioned. Before this group, one has to present his best self.

If Kia likes commoners, I'll lower myself to that level...At least for now.

Rising, he walked to where Brodie and Barris had spread out a map on a large stone. "Gentlemen, since we will be traveling together, I feel I should share the workload." At their attention, he gestured at the horses cropping grass. "I can share a watch tonight."

"Thank you, Relliq," Brodie interjected, "but Barris and I have some planning yet to do. We'll be rising early and moving fast tomorrow, so I suggest you turn in early. Barris and I can handle sentry duty."

Although the tone did not reflect any hidden meaning, it still brought heat to Relliq's neck. *Every time I try to get near Kia, that one blocks me. And now he rejects my offer of help?*

One plan after another on how to clear the other men out of the way occupied him during the meal and the rest of the evening. Sleeping potions will do it, he finally decided. And I'll use the one against the other. First, the smith. He may not have any powers, but he is too handy with that sword for his will to be left unbound.

Using the excuse of a moment of privacy, he walked to the edge of the woods and into the treeline where he could observe the others without being seen. He cast a spell of obedience and watched the purple haze surround the girl filling the water jugs. "Take the pill from your pocket and put it in Brodie's mug." When she didn't obey, he repeated the command. He kept up the mantra as the girl's hand moved inexorably towards the mug.

The haze shattered in a hail of sparks that shimmered for a heartbeat, then vanished. With a soft, "Oooh," the girl's hand jerked. Although he couldn't see it, Relliq knew the pill had gone flying. "At least," he snarled, "no one will see it in the tall grass." More disturbing was what happened to his spell. Someone had to have cast a counter.

But who may have done it? He dismissed the students. They were too young and too untrained to even recognize the compulsion spell, let alone break it. As he had earlier, he considered the archmage's mother. However, he realized she had been looking in the other direction when he cast the spell. And besides, she had no real power, he reassured himself. His gaze shifted to rest on Barris. As he had most of the evening, the other man sat on a saddle on the other side of the fire talking to Kia. The image came with the realization that unlike the others, Barris had only introduced himself with his name, nothing else.

Worry rose its head. Could Barris be a mage?

Arrogance took over the internal conversation. Even if he is a mage, he is at most untrained. No threat.

While the one thought brought reassurance, the sight of the other man with Kia returned the fire to Relliq's veins. A spell from Ysbail's book came to mind. I can modify it to my needs, he thought. Gathering his magic, he pictured it a glowing ball of blue, neatly balanced in his hand.

"Powers hidden, powers shown,
Barris to obey me alone.
No girl be thine, leave her now,
Ignore Kia until in your tomb."

On the last word, he tossed the ball. Blue ribbons unraveled from the sphere. They hovered for four heartbeats, then flew towards Barris to encircle him in a spiral of shimmering threads.

"Yes," Relliq breathed. "Now he will obey me... and Kia will be mine."

What was supposed to be an impenetrable web of obedience dissipated into nothingness, leaving not even a single spark in its wake. Curses spewed from Relliq's mouth. *Barris had only flicked a finger.*

Deep breaths to calm down and he reconsidered his plans. I will have to wait for the camp to settle before I try for Kia, he decided. This time the compulsion will work. I will summon her to the woods. I have the way of it now.

The sense of someone's eyes upon him pulled him from his reflections. Relliq looked up and saw Brodie looking straight at him.

He can't see me in the deepening shadows. Still, there is no need to take a chance.

Careful steps took him through the trees to where the students gathered. Without a word, he started gathering up limbs for the fire. His senses extended to their max, he listened to two of the boys excitedly talking about studying with the Oracle of Givneh.

"The Way is different from what the Oracle teaches," the taller of the brothers said.

"I don't care," the younger of the pair said. "As long as it gets me out of that stifling village. There weren't no teacher, no bard, no nothing."

"There are different ways to study," Relliq interjected. "For example, Ysbail likes to use potions and herbs. Her poultices take the sting out of the bites of the desert bugs that are near Montrat. Whereas, the Oracle uses the power of people to accomplish his goals."

"You worked with Ysbail?"

The look of respect on their faces returned Relliq to his normal attitude. "Yes, I taught her much." He dropped his voice. "She is a healer, and I am so much more." He gestured at the wooden sword stuck in another of the boy's belt. "You don't need that. It is worthless against magic."

No word was spoken, but the boy's tight expression made it clear he didn't agree.

He was older than the rest, reality whispered. Too old to learn something new. Focus on the others.

"Got work to do," the youth responded. He walked off, picking up branches as he went. Relliq watched him head towards the fire.

"And so do you."

Relliq spun at the voice at his shoulder.

"Hurry up and gather the rest of the wood," Brodie ordered. He pinned a glare on Relliq. "Everyone is turning in early."

The image of Brodie slowly sinking in a pit of quicksand formed in Relliq's mind. Ducking his head to hide his smile, he followed the boys back to the fire to dump his armload of branches atop the pile already collected.

* * *

Kia pulled the sleeping fur around her shoulders and scanned the camp. Brodie's slow paces patrolled the outer barrier. Low snores came from where Barris lay on the other side of the fire. Dal's mother sat on a saddle, finishing the embroidery on hairbands she said were naming day gifts for her granddaughters. A final check on the students and Kia lay down next the campfire.

The sense of gathering magic pulled her from her sleep. Her lips moved in a silent tracking spell. A silver cord went to the edge of the woods, then dipped down to kiss a boulder just beyond the wards Barris placed around the camp.

Nothing is there.

At least nothing vision can see, she corrected.

Another incantation, one her brother had her memorize, flickered into being. A second cord formed, only this time instead of stopping at the boulder, the cord glowed. Brighter and brighter the light became until the shadows beyond the stone withdrew to reveal a figure. Relliq!

Anger and fear mingled, each sending Kia's pulse racing faster. *How dare he spy on me?*

She tried to get up, to walk over and brace him, but her muscles wouldn't move. An attempt to call out to Barris resulted in nothing more than a grunt.

Hope flickered when Barris stretched and rolled over, then was quashed when he curled back under his sleeping fur.

Her gaze rounded the camp looking for help. It settled on Brodie rubbing down his mount. The stallion snuffled and nudged his rider. Ears flicked forward in a warning signal. His head dipped towards Kia, then swiveled at the woods.

Obeying Wirake, Brodie started walking towards the boulder. His steps slowed, then changed direction. A head shake and he resumed his slow walk to the woods.

No, Brodie, don't, Kia tried to cry. You're not a mage, not a match for Relliq. Her heart wept. *I can't help him.*

Another shake of his head came with another direction change. Instead of the slow walk of one sleepwalking, he raced to his sleeping furs.

Power surged through the Cyrcle of One when he pulled the long sword from beneath the bedding.

Yes, Kia cheered. She grabbed the weapon's power. In her mind she saw the blade puncturing the bonds holding her. *Eilidh, help Brodie.* Praying that Dal's mother would hear the silent cry, she repeated the call, throwing all her magic into the summons. Kia held her breath and watched as Eilidh laid her needlework aside and touched Brodie's arm. She couldn't hear what the other woman whispered, but Brodie nodded. And when he rose, he shook Barris awake and together, one with the long sword clearing the way and the other with his dagger restoring the wards, they walked another ritual sealing of the camp.

Kia released a stifled cry.

Eilidh hurried over. "What is the matter, my child? A bad dream?"

"I..." blankness filled Kia's mind. Where just heartbeats before the thoughts were clear, now they were muddy.

Dal's mother looked over to where Relliq walked from the woods. Her gaze darkened. "Do not worry, Kiansel. Tomorrow we cross the invisible bridge. You will be safe on the isle. My son allows no one to control another, talent or not, man or woman."

Chapter Nine

The horse beneath Kia slowed. Not far ahead, the grass turned into a field of boulders. A narrow path, just wide enough for a horse, wove through the piles of rocks. The site was on no maps, yet she knew the bridge to the Isle of Mages lay just beyond the obstruction. It was hard, but she resisted the urge to kick her mount into a ground-eating gallop.

A loud "hello" rolled over the rocks. She looked for the source and saw a line of four people who seemed to just appear. They had to have been there, she decided. Unnoticed and hidden by magic. It appeared nothing lay beyond them but the sky and water. Kia whispered a spell of clarity and saw a transparent bridge. A sense of welcome she hadn't felt outside of the temple warmed her. All the rigors of travel, of Relliq's constant stare, now felt worth it. *We're at the rainbow bridge—at the Isle of Mages.*

Streaks of fire flew from the upraised arms of the tallest of the welcoming party. In a blink, not only did most of the boulders disappear, but the narrow path widened into a smooth road, and the bridge and those on it appeared to grow in stature. No, Kia corrected. They didn't change size; they were in actuality just a few wagon lengths away. The distance had been an illusion to protect the wizard's land from outsiders.

Brodie's signal to dismount came as a welcome change to the saddle. Yet she knew it would have a downside. Before her feet touched the ground, yet another grumble came from Relliq. She waited, watching Brodie to see his response.

To her relief, he merely winked at her. "We'll release the horses that came from the vale to return to the herd. Those that came from Clan Daimh," Kia watched as Brodie pinned Relliq with a glare, "or elsewhere, will be guided to the stable. A wagon will collect the saddles and our possessions."

"Why do I have to walk?" Relliq's growl seemed inordinately loud compared to the setting.

The urge to take Relliq back to the woods and teach him a lesson washed over Kia. She couldn't tell if it came from Brodie or Barris. Ever since Relliq had joined the group, he had bombarded the other men with non-stop complaints about everything from the length of the ride to the roughness of the terrain. "Let me walk the way of the Oracle," Kia whispered. "And save my friend's knuckles."

Relliq's next growl earned him dark looks not only from Barris, but the students and Eilidh as well.

Seeing Eilidh and Barris strip the gear from their mounts, Kia did the same. She rubbed the mare's velvet nose. "Thank you, girl, for allowing me to be your rider. I'll see you later in the stable."

The animal made more comfortable, Kia turned to the welcoming party. A dark-haired man stood with his arm around a silver-haired woman, while two girls Kia estimated to be about fourteen turns waited a few paces to the side. Their features and interactions told there were a family. The well-worn loose breeches, tight vest, and leather neckband the man wore gave the appearance of a tradesman. Or, she corrected, the younger son of a chieftain from the Mtwan Mountain region. *The archmage himself welcomes us.*

Eilidh stepped forward and motioned Kia to join her. "Dal, Ellspeth, may I present Kiansel, daughter of Forsom and sister of Brantly, current holder of the title, Oracle of the Temple of Givneh."

Kia went to kneel only to have her hands clasped in a firm grip and be pulled to her feet. She looked up into Dal's twinkling gaze.

"Welcome, Kiansel, to the Isle of Mages." His low tone seemed to echo in her head before changing to spoken words. A smile tweaked his lips. "I don't know if you remember me. You were quite young when Brantly assumed his mantle, and neither Ellspeth nor I have had much chance to visit in person."

Before she could recover from the force of the archmage's personality, Kia caught the buzz of a conversation between him, his wife, and Eilidh. *And the topic is me. They approve?* Confusion almost broke the contact until the comforting serenity of a benison filled her soul. Even though it came from a new source, the familiarity of the blessing, something she had felt many times before from her brother, strengthened the mental link.

This time Kia had no doubt as to the source. It came from the archmage's lady. "Greetings, Kia," Ellspeth said. "And don't even think about kneeling to me." A smile removed any sting from her words. "Thank you, my dear, for coming." Her gesture took in the rest of those waiting. "Your help with the new students is appreciated. I know your presence comforted their parents."

Now both Dal and Ellspeth projected approval.

Kia bent her head. With her simple, "Thank you," all the fears of the trip to the isle and all the misgivings vanished. *The Isle is where I belong.*

* * *

A loud grumble about walking came from behind the watching students. Turning, Brodie headed towards the sound. He had not even taken two steps before Relliq roughly pulled off the horse's saddle, letting the stirrups scrape the animal. "Stand still, you worthless bag of bones," he growled as foam dropped onto his clothes. "It is bad enough you couldn't keep up with the others. Go back to the mountains." He smacked the horse on the rump and stalked towards the welcoming party. His shoulder brushed Brodie aside. As they had earlier, the fàlaire blocked his path.

Despite the urge to retaliate, the need to check on the horse took precedence. "Wirake will handle Relliq for now," Brodie muttered. He held out a hand and took a step towards Relliq's horse who skittered away.

"Easy boy," Brodie coaxed. Two steps took him to the shivering horse whose eyes whirled in fear. Slowly, Brodie took up the dangling reins. Gentle strokes to the animal's nose and neck calmed it. "Here, let me take this bridle off. You'll be more comfortable."

Although it trembled, it allowed Brodie to remove the bit from its mouth. Now he saw the reason for the horse's reaction to his approach. A hard hand with the reins had cut its mouth. A nod to Barris and Eilidh and a tilt of his head towards Relliq who waited for his introduction satisfied Brodie they would watch the mage. One problem handled, he turned his attention to soothing the shaking animal. When the horse quieted enough, he ran his hands down the horse's shoulder and flanks. It didn't shy away, but gave a low moan of pain. Rivulets of blood rolled down the animal's side. At first he thought a sharp edge of the stirrups had scratched the hide. Closer examination revealed numerous, deep narrow cuts.

Anger at the mistreatment of the horse filled Brodie. A wave got the archmage's attention. Brodie flicked his fingers to point out the whip marks and blood trail to Dal and his lady. She looked up at her husband, who bent to whisper something in her ear. He straightened, gave a miniscule shake of head and the mercenary signal for "later."

Whether the archmage called for assistance from the fàlaire who had claimed him for his rider or Tairneach was just out and about, the large gray stallion trotted up to Relliq's horse. Brodie watched the head stallion of the vale nicker at the smaller horse in what to his ear sounded like a comforting reassurance. A nod of his head towards the path the animals used to go from the pasture to the stable and Tairneach nudged the Montrat horse to walk with him.

Wirake's low whinny summoned the rest of the fàlaire who fell into a line behind him. He looked at Relliq, then back to Brodie. A flick of his ears sent a clear message. I don't trust that one. Should I stay?

"Go on, boy," Brodie called. "I'll be by later with a treat."

A toss of the mane and Wirake led the others in the head stallion's wake.

One task accomplished, Brodie allowed himself to deal with Relliq. His quick steps took him to a spot between the mage and Kia just as Relliq stalked by.

"Outta my way." Relliq's shoulder knocked Brodie so hard he stumbled a step. A step to regain his balance and he shifted to block the mage. Movement captured from the corner of his eye showed Barris sliding into a spot at his shoulder. At least, he thought, I don't have to worry about defending Dal or Ellspeth. Although neither of the pair wore a sword, their magic was more than sufficient to handle Relliq. *Barris and I will not be more than two steps away. And we are armed.*

Brodie fought down a smile and saw that Barris had given into the impulse. The other man's face held a look of anticipation, as if he welcomed a confrontation. Eilidh who had stood quietly by while her son greeted Kia also had an eager expression on her face. So, Brodie thought, Relliq had even annoyed Eilidh. Dal asked me to evaluate the man … and I have.

* * *

Relliq's snarl halted Brodie's musings. "Enough of this." He brushed past the others and stood at the end of the bridge. "Stand aside. I am Relliq, master mage from Montrat with a message for the archmage."

When those in front of him only paid minor interest, he hardened his tone. "My business is urgent. Either summon the archmage or take me to him."

The woman, whose name he hadn't caught, turned her attention to him. His skin rippled beneath her head to toe scan as if her vision pierced his scuffed leather vest to discern his true thoughts. The look the man beside her turned on him was worse. A gasp escaped Relliq's lips. It felt like the wizard stripped away all pretense to reveal the inner soul. Heartbeats later the feeling fled as quickly as it had come.

Amusement twitched at the watching man's lips. "So, Master Relliq, you have a message for me?"

At the drawled emphasis on "master," Relliq's arrogance vanished. *How could I misjudge so badly? I should have known. Eilidh is the archmage's mother. Of course he would be here to welcome her.*

But he made no overtures toward the old woman, logic countered.

How to recover and get into the archmage's good graces? No option other than obeisance came to mind. Bowing his head, he dropped to one knee. "Sorry, m'lord. I meant to say I am here to offer my services as an instructor."

"Lady Ellspeth's and my time is sparse for the next three sevenday. However, 'Apprentice' Relliq, you are welcome to stay. Quarters will be provided. We'll evaluate your abilities once the recognition ceremony is over and see what position you are best prepared for. Now, if you will excuse me, I would like to greet my mother."

"As you wish, sire," Relliq purred. Head down, he stepped back. Anger hardened his heart. *My time will come.*

* * *

Brodie released the handle of the bellows. A snatch of the heavy tongs from the bench and he pulled the iron rod from the glowing coals to lay it across the anvil. Carefully placed blows bent the narrow metal strip into a gentle curve. Satisfied with the hook, he set it alongside the other four to cool. A glance at the sun showed it was time for the promised lesson with fighting staffs. Quick movements and the tongs dropped onto their peg while the hammer went onto the empty anvil.

Voices, other than those of Denai and Elendl, came from a rock at the edge of the practice space. Relliq sat on a rock, supposedly instructing the six young boys gathered around his feet. It had been two sevenday since their return to the wizards' isle and while Relliq had made comments, no problems could be traced directly to him. If anything, the other man seemed to be lying low.

That was a blessing, Brodie thought. Even though her time at the school had been short, Kia had blossomed. Her powers had grown stronger and her personality more self-assured. *It was more than the company of other mages. There had been no more strange visits.*

"Follow my Way, and I will make you strong."

Relliq's words reached Brodie. As he had for the fast few days, whenever Kia was holding a lesson with the younger children, Relliq was nearby. Lately, his lessons had skirted the true teachings of the Way. He did so without actually crossing over to where either Dal or Ellspeth had cause to discipline him.

It won't hurt to keep an eye on him, Brodie vowed.

"We're ready, Brodie," Denai and Elendl called in unison from the other side of the forge.

"Coming." Rounding the corner he saw the girls had already arranged the students and set up the flat space beyond the forge for the class. Both Denai and her sister held a pair of wooden staffs that reached to their shoulders. The usual group of eight students had been added to by several of the girls that he had escorted to the isle as well as two boys that Brodie thought of as Relliq's followers. The brothers had been seen attending Relliq's unofficial lectures on life as a mage.

A bow to acknowledge his opponent and Brodie took the staff Denai offered. He demonstrated some basic moves. "Now, Denai, frontal attack." Wood cracked against wood in a block. Denai stepped back, spun the staff and whipped it down only to have Brodie tip the blow aside. Next, with Elendl and Denai working together, he showed how to defend against two attackers. One by one he worked with the rest of the girls in the class, pairing them up with either Denai or Elendl.

Gesturing the latest group to their seats, he called up a pair of brothers.

The tingle at the edge of his senses alerted Brodie even before Kia walked from the trees. His lips tightened. The boys tended to act more aggressively when girls were around, especially Kia. While they had sat quietly during the earlier sparring matches, Brodie swore he could see a plan to show off form between them.

"Once slowly through the moves, Fwlïaid and Gurrod," Brodie told the pair. "Then we'll spar. Elendl will monitor."

"What do you mean monitor?" Fwlïaid said. Attitude colored his tone.

As the older of the two brothers, Brodie knew he often initiated trouble, then let his younger brother finish it. "Elendl will make sure the rules are followed. This is a sparring session, not a battle. No strikes below the belt and when an opponent is disarmed, you back off until they recover their weapon and resume position." He raised his staff into the first blocking posture. "Now, Fwlïaid. Attack."

The youth twirled the staff above his head and rushed. "Kiiiyaa." A twist of his wrist sent the end towards Brodie's head to be pushed aside.

"Nice try," Brodie answered. "However, that leaves you open to this." Wood smacked across the boy's arms, then the staff whipped around to the back of his legs. With a cry, Fwlïaid fell backwards and measured his length in the dirt.

A shriek of "No," and the youth clambered to his feet. Four steps and he stood beside his brother, a hand on the younger boy's shoulder. A stream of fire left the tip of Gurrod's staff and flew in a straight line towards Denai.

Her yell of surprise came a heartbeat before the flame vanished an arm's length from her face.

Brodie took a step towards the boys. Invisible ropes wrapped around his legs. The hard impact when he landed on his back forced his breath out in a grunt. Anger aided battle energy and he fought through the pain and tried to rise. No matter how hard he strained, he couldn't move. He swore blue bands trapped his arms. A groan escaped. *I am a non-tal. Who will protect the students?*

Rage added a different question. Who attacked?

Behind Fwlïaid and Gurrod, Relliq smiled. He threw a two-fingered salute, then signalled the watching boys. This time, Fwlïaid threw a magical spear.

Fire flowed towards Elendl. A wave of her hand and the stream exploded into a shower of sparks a fingertip from the end of the staff. She stalked towards to the boys, her sister a half-step behind.

"Denai, Elendl, stop!" Brodie yelled.

Changing direction, Denai came over to him and bent down to help him up. "Back," he forced out. "Keep your focus on Fwlïaid and Gurrod," he ordered. Several deep breaths and he growled, "Call your parents."

Elendl nodded, but her fists remained clenched. Brodie could see the obstinacy in her frame and prayed she would obey. She turned to the watching boys. "You know the rules. No magic against a non-talent." Fear showed in her voice. "You could have killed Denai and Master Brodie."

"Denai is a mage," Fwlïaid snarled. "If she can't defend herself that is her problem. Brodie is no master. He's just a smith." His voice rose. "They are your rules, not ours. Our master taught us to use whatever advantages we can. That if you have magic, it is your right to rule."

"Our father will see about that," Denai and Elendl said in unison.

Although he didn't hear either girl cast a spell or make a ritual gesture, Brodie felt the force holding him to the ground vanish. A push off the ground and he scrambled to his feet to stand between Elendl and Denai. An anxious scan showed neither the students nor Fwlïaid and Gurrod had moved. *Where is Relliq?*

The shadow of a brown robe vanishing around a curve on the trail that led to the village answered the question.

Gurrod tugged at his brother's sleeve. "Let's go. We need to get to our master. He will protect us." The boys broke the tableau and ran down the path their master had disappeared on.

Denai took three steps in pursuit.

"Denai, don't go after them," her sister called. "It could be a trap. Father will be here shortly and until then we need to stay and protect the others."

Brodie sent a silent prayer winging skyward. *Ancestors beyond the veil, please make Denai see the wisdom—and need—of staying. I can't force her to if she decides to leave.*

Denai showed the same anger and obstinance, but returned to stand beside her sister.

The sound of someone running came from the cliffside trail settled the issue. The archmage crested the top of the hill a heartbeat later to race over to his daughters. At their, "We're fine, father," he spun on his heel in a fast scan of all the students. "Is everyone all right?"

Brodie held his breath until they chorused, "Fine, master."

Their answers might have satisfied, but the tightness in the archmage's face didn't lessen. The power of the mage's anger forced Brodie back a step. He felt the other man bridle the emotion and used the opportunity to take several deep breaths to harness the battle energy coursing through his own frame. In clipped words, the girls told about the attack.

"I thought I saw someone slinking through the woods," Dal said.

"Brodie won the sparring session fair and square," Elendl said. "Even though Fwlïaid cheated."

Denai stood with her hands on her hips. "Father, the attack was unprovoked. Fwlïaid threw a spear of fire towards me, then another at Elendl. If we hadn't been trained…" Her voice trailed off and her face paled. Two heartbeats later, her face flushed. "They and their master should be punished."

Dal pinned the watching students with a stern look. "What Fwlïaid and Gurrod did is not the Way. Those with talent have a responsibility to use it to protect and serve those without magic." His gaze softened. "Class is dismissed. No more instruction for the rest of the sevenday

93

to allow those who will be involved in the recognition ceremony to prepare."

With maturity beyond their turns, Denai and Elendl led their class off.

A tall, gangly boy hung back. "Master Dal?"

"Yes, Dollag?"

"Fwlïaid and Gurrod said their master 'Relliq' told them to attack Brodie. He keeps saying those with powers should use them." He hesitated and Dal encouraged him to continue. "Brodie did nothing wrong. He was winning fair and square. If anything he was taking it easy on Fwlïaid and Gurrod."

Dal's gaze hardened. Brodie remembered that look. He had been the recipient only once, when as a new recruit he tried to protect his troop leader against the archmage.

"There is something more isn't there?"

The youth hung his head. "Master Brodie didn't fall down. He was thrown... by magic. I was looking at Teacher Relliq at the time and I'm sure he cast a spell." He raised his gaze. His attitude was of someone about to be punished and to take it without a cry.

"Thank you, Dollag. You did nothing wrong."

"But I didn't stop him. And I didn't stop Fwlïaid and Gurrod neither."

"You may not have fought this time, but you provided necessary information. Besides you do not yet have your journeyman blade. I would not require you to fight with the odds of three against one, and one of them a much older man." Dal laid a hand on the youth's shoulders. Even though he wasn't in physical contact with either Dal or Dollag, Brodie felt the strength of the benison placed on the boy. "Go back to your quarters. The ceremony is soon. If you hear the invitation, don't be afraid to answer it. Your actions this day brought you honor."

Dollag was barely out of earshot before Dal turned. "Brodie, I think it is time you gave me your evaluation of 'Master' Relliq." His tone sharpened. "Then we will have a little chat with him."

94

Chapter Ten

Brodie did a scan of the area outside the lean-to that covered the forge. Ever since Relliq's attack he had maintained a high alert. Even though Dal had reinforced the protective runes around the forge and shed that contained workspace and served as temporary quarters when he wanted time alone, the impression of being watched persisted. A sigh and he returned his attention to the dagger, inspecting it for any imperfections. He didn't want to have to start over. The recognition ceremony was just a few scant candlemarks away, and his instincts told him the weapon would be Denai's journeyman dagger.

Both Denai and her sister had a crush on him and while he discouraged their romantic interest, he cherished them as friends. The fear he would have to talk to their parents worried him, for he didn't want to hurt Ellspeth or Dal. "The girls will grow out of it," he told himself.

He flipped the dagger, blade over hilt, and caught it in the air to test the balance. An instinct honed from creating weapons on the isle told him it wouldn't be the only blade he'd made that would find a new owner. Besides, Denai and Elendl, young Dollag's powers appeared to be emerging.

And there is one more, his heart encouraged. Kia.

Drawings of the blades he had designed for the soon-to-be vetted mages lay scattered across the workbench. His gaze fell on the rendering of the knife he felt would become Kia's. The blade itself was in the annealing oven cooling from the final tempering. He had seen little of her in the two sevenday since their arrival at the isle. He had been busy getting the weapons ready for the future mages, and she with her lessons. Sketch in hand he opened the drawer holding the trinkets and gems meant for the hilts. Unlike the other sketches, the space for the element remained shapeless. None of the bits and pieces or any of the stones matched the signature he saw in the iron. Runes for power and wisdom had already been etched into the metal and gleamed from the page in reflection of the energy embued by symbol and meaning. He didn't know what the key to unlocking the dagger's power would be, only that there was nothing to mate with the blade. "I'll know it when I see it," he muttered.

* * *

Kia wandered the beach, taking in the cool air. The waves, although gentler than those outside the protection of the headlands, imparted a serenity she needed. The closer the time came for the recognition ceremony, the more she sought time alone. Stopping, she watched the water sweep away her footprints in the sand. Like my life, she thought. Only a few prints remained, a reflection of her journey to the isle. And ahead? A blankness awaiting direction. "Or," she murmured, "a destiny to be fulfilled. At least I don't have long to wait."

Unless you are not chosen in this ceremony, contrariness added. Some candidates wait for turns before they answer the summons.

"I have already heard the call to the council fire," she whispered in a reassurance that was becoming less and less effective.

A wave rolled out. Amidst the reeds left behind, light glinted in the sand. Stooping, Kia brushed away the grains to reveal a piece of sea glass. Ripples in the surface polished by movement of sand and water reminded her of a horse's mane. Tilting it to catch the sun, it seemed like she looked into the heart of the stone. A perfect star flickered. Intrigued, she put it in her pocket.

Happiness and a strong sense of accomplishment filled the ether. Following the emotion, she turned and headed back towards the village. Once beyond a large rock pile, a sail became visible, as did the group of people standing on the dock. Blue ribbons ran from the upraised hands of a youth in the stern to the sails. Kia realized that the boy used magic to control the wind and move Ellspeth's ship. She and Dal had laid spells on keel and hull so that *Windmaster* could safely be used as transport and training vessel for those with powers.

The sails fell limp and the boy's look of concentration turned into a broad smile. Claps and cheers of "well done" rose from those gathered on the shore.

Dollag will make journeyman tonight, Kia mused. Then a worry niggled at her heart. *But will I?*

To pull herself away from the thought she focused on the two women standing at the wheel. Silver hair blowing in the breeze identified one as Ellspeth, captain of the vessel. Although she had never met her in person, the older woman could be none other than the First Seat of the ruling council of the House of Cszabo—and Ellspeth's mother, Mirrim. Word around the village was that the head of the House of Cszabo didn't get out of Stratven often, so her visit was special.

"Both grandmothers are on the isle," Kia mumbled. "It appears Denai and Elendl will get their blades tonight." *And their family will rejoice. Unlike mine. Neither my father nor the Oracle could make the journey.* Sadness that there would be no one for her when she stood before the bonfire just reinforced the belief she wouldn't make the cut and would be sorry she came. Again the archmage's summons to the isle echoed in her mind. As she had so often since she saw the images and felt the urge to come, she wondered, why her? None of her kin studied the Way. They were all dedicated to the temple.

No answer appeared and turning her back on the happy gathering, she headed down the beach to find a spot to be alone with her thoughts. Her unconscious walk took her around rocks and hunks of driftwood. She stepped over the line of reeds that marked the high water mark to avoid the waves that rolled onto the beach. It wasn't until her legs ached that she realized she had climbed the headlands and was at Brodie's forge.

"Excuse me, Brodie, a moment, please?"

When he turned she realized he had been searching in a drawer. "I apologize if I'm interrupting you."

"No problem, Kia. I wasn't doing anything important."

Despite the evenness of his tone, she swore there was an edge to it of something unspoken. She opened her fingers to show the sea glass balanced on her palm. "Lord Dal said if I find anything of interest, something that called to me, to bring it to you."

He held out a hand. "I'll see the glass is taken care of."

As soon as Brodie took the shard, a longing for it enveloped her and she almost snatched it back.

Brodie watched the conflicting emotions in Kia. Her need to have the glass pulsed with a life of its own. It took all of his control not to return the stone to her—or to take her into his arms. One he could not do without tainting the selection. The other reason was harder to acknowledge. *She is not mine to hold.*

"Thank you, Kia. Would you like some water? You look a bit parched."

Her startlement at the request told Brodie his distraction had achieved his desired effect. With her attention diverted, he set the stone atop the sketches. "It's time I took a break. Take a seat outside and I'll bring the drinks." Regret at not having a chilled bottle of wine to offer rose to be quashed. *I'll have to make do with what I have.* He followed and on the way out snatched up the water gourd hanging on a peg at the door and two mugs.

Whether it was the quiet of the cliffside spot or the rhythm of the surf below, Kia seemed to relax and Brodie relished the familiarity they shared.

"Brodie, I don't want to bother the archmage or Lady Ellspeth. But, you've been on the council isle for a while."

Kia's pause told Brodie what she was going to ask and his muscles tensed against the pain he knew that would rise.

"Can you tell me what to expect at the fire ceremony?"

"I can't answer as a mage." Anger teased at his tone and he forced levelness into his voice. "But here's what it appears as to a non-tal."

A candlemark later, after a quick hug and a soft, "Thank you. I feel much better," Kia headed down the trail to her quarters.

Although he usually ate with the rest of the villagers who chose the companionship of the communal dining hall, Brodie had no taste to be with others. The meat and bread he had brought for his mid-day meal remained untouched. It will do for the evening's, he decided. Time to break open the oven. The blades are now cool enough to be handled.

Soon the sketches were arranged in neat rows across the top of the bench. Leather squares that had never been part of a garment or saddle covered each drawing. From now on, no one would touch the weapons—except their intended owners. With another piece of virgin leather between his skin and the iron, Brodie brought each of the blades to the bench for one final examination. He didn't need to see the sketches to place the daggers on the correct covering square. As their creator, the imagined and the actual spoke to him. Next he pulled hilts from their storage box with the same care and soon each blade had a hilt next to it. Well-practiced movements wrapped up the items and soon filled the box at his feet.

Two steps took him to a storage cabinet, he opened the door and pulled a small box off the shelf. Made from wood of the kapuna tree that contained the heritage of all mages, Dal had presented him the box at the first council fire after Brodie took up the island's forge. Every time he filled the box he channeled the archmage's blessing, adding his own prayer that the items within would find their appropriate blades. Setting the lid aside, he riffled through the drawer of stone, shells, and other oddments that had been collected by the instructors and students, or others in the village. Unlike the blade and hilts which weren't handled until claimed by the future wizards, the element that would serve as their focus, and the key to unlocking the blade's potential, did not require the same protection.

Some of the items in the drawer had been handed down from generation to generation. Others, like Kia's, had been found in the local environment. When his fingers touched a piece he felt might be suitable, he dropped it into the box. A gold ring and a smaller silver one went in followed by a polished red stone. Some of the stones bore the roughness from when they came from the ground. Others were polished smooth either by grinder or the countless eons of fingers rubbing across the surface. The shell he had picked up the other day went in as did a green gemstone from Eilidh's ancestral homeland of Tarekus. Soon the box was filled with just enough space for one more item.

Light glinted off the piece of sea glass. Energy tingled his fingers when he touched it, and the image of the blade he felt would be Kia's appeared in his mind. Only where before had been an amorphous empty spot, now he saw the sea glass. Unfamiliar runes were etched in the stone and filled with silver.

Quick strokes and the runes were transferred to the sketch.

"Now to ask Dal or Ellspeth what they mean. Once I understand them, I can engrave them onto the stone." *Then the dagger will be complete except for one thing—for Kia to select it.*

* * *

Dusk came too quickly for Kia's unsettled soul. Like the others preparing for the ceremony, she had not eaten since midday, and then only lightly. As the candlemarks passed, she found it harder and harder to resist the urge to pace. Not even the warmth of the amulet given her by her father so many turns ago eased her nerves.

The sight of the dark blue velvet dress laid out on the bed only added to the tumult in her mind. The teachings of the Oracle embroidered in gold around the hem glowed in accusation of her plan to study the Way. A tug pulled her white robe of an acolyte out of the clothespress. Quick shakes removed the lingering wrinkles and soon it lay alongside the formal gown.

"The white of an acolyte is appropriate," she whispered. "After all tonight's bonfire is a recognition not just of knowledge, but of acceptance of power."

Fear rose with a discordant note. *But will you accept the Way? It means discarding everything the Oracle has taught you … everything you've learned at the temple.*

Denying your family, her heart cried.

To that Kia had no answer.

* * *

Slow steps brought Brodie down the trail to the village. Despite its small size, the box that held the elements felt as heavy as the one containing the blades and hilts. The sun hung low in the sky, and he knew that the wood had already been laid for the night's bonfire. Again, he wished he could participate. Ruthlessly, he drowned the sadness that came with each summoning. He wondered if Kia had eaten. Denai and Elendl had only eaten lightly at mid-day and fasted since so as not to upset the sprites dancing in their stomachs. The closer he came to the center of the village, the stronger the sense of an impending event grew. *No wonder,* he thought, *every resident of the isle is here.* While most conversations were carried in low tones, a sense of anger came from the back of the crowd. Taller than most of the residents, Brodie could see who would disrupt the event's serenity and solemnness—Relliq.

Working his way closer to the other man, he saw Elendl and Denai communicate with their silent language they had developed since childhood.

I will miss them when they go on their journeyman walk.

At the girls' wave, he changed direction. "Brodie, will you stand by us … sponsor us," Elendl said.

"Our grandmothers aren't coming," Denai added. Her voice sounded rough from crying. "Grand-dam Mirrim doesn't like magic. Grand-dam Eilidh is on the isle, but she hasn't answered the summons yet. She might not be a full-fledged mage, but she knew the ceremony began at full

101

dark." Her hand moved to swipe her eyes, but stopped in mid-stroke. "Maybe Mirrim stopped Grand-dam Eilidh from coming?"

Brodie's scan of the crowd didn't reveal either Ellspeth's or Dal's mother. *I can help ease the girl's worries. They'll need all their concentration tonight.* "Nothing on this side of the veil would stop Eilidh or Mirrim from standing with you tonight," he whispered. "I can't sponsor you, but until your grand-dams show I would be proud to wait with you."

Moments later the crowd parted to create an aisle. Dal's mother entered on Mirrim's arm. The cut of Eilidh's hunter-green gown and the embroidered silk trim on the bodice and sleeves reflected a style long out of fashion at court. A chain of silver-filigreed rosettes and beads circled the older woman's upswept hair. Even though as head of the House of Cszabo, Mirrim could afford the most current fashions, she too wore a vintage dress, which harmonized perfectly with the one worn by Dal's mother. Brodie recognized the crest of Mirrim's vessel, *Northern Pearl,* and that of Ellspeth's grandmother's ship, embroidered in gold on the cuffs. By wearing her own mother, Rima's, bridal gown, Mirrim not only symbolized continuity but showed the family association with the sea. And Brodie, mused, Denai's heritage. Ever since her childhood, Denai had a special affinity for the deep blue, and he knew of Mirrim's hope that her granddaughter would one day command a ship.

As the women approached, he leaned forward. "Don't let logic or the wishes of others hold you back," he whispered. "If you hear the call, feel the summons in your bones, follow it."

The girls' hopeful look contrasted with the sense of foreboding that colored his soul. He visualized the premonition as a dark knight and ran it through with TânOer. A squeeze to their shoulders and a bow to Mirrim and Eilidh, he stepped back, picked up the box from where he had left it and moved to his position at the edge of the crowd to await his part in the proceedings.

Silence fell over the square. Ellspeth emerged from the council tower. The only sound was the soft swish of the gown around her ankles. Firelight glittered in her hair and on the circlet around her neck. Barris followed behind her in single file. A second man, slightly taller and more tanned, left the tower with the even taller, Dal bringing up the rear of the procession.

It would be a special ceremony with both Barris and Nobyn in attendance, Brodie thought. At the most only one of them participated. The pair were Ellspeth's and Dal's first apprentices. Now masters, the men divided their time between teaching at the school and travelling the countryside.

Ellspeth offered an incantation that although soft carried to the crowd. A whoosh and fire appeared in the heart of the pile of wood laid out in the heart of what used to be a large grindstone. She stepped up to the fire ring. "Fire, earth, and magic be divided on the stone. So too will be blade, hilt, and token until selected by their chosen one." With a nod to her former apprentices, Ellspeth, Barris and Nobyn placed their blades on the millstone separating it into three segments. Dal and Ellspeth moved to stand on one side of the fire, while the two men separated to opposite corners to form a human triangle.

A prayer that his work be well received that night, Brodie unwrapped the first of the blades to be selected by the journeymen and placed it within the first marked section of the fire ring. Four blades were unwrapped, presented to the fire and laid in a parallel line. Although they were identical in size and shape, some instinct told him the next three blades didn't belong in the line. Instead he arranged them as divergent lines radiating outward from their bases. The rest of the blades formed an inverted star. Satisfied with their placement, he took slow steps to the section of the stone marked by Barris and Nobyn. Deft movements set the hilts out in neat rows without even a single snick of metal on stone to mar the gathering silence. After a deep breath to cancel the rising tension from the crowd, he spread the elements in the remaining empty section. Bowing his head, he again offered a prayer, took a step back, turned and retreated to stand at the edge of the crowd watching the gathered hopefuls.

Before the tension became unbearable, the sea breeze carried Dal's deep tone across the square. "Welcome to the council fire of the School of Mages. All, whether a student of the Way or not, a holder of powers or not, are welcome to cast their wishes into the fire." His words went on, not by voice, but by mind. *Let all who hear the silent summons approach the fire.*

The words echoed in Brodie's soul. *How can I hear Dal?*

It's just a reflection from the weapons, reality answered. The creator of the metal would have an affinity for the blades it is transformed into.

Four boys and a girl took a single step forward. One of the boys halted, then with a shake of his head returned back to his place. Disappointment filled his face. The others, their faces tight with concentration, silently circled the grindstone. Their fingers hovered over the blades and one by one the to-be-vetted mages selected the slivers of metal that would soon serve as the focus of their powers.

Brodie clenched his hands against the pain caused by the joy on their faces. The skin tightened over his knuckles as each student knelt before Dal or Ellspeth, who blessed the dagger and traveler.

Denai reached out to Elendl standing beside her and entwined her fingers with her sister's. Although no one said a word of encouragement, Brodie felt the sense of anticipation grow from those watching, especially the girls' grandmothers. Ellspeth and Dal's straight posture spoke of controlled worry ... and pride.

At Dal's slight nod, the girls looked at each other and walked to the bonfire.

Yes, Brodie wanted to cheer. He suppressed the urge and like the rest of those watching held his breath.

Elendl circled the fire, heading unerringly towards the dagger Brodie knew Ellspeth had carried as her boot knife during her time at sea. With the same lack of hesitation,

Elendl picked up a hilt and the green stone that was her grandmother's. A sense of continuity and of the connection between generations rose as a shimmering ribbon in the fire's smoke.

Denai almost ran to the blade Brodie had just finished that morning. Then she took two steps and snatched up the pink shell with the whirls that had reminded him of the Cyrcle of One. Almost as an afterthought, she reached out and picked up a hilt. Her precious items clutched in her hand, she walked with a new maturity to join her sister. Their happiness was so strong Brodie knew it radiated to everyone in the crowd.

A single scowl showed amongst the smiling attendees—Relliq.

Brodie watched for several heartbeats before making a silent vow. *Dal and I will have to talk about that one... and soon.*

Elendl and Denai's shift to stand before their parents pulled him from his thoughts. Elendl kneeled before her father, offering the blade, hilt, and stone. Denai mirrored the actions to her mother.

Although neither Ellspeth nor Dal allowed the pleasure they felt an uncontrolled rein, Brodie sensed their happiness join the rest of the good wishes rising from the bonfire. Hilt slid into the blade, and their token of magic, whether the shell or stone, clicked into its setting. Their hands on their daughters' heads, both Ellspeth and Dal moved their lips in silent blessing.

The warmth of a benison filled Brodie. Confusion soared in his mind. *How could I feel it? I am not a mage.*

It is because of my closeness to Denai and Elendl, he rationalized. I've known the girls their entire lives.

Once again the hope that he could have powers, even just the tiniest spark of one rose. Before the wish could be consigned to the fire, he smashed it into fine sand and, determined never to see the light of day, buried in the deepest part of his heart.

Chapter Eleven

Dal's words echoed in Kia's mind—and her heart. "Let all who hear the silent summons approach the fire." Fear at not being selected held her in her quarters. Finally, she couldn't delay any longer. She still had to attend the bonfire, if only for her students. A silent prayer and she walked out the door into the setting sun. "To what," she whispered. "Failure or my destiny?"

Her robe swished with each step, proclaiming the reasons not to try.

The others are so young. I'm too old to be an apprentice. Magic does not come easily.

"You are the descendent of a mage," her father's words roared over the arguments. "Powers are not restricted to those who study the Way. They also run through the veins of the oracles. You have the heritage of both. Go and see which fits you best."

Used to obedience, she heeded her father and gave into the burgeoning desire. Her steps quickened until she reached the edge of those gathered. It seemed more than the parents of those answering the call packed the small square. Every single resident of the village, as well as the retired sailors who manned *Windmaster,* waited.

Before Kia could figure out how to get through the crowd, it parted. A deep breath and she moved through the narrow path. Still unsure of her worth to be a supplicant, she stopped at the edge of the open space that surrounded the fire ring. Her vantage spot provided a clear view as fire came to life in the cold wood.

But more than the dancing flames called to be possessed. A tingling in her hands made her look down, only to see her fingers curled as if they held a weapon. Her gaze lingered on one of the blades laid out on the stone. It demanded to be possessed by her. To fight the lure and maintain control, her fingers tightened into a fist until the skin became translucent.

A sense of encouragement and belief in her lightened the darkness.

My father isn't here, nor is my brother. So who?

Looking around the crowd, she saw Eilidh's nod and knew it was Dal's mother who had sent the support. The older woman had a sad, wistful expression that disappeared as Kia watched.

"There are those who wish to respond but do not yet feel free," Dal called with both voice and mind. "Let anyone who hears the summons of the fire, come forward."

A rustle went through the crowd as some shifted from foot to foot.

Dollag left the students he had been standing with. His first hesitant steps grew surer the closer he approached the fire. Pride in her student fought with worry that he would select "her" blade. Anger rose over the other emotions. They are unworthy of the Oracle, Kia reminded herself and sought a more harmonious center.

Within heartbeats Dollag had blade and element in hand and presented them to Dal. As the boy rose from the blessing to stand between Dal and Ellspeth's first apprentices, Kia felt the archmage's approval of the new journeyman and added her own silent well-wishes.

Don't be afraid. What is meant to be is meant to be. You are a mage.

Who wants me to accept the call, Kia wondered. Her gaze went from mage to mage. Warmth and acceptance came from Ellspeth. Dal's wink encouraged even as she wondered if she had really seen it. Barris and Nobyn's attention remained on those who had not yet answered the call. Neither of them had spoken to her. Finally, her gaze lingered on Brodie. At his smile and gesture to the fire, Kia acknowledged reality. *I can't fight my own urges and the pull of magic.*

The glow she had seen emanating from the fire ring turned into a solid beam that reached to the stars. Three steps and she was at the summoning light. A whispered prayer and her fingers wrapped around the blade at the base of the signal. She swore the knife hummed in happiness, welcoming her. *Just like TânOer.* Her steps to where the hilts were laid out were surer. She moved her hand a few inches above the displayed pieces until the blade she held sent an answering chord. Picking up the hilt, she realized it had an empty circle. It awaited an element.

A column of pale green light leaped skyward from the other side of the millstone. Without conscious control, her feet took her around the bonfire. Its warmth chased away the night's chill and that of the action she was taking. The blade called to its missing piece. Surprise stopped her in mid-reach. The element whose signal she heeded as the blade's mate was the sea glass she had found. Only now it had a flying bird incised on it.

Again she sought Brodie in the crowd. You did the artwork? she mouthed. His slight nod shy smile answered. The tilt of his head told her the next step.

With slow steps, Kia circled the stone ring. Her path ended in front of Ellspeth where she opened her hand, leaving the makings of the dagger balanced on her palm for the older woman to see. "Mistress, I come to you as a seeker of the call. I beg your blessing."

Ellspeth slid the hilt over the blade, then pressed the sea glass into its setting. "I am so happy for you."

From beside his wife, the archmage's deeper tones added, "As am I."

Their touch on her head was so light, Kia almost thought they were rejecting her petition.

But their words were of approval, reality countered.

Confusion almost blocked out Ellspeth's blessing.

"Kiansel, daughter of Forsom, may your ancestors beyond the veil guide and protect you from this day on," Ellspeth whispered.

Power surged through Kia.

Dal's formal acceptance, though spoken loud enough to carry to the entire crowd, was by no means any less intimate or heartfelt. "By the power of the archmage, holder of the master spells, I welcome you, Kiansel, daughter of Forsom, and brother of Brantly, holder of the title of Oracle of Givneh, to the Brotherhood of Mages."

Ellspeth took Kia's hands in hers and leaned down. "Your father would approve."

A blue glow surrounded Ellspeth's hands, then spread to include Kia's. She felt the strength returning to legs that just a moment earlier she swore would not keep her upright. Kia fought down a gasp. The signature in the magic was not the archmage's lady. Instead, the one behind this second blessing, a benison colored by pride, was from her father. The last of her resignation vanished as a green ribbon wafting upward in the smoke of the bonfire.

I am a mage, Kia's heart exclaimed.

* * *

Relliq fumed. His ire grew with each person who stepped up to the fire. *What is going on? I didn't hear any summons.*

Maybe the call was just for apprentices, pride argued.

"I deserve a master's recognition," Relliq hissed. "This is only a journeyman's call." Memory of the last time he tangled with the archmage rose and he took a calming breath. "I will wait my turn." *As long as it is not too long.*

"As the flames die down, so does the night," Dal intoned. "If any want to heed the invitation, do so now." His tone softened. "If doubt or some other reason holds you back, there will be other fires."

Relliq's soul froze to glacial ice. The archmage had just issued the final call. Anger that he had not been personally invited to the fire, let alone participate as an instructor, raced through his veins. *I am a master. Yet I am to answer a lesser summons?*

Even though he had not heard the silent announcements the others had, one thought rose above the rest. *Since I'm here I might as well make my mark.*

His boot heels on the flagstones sounded with each strut to the stone table. Only a few blades and elements remained. Randomly, he picked up a blade and a black crystal with a rune incised into it. "These will do," he muttered. "They look appropriate for a master."

Now for the next step. Who to ask to use their magic to blend the pieces into a tool suitable for a wielder of powers. Nothing in his studies had ever mentioned the possibility of two equal archmages. *And I still don't fully know his lady's role in the world. Still she would be the easier of the pair to manipulate.* Schooling his expression, he presented the dagger to Ellspeth. "Mistress, I come to you as a seeker of the call. I beg your blessing."

At her glare, he knelt. Anger at this second insult sent rivulets of sweat rolling down his back.

Unlike the other submissions which she instantly accepted, Ellspeth held it up for a close examination; then with a tilt of her head inquired the archmage's advice. Although neither spoke a word, Relliq swore some communication went between them. Regret filled her face. "I am sorry, Relliq. I cannot approve this union."

The soft tone of her dismissal didn't take away the heat her words caused.

"But... but... I heard the summons to the isle," Relliq began. He rose to his feet and gestured at what should have been his. "Those are worthy of a master."

The archmage took the blade and stone from his wife. "Which you are not yet, Relliq."

Although Relliq knew the low words could not be heard by the rest of those watching, embarrassment added to the fire in his heart. A spell to curse the pair in front of him leapt to his lips. For an instant, he swore no man stood before him, but a pyramid of lambent energy that absorbed the spell and cast it aside as a butterfly on the wind.

"Coming to the Isle is not a guarantee of acceptance at the fire," Dal explained with the tone of a teacher to an errant student. "You are welcome to try at the next recognition ceremony after you've further studied the Way."

Pulling himself to his full height, Relliq locked gazes with the archmage. A slight nod of his head and he slinked into the darkness beyond the fire. Instead of going to his quarters, he stopped in a shadowed walkway between two buildings. No light came from the windows to betray his presence.

The memory of the benisons bestowed on the new mages kept him from leaving. He circled the power, a moth gathering strength from the blessings, especially the ones Dal and Ellspeth gave their daughters. *Their powers will be an asset when I take over as master of the school.*

But they are too young, reality whispered.

Firelight on brown curls presented another option. *Kia isn't. She will be a suitable mate. Having powers will make her even more so.* "And I will train her in the proper use of her talents."

All the anger he had suppressed vanished. "I will possess power," came out in a raspy growl. "And Kia." A smile twitched his lips. *The archmage will pay for embarrassing me. He will come begging when his daughters are my students.*

Silent steps took him away from the fire.

* * *

Brodie watched Dal and Ellspeth welcome the new mages to their powers. Altogether twelve apprentices acquired their journeyman blades. From what he could see, only three blades and a handful of elements remained before the fire.

"May Lady Ellspeth and I have another moment of your attention," Dal called out. In response, those watching quieted. "Ellspeth and I have an announcement." A wave brought Denai and Elendl to them. "There has been talk about my lady and I being prejudiced about Denai and Elendl's powers. And you're correct."

Laughter rippled through the crowd, then died down. "I swear on my honor as archmage, that they have not received any awards they did not earn. In recognition of their, and the others who claimed their blades tonight, new journeyman status, and to allow them and their parents and sponsors a chance to breathe, the following assignments."

111

Brodie held his breath. He knew what was coming and hoped that the girls would be happy.

Dal looked at Denai. "Denai will sail with her grandmother, Mirrim, First Seat of the House of Cszabo, on *Northern Pearl* and accompany her on whatever land trading caravans Mirrim deems appropriate. Dollag and two of the girls will go with them to spend a turn studying with Voan and Jesmen in the Southern Sea. For the time being, Elendl will continue to instruct here on the council isle, and travel around the land as needed. Those of you who will be going to learn what insight the Oracle of Givneh can provide already know your journey."

Ellspeth pointed to three of the new journeymen. "The restriction is now lifted. You can now share your news." She smiled at the squeals as two girls hugged each other. And at the hugs they gave a lanky boy standing near them. "All instructors, the new journeyman—and their families," she emphasized, "are invited to a celebration. Wine suitable for the occasion has been brought from the cooling cave. Refreshments have been prepared by Murdo and will be available in a few moments." Her smile broadened. "I've tried them and they are not to be missed."

Brodie had hoped to avoid the gathering and tried to slip away. He hadn't gotten more than three steps before the crowd blocked his way.

"Master Brodie, thank you." He turned to see Denai and Elendl, their eyes glittering with excitement. They tugged Kia in their wake.

Brodie noticed a new self-assuredness in both her and the two girls. Although, he admitted that Denai and Elendl can still revert to acting their actual age in a blink when the situation is appropriate. "Congratulations, Denai, Elendl. You have both earned it." A chaste kiss on the cheek and a firm hug followed.

"Have you seen Kia's dagger? The artwork is gorgeous," Denai babbled.

Her sister shook her head with the attitude of a long-suffering older sibling, despite there being mere minutes difference between them. "Of course, Master Brodie has seen the dagger. He created it. And I thought I saw his fine hand in the runes worked in the stone." She cocked an eyebrow. "What do the symbols mean? I've never seen them before."

"I know," Kia said.

"Please, Kia, what do they mean?" the girls chorused.

The reverence with which Kia handled the blade told Brodie that she would do well. "The symbols are from my home." Her finger traced the top part. "This is my heritage, an ancestress who was a mage." Now her smile broadened. "And the rest are the Oracle's signs for wisdom and charity." She leaned in and Brodie wondered if it was for a hug or a kiss. His heart soared when she did both.

Kia is just a friend, his heart warned. And now she is also a mage.

Barris' hand on his shoulder prevented any more outward appearance of emotion. "Hey, Brodie, share the wealth."

A final hug to the girls, a wave to Kia, and Brodie backed off to allow his friend to take his place.

What about Kia? His heart asked. She needs a friend tonight. Go to her.

Barris will comfort her and make sure she enjoys her evening.

Brodie wove his wave through the crowd of well-wishers, adding his own congratulations to the new journeymen. A final look over his shoulder showed Barris and Kia being pulled from person to person by Denai and Elendl. The pain of not being a mage became too great and he headed into the darkness. I'll sleep at the forge tonight, he thought. The stars will keep me company until the dawning.

Rest eluded him. The satisfaction of making the daggers—and their new owners joy in them—was countered by other memories of the evening.

His thoughts swirled. I have no powers. Yet not only did I hear Dal's invitation to come to the isle, but also the summons of the newly-fledged mages to the council fire.

Dawn came with a peach glow that heralded a sunny day without storms. But it did not reflect the chaotic whirl of Brodie's thoughts. He paced the workshop, stopping on each round to look out at the ring of pillars that served as a summoning landmark. The questions that had prevented rest the night before also stopped him from working the forge. At least, he thought, now that the ceremony is over there is no urgency to make any more daggers. A silent vow formed to find out how he heard the unspoken calls. *Dal is the archmage, he will know the truth.*

Finally, the frenetic energy overcame even his reserves and he laid down. Warmth on his face finally lured him into a cottony darkness. Dreams of his rides with Kia alternated with the memory of watching the sunset with her.

He woke to see the sun dip below the horizon, taking with it the last of the day's warmth. Although the sky was clear, a fog formed over the water. Brodie watched it roll up the headland and into the lean-to. The cold mist that swished around his feet reminded him of another day … and another fog. A decision to talk to Dal pushed aside all thoughts and he headed down the inland trail. Shadows that seemed to move quickened his pace. He didn't slow his breakneck speed until he reached the outer buildings of the village. And it wasn't until he entered the council tower and was surrounded by the protective runes that he relaxed.

"Come on up to the council room," Dal called down the stairs. "Ellspeth is out with our mothers." His expressive shrug showed his relief at not being there. "They are helping Denai select her gear for the trip. Then they are planning on helping Elendl plan for her first walkabout." Whether it was his expression or the archmage anticipated the meeting, he shifted from father to archmage. "What brought you to darken my doorstep?"

How to answer, Brodie pondered. A single word escaped. "Relliq."

"That one." The grimace vanished from Dal's face and he gestured to a chair. "Your timing is perfect. He is to join me in a candlemark. Since you're already here, what are your thoughts of him as a man?"

In clipped tones, Brodie provided both facts and impressions of the trip after Relliq joined them. "I can't prove it, but I believe he cast a spell on both me and Kia." The memory of walking towards dark woods faded into that of tendrils of fog clutching at his legs. "I also think he was the one that controlled—or at least created—the fog that almost killed me." Now it was Brodie's turn to hide embarrassment. "Dal, I admit I don't like the man and that may have colored my evaluation." His gaze rose to meet Dal's piercing one. "But I don't think so."

Dal stood and started pacing the room. His fingers traced the rune for wisdom on the stone embedded in the windowsill before returning to sit on the corner of the desk. "Your emotions do not color your impressions. If they did, you could not create the journeyman daggers. The metal must be worked without malice or anger. And you are not wrong about either the man's character or his being behind several incidents—including the fog attack."

He paused as if deciding how much else to divulge. "My mother may not be a full-fledged mage, but she has a long ear. Many a child in our clanhold learned too late their misdeeds had not gone undiscovered. And she too believes that Relliq attacked you—and is Kia's stalker."

Rage surged through Brodie. His jaw tightened. *I don't have powers, yet one who does dares to misuse them?* His heart thundered a command that overrode all else. Kia must be defended.

Footsteps on the stairs had him out of his seat. Back to the wall, his hand dropped to his boot and came out with a dagger.

"Put the blade away, Brodie." Dal commanded. "We have nothing to fear from Relliq."

A wave of arrogance preceded the mage into the room.

Brodie hid the knife behind his leg and shifted his weight. *If Relliq is stupid enough to attack Dal, I'll be ready.*

* * *

115

Each heartbeat since the boy relayed the order to report to the council chamber allowed the anger to build. The clack of Relliq's bootheels striking the stone floor sounded in the stairs. The urge to shuffle to approach the archmage's office in silence added to his feeling as an errant child summoned before the schoolmaster.

Stalking into the room, he jerked to a halt only two steps past the threshold. Not in any display of respect, but at the sight of the smith leaning against the wall. Why is that non-tal here, indignation hissed. This is to be a meeting of those with powers.

Calm down, reason ordered. Remember the ease at which the archmage countered the spell at the bonfire. More can be learned from open ears than loud growls.

A deep breath and he tilted his head in a bow. Beneath his lowered lids, he watched for a reaction to the obeisance. "You summoned me, archmage?"

"Yes, Relliq, I understand that you continue to refuse weapons training, either with Brodie or Murdo."

Relliq scanned Brodie from head to toe, then turned dismissively away. "Sire, swords are useless before a strong-willed mage. I don't see the reason to lug around steel when one can wield magic."

Dal shook his head. "Sorry, I forgot you don't yet have a journeyman's blade. Once you're further along in your studies, you'll realize that steel and iron can enhance your powers." A smile twitched his lips as if some happy memory surfaced.

Determined to find out what it was, Relliq tried to read the archmage. His spell stopped at the edge of the desk. But how? The archmage didn't move a finger, whisper a spell.

The room must be enspelled, logic provided. And the desk has been used by generations of mages. Their powers imbued the wood, acted as a block.

"Apprentice Relliq."

The other man's words and tone pulled Relliq from his thoughts.

"My initial thought since you left Montrat so precipitously was to send you back there. However, various facts have come to light. Ysbail and I both agree that you are not suited as a healer. You refuse to adhere to the tenet, 'Do no harm to those without powers.'" His tone sharpened. "Since you reject the basic disciplines of the Way, you are being relieved of teaching duties. You will be sent to the Oracle of Givneh for additional studies."

What control Relliq held on his emotions loosened. "No, I am an instructor. Fwlïaid and Gurrod need me. Under my tutoring, the boys have made sufficient progress to justify my taking over all their training, rather than wasting my time educating the five-turn-old children and those whose powers have been constrained."

Although Dal's voice remained level, it projected a restrained force. "Relliq, you've been given several chances to change your attitude. Either do so now or I will adjust it for you. And the lesson will illustrate why steel can prove more 'educational' than magic."

In an instant he transformed from an ordinary man back into the archmage. "What you are teaching is not the Way. The choice is yours. Go to Givneh or have your powers bound forever."

The dark look in the other man's eyes stopped the retort on the tip of Relliq's tongue. "I...I yield. I will go to Givneh tomorrow." At the wave of dismissal, he spun on his heel and walked from the room.

Rage at being disciplined like a first-season student mingled with the humiliation at how easily he allowed himself to be bested. "That will not happen again." Only three steps from the tower he stopped and looked up at the window of the council chamber. "I thought the archmage would be different. Now I see he is just as weak as Ysbail. Things will be different when I am archmage."

Chapter Twelve

A push sent the plate to the other side of the table. "I can't eat any more of this slop," Relliq growled.

"Master, does the food displease you? I can bring a biscuit fresh from the oven. Maybe some beef? Sliced thin?"

Relliq looked over his shoulder. As he suspected, it was the old man who worked the food line who had spoken. "Thank you, Solit, nothing more." He gestured at the empty seat on the bench next to him. From his second day at the temple, he had cultivated the greybeard as a source of food—and information. "Sit, rest a few moments. The next group of pilgrims won't be here for a half candlemark, more than enough time to get the food ready."

The other man looked at the plate, wistfulness on his face. Although there was no sound, Relliq swore he could see Solit's thoughts. From what he had found out, despite the cook's thin frame, he ate everything and anything he could get his hands on—and was still hungry. Food was a lure. *It is time for all the treats I've brought him to pay off.*

"Please, Solit, eat what you wish. I already had a full meal." Relliq leaned in close, pulled a cookie he had purchased in the town from his pocket and offered it to the other man. "This is from my private stock."

A scan of the room showed only a few pilgrims and none of them were paying attention to anything other than their food. Now is a good time, Relliq thought, to get the oldster talking. "Solit, I heard a tale in the dormitory."

The glitter in the oldster's eyes revealed an intelligence normally hidden—and a curiosity. He had already shown a proclivity for gossip, both receiving it and spreading it.

"One of the boys who came from a town in the south whispered about a mage of power, a man called Bashim."

Where before there had been interest, fear flickered across the oldster's face. "We don't talk about that one. He be a rogue." He turned back to push the sole uneaten cube of yellow root vegetable around the plate with a spoon.

"Please," Relliq whispered. "I won't tell anyone." He leaned in close. "I know some mages and need the information." To ensure the other man's compliance, his lips moved in a silent incantation.

Lips be loosened, tale be told.
Tell me what I need, o man who's old.

Relliq saw the man resisting. For a heartbeat, he thought the oldster had beaten the spell. No, he swore. I will not be denied. A breath and he repeated the spell along with an additional compulsion. "Now tell me about this mage."

Solit stilled. His shoulders slumped and his eyes glazed over. "The one you speak of was named Bashim. He tried to kill every wizard in the world other than himself. Then he took over the temple, turning people into slaves."

"Tell me more," Relliq whispered. "How did Bashim do this?"

"I can't answer about the murder of the wizards, but as far as the temple, all I know is that after someone attended a service, Bashim would have a private meeting with them." The oldster shivered so hard the loose skin under his chin shook. "After that they would obey. Women went willingly to his bed and men to war for him."

Images raised by the old man sent heat racing through Relliq. *No more cold beds.* He envisioned himself in the Oracle's quarters. A woman lay in the bed, her long, blond hair splayed across the pillow. She lifted the sheet in beckoning. "Come to me, my love. I will make you happy."

Relliq recognized her as one of the women who frequented the dock-side taverns in Berife and went to the upstairs rooms for a few coppers. She had entertained him for several nights until the storms lifted and he couldn't delay the journey to the temple.

His astral-self drifted closer to the bed.

The woman rose to her knees, the covering falling away. "Command me. I am yours."

This is what I need. And when I am done with this one, Kia will be mine.

A low murmur went through those in the room. Even though he didn't hear it in his mind, Relliq recognized the silent call for the evening service. He stood and waited as the others filed out. Slow steps took him to a position at the end of the line. The short line he was in shuffled from the dining hall and merged into a longer line. Hall after hall, people joined the procession. No matter how hard he tried to advance in the line, he found himself blocked and shifted farther back as others moved ahead of him.

Angry thoughts swirled as he watched the procession make its way. The official bells summoning the temple's residents to service hadn't even rung. Days before when questioned, the oldster had mentioned a silent call. *Why don't I hear the call? I am a mage.* Then he remembered what else the man had said. The Oracle's words were only heard by, "those fully accepting the teachings of the temple."

Following the example of those around him, Relliq stared at his feet. Each shuffle swung the hem of the white robe of an acolyte. "I should have the black robe of a bishop." He cast a sidewise glance at those in the next line. Each, regardless of their sex or age, had a look of anticipation and a smile. *I am not one of the Oracle's sheep. Unlike those fools, I know the truth.*

The last two people between him and the door entered the audience hall and Relliq schooled his face into an expression of piety. Warm, welcoming light beckoned him into the room. The back corner where he ended up was a different spot than he had been at before. Instead of listening to the choir and the speech by one of the elders, he used the time to study the murals on the wall. Armed with the new knowledge obtained from the kitchen worker, he looked at the paintings with a different eye. Frustration rose when no insight was gained.

A hush fell over the room as the Oracle entered from a door near the stage. As usual, the temple leader wore the white robe of an acolyte. Four sentences into the sermon, Relliq tuned the man out. *I've heard enough preaching about charity and helping others. The rule should be "help yourself before you help others."*

He tried to decide whether the archmage or the Oracle had the most power. His first thought was that the archmage was hampered by the rules of the Way, whereas the Oracle made his own rules. Then he corrected himself. *The Oracle is as weak as the archmage. But there is one difference. If I am the Oracle, I make the rules. Then the wizards will follow me.*

* * *

With the large group of newly-arrived pilgrims, it took a sevenday before the hallways quieted enough for Relliq to stalk from his room other than at meals or services. He stopped at each intersection to listen for guards returning from their late night patrol or for early risers. His nerves tingled by the time he reached the library. A final look to ensure he was unobserved and he pushed open the heavy door. The panel swung open with nothing more than a sibilant hiss of air moving. Inside the large anteroom, door after door led to even more chambers where volumes ancient before time filled the shelves. "At this time of night no one will be here to monitor what I look at," he chortled. In a low tone, he cast the spell he had used earlier on Solit. A ball of shimmering thread that pulsed with life appeared in his palm. "Bashim is the one I seek, show me the book I need," he whispered.

The orb rose and floated down an aisle between shelves. Relliq raced after it. His footsteps echoed off the high ceilings. Turn after turn the ethereal guide led him deeper and deeper into the library. It hovered, then tried to go further. A screech came from the ball as it bounced off a door.

"I'm coming. Wait for me." Relliq swore the ball blinked impatiently. A lift and twist of the lock and the door swung open to a black void. "I can't see," he snarled. "I need light."

A light appeared in a lantern above the door. Before Relliq could move, a glow appeared in another, then a second, and a third. He stood watching as hundreds of lanterns ignited to reveal the true scope of the temple's archives. Beneath each light a door awaited exploration. "An endless hall," he breathed, "full of secrets and no one to stop me from learning them all."

The seeker ball flew back to Relliq. It hovered before his nose before resuming its flight down the hall. He followed along, more slowly than before. This time, his footfalls were only soft scuffles and didn't disrupt the silence of the archives. The light above one door changed to a brilliant blue and the orb went through. It danced on the threshold until he entered the room, then repeated its aerial antics before a book. The volume looked like it was held together by nothing more than spider webs.

With no hesitation, Relliq reached out and touched the edge of the book's cover. Magic tingled his fingers and worked its way up his hands. "Finally," he breathed, "I can study a real book of magic. And it's not that weak discipline, the Way."

Pulling out the book, the image of a city floating in the air above a lake appeared on the cover. "This isn't what I want." A shove returned the book back to its place.

A hiss accompanied the seeker ball's return to hover in front of Relliq's nose.

His swat sent the orb scurrying away. It hovered for a heartbeat, then zipped back to the book. Back and forth it flittered between book and nose. Trust in his magic overwhelmed the disbelief and he pulled down the book. The same image of the city reappeared. Sitting on the floor, he started turning the pages, stopping when a phrase or spell caught his attention.

The tale of Belrum, founder of the School of Mages, unfolded. "Belrum may have founded the school, but he didn't put the restrictions on it that the current archmage does." Relliq's words, despite the softness of the whisper, echoed in the room. "I must find this lost city the book describes. Even if neither the gold goblets encrusted with precious stones nor the bags of silver coins remain, a site that old would still be a source of power."

Clicking made Relliq look up. A pale blue star shone in the core of the seeker ball. While he watched, the color darkened with each pulse. Between one breath and the next, the spectrum changed to a deep burgundy. A whispered curse escaped Relliq's lips. He had lost track of time. Since he didn't hear the silent summons to the services, there was no way for him to know when the halls would fill. Or worse, someone enter the archives. "I haven't found what I want," he told the sphere. The book tucked under his arm he slipped out of the room. Two steps and the book vibrated in his hand. The closer he got to the anteroom, the harder the tome shook.

"No one told me there were restriction runes," he wanted to yell. Instead he reduced the scream to a hiss. Retracing his steps, he worked his way to a secluded chamber off the main library. A glance around the room revealed a half-empty shelf behind the door. "That's a good place to hide my treasure until I have more time to read it more thoroughly. No one will look there."

The next night he created a reminder spell so he'd wake when the halls were clear. This time the seeker ball went to a different volume in an even older section of the archive. It told the tale of a mage who opposed Belrum. Relliq eagerly read how the mage increased his powers. Not by use of element or token, but by accessing a human energy. After a battle by sword and magic which left Belrum severely wounded, the opposer's powers were bound and both men rode off into the desert.

"This is just another reference to the lost city," Relliq cursed. "This isn't what I want. Where is the secret to controlling others?" He called forth the seeker ball, one more time. The ball led the way between racks and racks of parchments to the oldest section of the archives, the one the gray-bearded gatekeeper had said contained the journals of recent oracles. It hovered before a small, leather-bound volume and issued a discordant hum that set Relliq's nerves on edge.

A deep breath to slow his racing pulse and he reached up and grabbed the book. At first it didn't move as if it was stuck. A tug and a sheet of paper that had been hidden beneath the book slid off the shelf. The sheet floated to the floor, landing writing side up and revealing a single word written in a tight script–Bashim.

"This is the journal I need," Relliq crowed. "It must contain what Bashim found… the ability to control others."

The prospect of gaining power energized his fingers and he eagerly scanned a page. However, after the first dozen pages, the time he spent on each page dropped. The rows of statistics telling the number of people served in the community or records of how many pilgrims arrived at the temple bored Relliq until he wanted to cry. Still he forced at least a cursory look of each page until the handwriting and the content changed. Instead of notes of barrels of grain produced, page after page contained the ancestry of livestock and local residents. Supressing a yawn, he considered returning to his quarters, except the tight script held him captive. The name at the top of one list caught his eye. It pertained to Iago, the wizard who fought Belrum and lost. Marks behind the next three names indicated a descendent.

Relliq smiled. Iago might have disappeared, but not before he left behind a son. He continued tracking the ancestry chart. His finger traced the faded entry with a finger and saw the annotation, horse trader. *My mother had told about an ancestor who had raised horses. This man is my ancestor. He is a descendent of Iago.* Pride filled Relliq. *Then so am I.*

Encouraged he continued tracing the man's genealogy. One branch led to a dead-end, so he retraced the familial lineage down a different path. A name had been written at the bottom of the page, then crossed out—Bashim.

Shock mingled with surprise and raced Relliq's pulse. *Bashim is a kinsman. Mages have been in my family since the dawn of time.* His lips pulled into a rictus of a smile. *Me, not that weak-willed Dal, deserve to lead all our kind... and I will! His power will be mine.*

* * *

Relliq stretched. Bones creaked and muscles protested the movement. He had read the entire night... and still hadn't found a means of getting the books out of the archives. Even if the old man who sat at the entrance to the library was at his post, he wouldn't allow the removal of an oracle's journal without a written note. *And I can't get that.* Frantic thoughts searched for the means to achieve his goals. *I may not be able to remove it yet, but I can read it in here.* After a vow to return after morning services, he headed to the dining hall to quiet the grumble in his stomach.

A surprise summons from the Oracle prevented his return to the library. Despite the urge to return to his study of the journal, Relliq fought to keep the proper expression of piety and stood patiently all during the briefing for the trip to take healing potions to a small village in the desert stricken by an unknown illness. Organizing the supplies and foodstuffs took until after the evening meal. Frustrated by the delay, he headed to the library and pushed open the door into a changed library. Sunlight brought in by mirrors filled the room with an orange glow. Students filled every table. Elders led small groups in quiet discussion.

Excitement raced Relliq's pulse. At least I now have the means to remove anything I want from the library... and the archives. He pulled out the folded note bearing the Oracle's instructions to provide anything he wanted. "I don't think the Oracle meant for me to use it this way," he chuckled. "But since I have it, I might as well use it."

Soon the books he wanted to study further were piled high on a table. A glance over his shoulder to ensure no one paid attention to him and he slipped into the side room where he had stashed the journals gathered on previous nights' explorations. It took three trips to get them all to the front desk.

The oldster raised an eyebrow and opened his mouth to object.

I know how to handle this one, Relliq thought. He just smiled and showed the writ. "You can check with his eminence if you wish."

"No, sire. That is not necessary. It was just that it is unusual for someone to take out so many books at one time."

"I am not the usual student," Relliq crowed. "I have a special task from the Oracle."

Whether it was his tone or the words, the oldster waved over a youth. "Help Acolyte Relliq carry the books back to his quarters."

Not even the emphasis on "acolyte" dimmed Relliq's excitement. *Finally, progress. And soon the archmage at my feet ... and Kia in my bed.*

The lure of the bed in the corner faded beneath the siren call of magic. Excitement, both at escaping the dull life and the prospect of achieving his goal of power, prevented any sleep. Even though he had to leave just after dawn, he stacked and re-stacked the books, deciding what he could take with him. Something drew him to a book wrapped in a cloth, tied with a purple ribbon. His fingers grazed the cover. Power, that of constrained magic, surged through his hands. A magical and physical seal had been applied to the ribbon. He looked closer. The journal wasn't from the current leader of the temple, but the one before. Entries recorded the arrival of new pilgrims, of hard-faced men who although they went through the motions never fully accepted the discipline. Script that appeared as if the author had hurriedly jotted down the words added that the leader of the men was a disgraced mercenary named Ruaridh and the one he obeyed was Bashim.

Jagged edges showed where someone had torn pages from the binding. There were so many blank and missing pages that Relliq flipped to the back of the volume and started working towards the front. Two dozen blank pages filled the last third of the volume. He searched the pages by vision and by rune to make sure there weren't any hidden messages.

A pattern soon revealed itself. The invisible runes held a message in the wizard's code. "And I can read it," Relliq gloated. "Even though the archmage didn't want me to learn his secret language, I taught myself it anyway."

Piecing together the runes and translating them took so much time he sensed the first silvering of dawn before he had copied down less than a quarter of the symbols. Just one more page, he promised himself. Then I'll eat and head out on the Oracle's assignment. His harsh laugh told of another thought. "Nothing says I have to return."

The next page revealed not the usual rune, but a paragraph that flamed red, as if its writer poured his lifeblood into the warning.

"I've found it," escaped as hissed words. "Found what was not meant to be read by any other than a future Oracle. Bashim used loyalty, love, and fear to boost his powers." Satisfaction colored his mind, yet the sense of something more dashed the exultation.

"Powers beyond ken, powers of stone,
Show me the secret hidden in this tome."

No tight script showed. Instead, the gray haze of another protective spell blurred the words. "No," Relliq cursed. "I will not be denied." Repeated calls for the message to be seen resulted in only two more words. *Blood sacrifice.*

His thoughts were a chaotic mixture of anger and determination. *Now I know what I need to gain the power I want. First I take the Temple, then the Isle.* His fist tightened at the memory of how he left the School of Mages. "The archmage will kneel before me … or die."

Chapter Thirteen

Slow steps took Brodie along the beach. The recognition ceremony was over, so even though he scanned the ground it was more in reflection than actual search for tokens for a dagger's hilt. After the excitement and anticipation of the council fire over, malaise seemed to hang over the isle. Only Ellspeth's bright beacon of her powers and Dal's determined good humor kept the darkness of depression at bay.

But he knew it was only a stop-gap measure. All too soon the shortened days and colder temperatures would restrict most of the residents to the immediate environs of the village. No more students studying in the grassy verge outside his forge, no more outdoor weapons training. Sessions would continue, however they would be smaller and in the practice ring of the stable.

A sigh escaped Brodie's soul. His life seemed particularly empty. Those who were going to the Temple of Givneh had set off that morning. Ellspeth and Denai had sailed *Windmaster* on the previous evening's tide to meet up with Mirrim's ship and to transfer those continuing on to the Southern Sea. Even though *Windmaster* had returned with the dawning and the vessel gently bobbed in her usual birth, the shadow of the missing hung over the isle.

A faint call impinged on his senses. It wasn't Ellspeth or Dal. And it didn't carry the tone of either of their girls. But the touch still felt familiar. He opened his mind to the mage's contact and with it came recognition—Kia. He knew she didn't like mindspeech. It was still too new to her. When she did reach out, she would be off by herself so she could use her voice to boost the connection without anyone hearing the conversation—or being thought crazy for talking to herself.

"My mare told me she wants to get out of the paddock and go for a run. Ellspeth said the weather would be nice this afternoon." A tentativeness entered Kia's tone. "Rielle asks if Wirake could accompany her."

"I'll ask Wirake. I'm sure he'll agree." Brodie dropped his mental voice to a conspiratorial whisper. "He's been fussing lately to take a run also." He left unvoiced the question if he was going to be invited as well.

Kia's hesitancy deepened. "Brodie, you're welcome to join us."

Swift thoughts finalized the arrangements. As soon as Kia ended the contact, Brodie headed for the communal kitchen to ask Murdo for a travel meal. The former mercenary was as adept with a pot and oven as he was with a sword.

"I'll prepare something special," Murdo said. "Kia deserves happiness; even if it is just food and wine while watching the sunset. It will be ready in half a candlemark."

True to his friend's word, the meal was ready within the allotted time. A wave of thanks and Brodie slung the saddlebags over his shoulder. The food sent over by Murdo weighed down one saddlebag and the bottle of wine Dal provided from the storage cave had been carefully stored in the other.

Shadows made by the sun directly overhead chased Brodie's steps as he returned to the stable. He had already set out both his and Kia's saddle on the paddock fence. Rielle whinnied a greeting and galloped over. Her ears flicked forward in a subtle request for a pat. Heavy hoof falls announced Wirake's arrival. The stallion stuck his head over the rail sending a whiff of oats into Brodie's face.

"All right, you greedy glut," Brodie said with a laugh. He dipped his fingers into a pocket and came out with two sugar cubes. A quick shift had one in each hand.

Wirake snatched the one cube, then tried for the other one.

Brodie pulled his hand back. "Uh... uh. One for the road and that is it, Wirake. The other is for Rielle."

Wirake's snort was a clear message. *If that is all you have, it will have to do.* He backed out and the mare stepped up and gently lipped the cube from Brodie's palm.

Laughing at his stallion's behaviour, Brodie saddled Wirake and tied the saddlebags into place. Well-practiced movements placed blanket and saddle on the mare and tightened the girth.

"Thank you for saddling Rielle," Kia said from behind Brodie's shoulder. She stood at the gate. A scan took in the split skirt several of the women had taken up as riding garb. A tug lifted the lockbar and she swung open the gate.

A toss of his mane and the stallion pranced out.

Kia's laugh mingled with Brodie's at the fàlaire's antics. Her smile grew when the mare walked from the paddock and knelt, putting nose to knee in an elegant bow.

"Why don't you do that, Wirake?" Brodie said in a mock growl. His answer was a bump to the shoulder that nudged him back a step.

Kia's chuckle helped ease Brodie's sense of loss. *Kia is a friend and can remain so even after her powers grow.*

"Be nice, Wirake, or Rielle won't let you join us." Kia admonished the stallion.

Wirake gave a sharp exhale. *I'll be coming if you want me to or not.*

The mare spun and flicked her tail. She coquettishly looked over her shoulder as if to say, *Behave and maybe we'll run together.*

Her actions filled the air with more laughter.

"Then let's go," Brodie said. He gestured at Rielle's saddle. "Kia, if I may?" At her nod, instead of the customary cupped hands used to assist in mounting, he placed his hands around her waist and lifted her into place. A deep breath pushed back the shock that ran through him at the contact. He stepped back with a bow in apology of the familiarity. Leather squeaked as he put a foot into a stirrup and swung one-handed into the saddle.

The fàlaires' slow trot allowed time for thought and to take in the scenery. And for Brodie, the occasional side glance at Kia. Each time, her smile was broader and broader, and he swore she seemed to come to life. Once the fàlaire crossed into their favorite pasture, Wirake whinnied a command to Rielle. Their gait slipped up to a canter and side-by-side they raced through the tall grass. Occasionally, either the mare or the stallion would pull slightly ahead. The one left behind would bugle a command and take a leap forward. Once they were again nose to nose, the fàlaire matched each other step for step.

Kia's laughter at their antics filled the air.

Brodie let a smile reach his lips. He stored the happiness and sense of belonging, both stronger than ever he'd felt before, in his heart as protection against the dark, lonely future he sensed was coming.

The stallion and mare worked their way back and forth across the pasture until Brodie called a halt to their racing. "To the beach, Wirake. Time for you to cool off."

Although they obeyed the command, neither fàlaire nor rider wanted to end the outing and they continued quite a distance along the beach. The fàlaire splashed through the waves until Brodie, tired of holding his feet up along Wirake's neck, told the stallion to slow down or let him off.

Wirake stopped and looked over his shoulder. His whuff communicated a clear message. Well, if you don't want to get wet, get off. He turned and trotted above the waterline and stopped.

"Why don't we strip Rielle and Wirake of their saddles and tack and let them run free for a while," Brodie said to Kia. "They'll return when it's time to go back to the village."

"What about the evening meal?"

"Wirake and Rielle can wait for their oats until they're back at the stable." Brodie pointed at the saddlebags behind him. "Our meals are in these."

"In that case, I agree." Kia's attempt to stand in the stirrups showed the toll the trip had taken. Her legs wobbled and she sat down hard on the saddle.

"Not far now," Brodie encouraged.

A few steps later they stopped at a natural shelter carved in the rock by the action of sand and water. Brodie waved at two flat top rocks that formed a bench and table. A fire had been laid in a shallow circle hollowed out by the repeated crash of waves. "Dinner at the finest inn on the isle."

Kia's lilt bounced off the cliff, "You planned this? How? We only decided to ride this morning."

Reveling in her pleasure, he joined in with a chuckle. "Not a real plan. I've walked past here from time to time. I thought it would be the perfect place for a picnic and stacked some driftwood to dry."

Swishes of their tails showed the fàlaires' impatience with human talk. They shifted from leg to leg while their saddles and bridles were stripped and set on a rock. Brodie slapped Wirake on the neck. "Go. Just don't drink the sea water."

Wirake's nudge to Brodie's shoulder sent Kia chuckling again. She rubbed the mare's nose. "See you later, Rielle."

The fàlaire galloped off, romping in the surf. They pranced in the water, spun to race onto the sand, then back into the waves.

"I'll start the fire," Kia said. Holding her hand above the small pyramid of wood, she whispered a soft incantation. A spark appeared within the heart of the driftwood and a heartbeat later flames raced up the branches.

The happiness on her face at what was normally a minor act of magic added to Brodie's pain. Turning away so she couldn't see the emotion, he folded the blanket he kept tied behind the saddle into a cushion. It only took a few moments to unpack the dinner and set it on the rocks at the edge of the fire to finish cooking. A flick of his knife undid the seal of the wine. White liquid splashed into the glasses and he handed her one. "With the archmage's compliments."

He sensed Kia's intense gaze and wondered at her thoughts.

She is a mage. I am a non-tal. We can be nothing but friends.

Murdo had pre-cooked the food so that only a quick browning was needed. A taste to verify it was hot enough, and Brodie scooped it into the dishes, handing it to Kia with a courtly bow. Taking his own plate, he sat down beside her, soaking in the serenity she projected.

Dishes washed and the last of the wine in their glasses, Brodie nodded at the fàlaire frolicking further down the beach. "Do you want to leave? I can whistle for Wirake." Even as he asked, Brodie prayed that Kia would refuse.

Her head tilted. "Rielle seems to be enjoying the outing. If you think we can find our way back to the stable in the dark, why don't we watch the sunset?"

Ducking his head to hide his pleasure, Brodie draped a blanket over her shoulders. "So you won't get a chill."

She leaned into his shoulder and with his arm around her waist they watched the sky turn a burnt orange. They didn't move even after the sun sank beneath the horizon and stars filled the heavens.

* * *

Dust covered the horse and rose with every hoof fall to coat Relliq's clothes. It infiltrated his nose and made each bite of food or drink of water taste like sand. I'd take another sip of water, he thought, but Wemsig is deep in the desert and to a section I haven't been to before. The water has to last until I get to the village. *I bet it doesn't even have a tavern, let alone mugs of cold brew.*

He considered using the reins as a crop to make the horse go faster, but knew no amount of whipping would make that happen. Even if it did, the packhorse following behind at the end of the lead rope would still slow them down. Which would just create more dust. "Why did the Oracle assign me this nag as a mount? There were many fine animals in the stables, yet I have to ride this old sway-back."

Why is the Oracle punishing me?

Maybe he's not, pride piped up.

Consideration of the thought occupied him and helped pass more candlemarks. "After all," he muttered, "the Oracle did send me out alone." Another idea cheered him up even more. "I'm out of the temple. Now I can study Bashim's journal without anyone interrupting me."

For more wagon lengths he debated not returning to the temple. Memory of the books of spells hidden beneath a loose floor stone shattered the idea. *I haven't had time to read them all, let alone learn the secrets of their magic.*

A panicked whimper pulled Relliq from his reverie. The blue sky had disappeared and a black cloud filled the entire area between horizon and sky. The pack animal reared, pulling the lead rope from Relliq's hand. His skin burnt from the rough fibers, he couldn't keep his grip on the rope. A final tug and the animal galloped off.

A change in the wind announced the dust storm's direction—straight towards him. The flat, open desert offered no sanctuary. There were tales of those who had their mounts lay down as a windbreak. And just as many, where the horse broke away. The only sure way to ensure the animal didn't run away would be to slit its throat. "Leaving me stranded, to walk to the village," Relliq growled. The horse beneath him tried to spin on its haunches. A hard tug on the reins turned its leap into a spin. Before he could prevent it, the animal snatched the bit in its teeth and raced towards a gray spire in the distance.

Wind-whipped sand pelted both horse and rider. Gusts clutched at Relliq's clothes. His hat had long since vanished into the storm. Eyes closed against the sting, he lay flat against the horse's neck. His arm mechanically rose and fell as he encouraged the exhausted animal onward. Relliq opened his eyelids a slit. Through the blur of tears, the spire passed by in a flicker of black. A darkness which in turn widened and deepened, then revealed itself as a rock wall.

The turbulence weakened. Head down, the horse plodded on.

A black slit appeared in the rock wall. The horse staggered in. It stopped and hung its head between splayed legs. As exhausted as his mount, Relliq remained draped over the animal.

Long candlemarks later, the howl of the wind penetrated his storm-bruised senses. He slipped from the saddle. His legs gave away, refusing to bear his weight. Damp stone chilled his skin … then blackness.

* * *

An eerie silence pulled Relliq from his stupor. Strained muscles left unused too long felt locked in place. Rubbing grit from his eyes didn't provide any details of his surroundings. The stygian dark of the underground remained.

He sent his mind back through his memories in search of where he was. Vague images of a whirling cloud of sand overtaking him shifted to one of a black slit in the cliff face. His senses told the moon was just rising, which meant three candlemarks had passed. A whispered incantation called forth magelight. The shadows cleared, revealing the refuge as a cave. *And I am not the first to use it*. A stack of branches and twigs in the corner told of previous habitation. Crunching from along the back wall told not only his horse's location, but also that of the packhorse. And that they had found something to eat.

Dry lips reminded him of a need more urgent than fire. Stiff fingers pulled the canteen from its holder. Sloshes provided the bad news. The container was almost empty.

"I would find a traveler's shelter with no water." Relliq's words echoed off the walls. They brought forth the faint memory of the shimmer of water before the dust cloud's approach. He hoped the lake wasn't a desert illusion. Pulling his scrying crystal from his pocket, he cast his senses out into the storm that again howled outside. He couldn't even tell if the sun was in the sky or if stars glittered in the heavens. Beyond the cave entrance nothing existed except a cyclone of sand that whirled to the sky, and as far as he could tell, all the way to the distant horizon.

The blankness of the crystal brought forth memories of other searches. "I may be alone, but I don't have to be *alone*." At his words, the munching stopped, and Relliq saw the horses flick their ears before returning attention to the few grains of feed they had found.

Crystal in hand, he called forth Kia's image. Unlike his other attempts since leaving the temple when the stone remained unchanged, this time her image shimmered into being. "Yes," he chortled, "she's outside the protection of the wards of the isle."

Tilting the stone back and forth, he focused on Kia. This time he sensed the sea.

The impression of another presence intruded.

Kia is not alone. Rage flared at the identification of her companion. "She's having dinner with the smith." Relliq's words bounced off the stone walls. "That one will be the first man to bow to me. His devotion will feed my power." Emotion twisted Relliq's lips into a rictus. "Then Kia will stand by my side." Heat from the memory of the previous night's dream crept down his back. "If she refuses, there are others."

* * *

Kia stood before the door to the office used by Ellspeth. A rap of her knuckles on the office door resulted in a light "Enter." Despite the tone, Ellspeth's call sent the fire racing along Kia's nerves again. She hesitated. How to tell Lady Ellspeth about that night on the beach? She would want to know about Brodie—and his feelings for me.

And yours for him, her heart snuck in.

At the repeated invitation, she pushed open the door.

Ellspeth looked up. "Come in, Kia." She gestured at a chair. "I'm glad you're here. I've been meaning to ask you over. We haven't had much time to get acquainted." The other woman shrugged. "Some days I feel it is a case of the teacher being only two steps ahead of their students."

"More like one step," Kia said.

"Don't sell yourself short. I've seen the student's improvement since you came to the isle." Ellspeth's smile conveyed more than confidence, but a surety of the belief. "Dal and I do appreciate your agreeing to be an instructor here. I know it is quite a change for you, being away from your family and the temple."

A shadow flickered across her face so quickly Kia thought she had imagined it. What had happened to the archmage's lady in the temple? It was a place of hope and charity. Her thoughts swirled. I know neither Dal nor Ellspeth have an issue with Brantly. They helped bless his ordination. Then she remembered that Ellspeth's first time through the golden gates was not under Brantly, but the one she had only heard about in whispers—the false oracle, Bashim.

"Lady Ellspeth, I need some advice."

White hair swayed when the woman nodded in understanding. A smile twitched her lips.

"You know?" Kia stuttered. "Does Lord Dal know also?"

"I keep few secrets from my mate," Ellspeth laughed. "You'll find out that the fàlaire are not above participating in—or manipulating—the lives of those they've chosen as their riders. Rielle told my mare you were feeling lonely. My mare bespoke Tairneach. They came up with a plan. Rielle would ask for Wirake's company on a ride."

Enlightenment dawned on Kia. "Which means Brodie would come also." She shook her head. "Lady Ellspeth, you're telling me Rielle set me up on a date?" An unladylike snort escaped. "No more treats for that one."

Ellspeth's amused lilt filled the office. "You should ask Dal about some of the shenanigans Tairneach has pulled. Especially the night he hid in the darkness outside our camp." Her shrug showed there was more to the story she wasn't going to tell. "Of course, that was before I knew fàlaire, especially the head stallion, had a kind of magic of their own." Her expression brightened as if the story brought forth a fond memory. "And there is the tale of when Dal and Taer were trapped on a cliff edge. Taer leaped into open space and sprouted wings like a great hunting bird." Ellspeth's chuckle deepened. "Dal had no idea Taer could fly... or more accurately glide like a hawk on the wind."

Realization the other woman shared not only a secret—but insight into the archmage warmed Kia. Which left unanswered the question. *Of all those on the isle, why did Rielle arrange for Brodie to join us? Did she want a romp in the surf with Wirake? Or for me to be with Brodie?*

A mental note to have a talk with the mare, aided by a handful of sugar cubes and orange roots to obtain her cooperation, and Kia shifted her thoughts to another problem that required handling—her stalker.

I should talk to Lady Ellspeth now, she thought.

"There is nothing to talk about," a voice whispered in her mind. "Forget, little wizardling. Forget."

The other woman stretched in a leonine move. "Sorry, Kia. It's not your presence. It's just been a long day. I sense something else, but a hesitance as well."

Where just a moment before, her thought was clear, now she couldn't remember what she had really come to talk to Ellspeth about. "It is late. Can we speak tomorrow?"

"Of course, child. Would you like Dal there as well?"

Kia stared at her hands. "I wouldn't want to impose."

"No imposition, Kia. You have my word." Ellspeth gestured at the tower around them. "Dal and I promised your brother to care for you as if you were our own daughter." Her chortle bounced off the walls. "And while we're happy you accepted the call and found your journeyman dagger, to tell you the truth, we're even happier you're not like Denai and Elendl." She leaned in closer and in a conspiratorial whisper added. "They are my daughters, but they can be a handful."

Rising she guided Kia to the door. "Sleep well, Kia, daughter of Forsom, sister of Brantly. Till the morrow let no trouble cross your shadow."

Soft steps took Kia from the room. A heartbeats hesitation at the door to the outside, a deep breath, and with the benison wrapped around her as a shield, she crossed the threshold.

Chapter Fourteen

As it had the evening before, the impression of being watched remained strong. Repeated looks over her shoulder failed to reassure Kia until she slipped into the shadow of a tree and listened for footsteps in the darkness. She could feel the presence even though no one was in sight. For long moments, she cast her senses into the night. Only the sound of the gentle breeze that ruffled her hair returned.

A deep breath and she squared her shoulders. "This is ridiculous." She kept her tone soft, in contrast to the strong emotion the words implied. A ten count later she left her hiding place and headed to the light shining from the entrance to the council tower. She knew it came from the lower room the archmage used as a private office, but not who the occupant was. Dal or Ellspeth?

"It doesn't matter," Kia muttered. "Either one will be able to help."

The lantern's glow quickened her steps. She didn't slow down until her foot crossed the tower's threshold. Breath gushed out at the watcher's sudden presence. "Come to me, little wizardling," whispered in her mind. "Join me and live." Her muscles froze. She couldn't move, couldn't get to the safety of Ellspeth's office.

"Kia, what's wrong? You're shaking."

Ellspeth's scared words broke through the thrall, freeing Kia. Her fingers clenched into fists so tight, the skin turned translucent. "He's here," she stammered. The rest of her words died in her throat.

"Not for long," Ellspeth snarled. Her fingers flicked in a ritual gesture of protection. Yellow beams flew from her fingers to cover her, then spread into a protective dome over Kia. Golden threads interwove between the lighter-colored ribbons to form a solid shield.

The ethereal link vanished. A gasp escaped through Kia's tightened lips.

"Better now?" Ellspeth pressed.

"Yes, mistress."

"Then let us get you into my office."

With the other woman's support, Kia staggered into the room before slumping bonelessly into the guest chair next to the desk. Three more heartbeats passed before Kia felt able to speak. "Mistress, I am new to magic, at least the formal kind taught in the school."

Ellspeth perched on the edge of the desk, waiting. "Go on, child."

The words rushed out. "Does the feeling of being watched ever go away?"

Now Kia knew she didn't imagine the other woman's reaction. "Unless you announce yourself, it is considered bad form to spy on someone," Ellspeth said. "Except in an emergency, most would ask for approval to visit by crystal. And at the very least would announce themselves." Her voice softened. "Kia, my mate mentioned an unknown observer at the temple."

"And on the trip here," Kia added.

"We'd hoped you would find peace here on the isle, that the protective wards placed around it would block any unauthorized intrusion." A stray silver lock escaped its knot as she shook her head. "Your mutter a few moments ago, whoever penetrated those at the temple, did so here at the isle." Anger changed the color of her eyes from green to steel gray. "And the tower itself."

"Could it be one of my students?" Despite voicing the question, Kia prayed the answer would be, "no." She liked the boys and girls in her class. "The nightly visits had stopped until recently."

Until the ride with Brodie, worry hissed. Maybe he is your stalker.

No, Kia reassured herself. Brodie is not a mage. Even if he was, he is too good a man. He would NOT stalk.

So who? worry pressed.

Ellspeth read off a list of the active mages. "There aren't that many with the ability for the level of advanced scrying needed to reach you here. Barris and Nobyn are the most experienced." Her eyebrow rose in questioning.

"No, mistress," Kia reassured the older woman. "I know their mental touch. It wasn't them. Your and the archmage's first apprentices are friends." Only one name stayed with her, Relliq.

A soft rustle reminded Kia, Ellspeth waited for a response. "I felt the watcher when I first arrived. He went away after the recognition ceremony." Kia stared down at her hands. "I felt it again on the beach the other night. Now it's almost constant."

Ellspeth's eyes held sadness and an understanding. "Many seasons ago, when my powers were just awakening, there was a rogue wizard who haunted my dreams. I couldn't sleep without hearing, 'Come to me, little wizardling.'"

Shivers racked Kia.

"Sorry, child," Ellspeth's soft tone whispered. "I didn't mean to upset." She came around the desk and engulfed Kia in an embrace. Warmth from the other woman surrounded Kia until the shakes passed.

"You didn't, mistress. It was just that your words sounded so familiar."

"The one who spoke them to me is dead." Ellspeth loosened the embrace, then tightened it again when Kia tensed.

Kia heard the surety of knowledge in the other woman's tone and forced herself to relax.

Ellspeth took a step back, snagged a chair and pulled it next to Kia. "So, my dear, let us focus on yours."

In the flickering candlelight, under Ellspeth's encouraging nods and warm clasp, Kia recounted every occurrence of her unseen watcher. No detail, from time of day to phase of the moon, was left hidden.

Finally, Ellspeth called a halt to the questioning. The moon shining through the tower windows told of time passed. "Kia, Dal and I both agree. Brodie will escort you to your cottage. He may not have active magic, but his strength can help reinforce yours." The hand she laid on Kia's shoulder felt warm and reassuring. "My dear, I understand you've been introduced to TânOer?"

Too exhausted to speak, Kia just nodded.

"Then, Kia, you'll have another weapon at your disposal. The magic and power inherent in the sword can also serve to boost your own. Do you remember your brother and father's instructions on how to do so?"

Again a silent nod.

Ellspeth opened the door to reveal Brodie leaning against the opposite wall.

He pushed off and swept an arm out in a bow. "May I escort you home, m'lady?"

Kia smiled. Brodie's mere presence helped restore some of the energy lost due to the workings. "Very well, m'lord. But be warned I don't bestow my favors lightly."

Memory of the low voice and the power within it still haunted her enough she didn't object to Brodie's arm around her waist as he guided her to the outside. One step past the tower's protection, she tensed, expecting to hear the stalker's call. She grasped the incantation Ellspeth had taught her, and wrapped the golden threads tightly around her as a cape.

No sounds other than those of the night reached her ears—or her mind.

* * *

Winds howled outside the cave. Just beyond the entrance, columns of sand wheeled and pirouetted. Relliq watched the otherworldly dance. Anger mingled with dread. Desert storms were known to last for days. Some lasted season after season until the dunes swallowed up entire cities. Water wouldn't be a problem. Although the trickle of water into the basin in the back of the cavern was slow, it was steady enough to keep both the small basin and the larger trough the horses used half-way full. Food for himself and the horses was a different issue. What grain had been left in the cave was almost gone. "And," he snarled, "they didn't leave any real food. Just a small bag of meat so dry I had to soak it for three candlemarks in hot water to make it the least bit edible."

Once again Relliq heaped silent curses on the leader of the temple. "It was only supposed to take me a sevenday to reach the village and I was only released supplies for that length of time plus an extra day or two." *I've already been trapped in this hell-hole for five days.*

Panicked whinnies from the improvised stable pulled his thoughts away from the storm. Hoof falls on stone quickened his steps. Where before the horses had been only skittish, now their eyes whirled in fear. Even hobbled, they struggled towards the back of the chamber. The scream of the wind overwhelmed those of the animals. Repeated soft calls of "easy boy… easy boy" and he was finally able to grab the tether ropes. Three loops through a hole in the rock made it harder for them to escape.

"Just stay here, boys," he told the prancing animals. "It's safer here than outside, and you wouldn't want to get stuck in some twisting passage." A twitch of his fingers and a ball of orange magefire formed in his palm. A toss and it landed on a ledge to cast the space in a warm glow.

With a second ball floating ahead to lead the way he raced to the entrance.

A strong gust shrieked a banshee warning. Before he could move, sand stung every inch of exposed skin. In a long leap he took shelter behind a rock. The precariousness of his situation grew more apparent with each look. The sand that had only been a few grains deep a candlemark earlier, now reached to his knees. Thoughts whirled, seeking a means of barricading the entrance. Each option was reviewed and discarded. The only thing large enough to stop the inflow of sand would be one of the horses. At the rate of the drift's growth, it would take both horses' carcasses just to slow it down. "And if I kill them, I'll have to walk across the desert," escaped in a growl.

The retreat deeper into the cave to where the larger chamber split from the narrow slot to the outside offered no real respite. From the more protected spot he watched more sand blow in. Curses bounded off the walls. No longer knee high, the pile of sand against the wall came to his waist. If the storm continued much longer, the drift would block the entire entrance, trapping him.

Snatching up a y-shaped branch from the woodpile, he slid a shirt over the two arms to create a makeshift shovel. Push by push, he moved the sand out of the way until his back ached and blisters covered his palms. Breathing deeply, he stopped to rest.

"No... no... no!" Although he had a walkway clear of sand down to bare stone, it was only an arms'-length long and half that wide. No progress had been made in clearing the entrance. "If brute force won't work," he muttered, "magic will."

"Winds be calm,
And no more blow.
Sunshine return,
Selah, make it so."

For a long moment, Relliq's senses pierced the darkness outside. Instead of the expected silence, if anything, the wind sounded louder. The mountain seemed to shake under the storm's fury.

A different spell, one to control the wind's direction rather than ending the storm followed. He tried incantation after incantation and every magical gesture in his repertoire. Each was as unsuccessful as the one before. The more energy he fed into the workings, the more exhausted he became, and his efforts only seemed to feed the unnatural weather. Rather than fighting the storm, he considered something different, a protective spell. *Magic might not stop the storm, but can create a wall across the entrance. I'll have to angle it. Otherwise I would only be creating a temporary barrier and the dirt will still be there, only a little farther from the slot.*

In clear tones, he called out the incantation. The miasma in front of the opening lightened. Three steps took him from behind the stone windbreak. He stopped and raised his arms, his hands together, fingers pointed towards the wind. A spark of heat flared between his palms. Relliq threw strength into his magic, and the fire spread to form an orange glow to encompass his entire body. The radiance expanded out in a wedge. The winds broke apart like a wave going around a headland. Closing his eyes in concentration, he held the bulwark against the weather.

No pellets stung his face. Emboldened, Relliq edged towards the outside. The closer he went, the harder it became to hold his magic together against the weather's fight. His legs shook and a heartbeat later, he sat down hard. Like a living thing sensing weakness, the storm pounced. The wind picked up intensity. The block flickered, then resumed when he fed more power into it.

A shift put his back against the wall. "Sitting is more comfortable than standing," escaped in a mutter to be snatched away by the winds. A few wiggles to get comfortable and he resumed his vigil. The orange glow of his spell formed a shimmering dome. Relliq prayed the sand piling atop it wasn't too deep. Otherwise when the spell ended, even without the storm feeding the drift, the entrance could be buried.

For long candlemarks he held the fragile protection against the howling winds. Whenever his magic wavered, the storm attacked and he had to throw additional power into his spell to regain lost ground. After what felt like days, he watched pillar after whirling pillar stop its frenetic dance. The sand that had lain above the invisible barrier fell to the desert floor in a cloud of dust. Exhausted, his hands dropped into his lap. His eyelids closed.

* * *

An unearthly stillness tugged at Relliq's senses. Deafened by the hours of fighting the tempest, it took several moments to acknowledge the silence. He opened his eyes, not to the gray haze of the storm, but to the blackness of night. An occasional star peeked through the scattered clouds. The wan light of the twin moons, Neba and Shartle, appeared in the heart of his crystal. A brief incantation revealed the storm's current location. It was close enough to spin and return to bury any unwary traveller. Curses learned in the back streets spilled from his lips. "And, it's heading straight for Wemsig."

Reasons to continue onto the village fought with those to head back to Givneh.

Self-preservation voted for the security of the temple.

Pride said the way into the Oracle's favor was to complete the assignment.

Exhaustion held the winning vote. Rest for now. Nothing needs to be decided until tomorrow. Wrapping a blanket around his shoulders and setting his back against the wall, he slid to the floor and sank into the cottony warmth of sleep. The beginnings of a dream flickered in his mind. Sunlight burnished a pair of tall metal gates a golden orange. A tall, thin man walked through the opening, stopped, and turned to look back.

As Relliq watched, the scene shifted. He looked down as if from a great height. The city now appeared in the center of a great basin surrounded by steep cliffs. Streams rushed from crevices in the cliff walls and water lapped at the city's walls. A blue dome formed over entire valley, including the city. The water didn't recede. Instead, the city appeared to sink beneath the waters until even the tallest spire vanished beneath the still surface of the lake.

Dawn showed the man walking in the desert. Footprints led deeper into the dunes until they vanished at the horizon. Behind him, smoke rose in a twisting column from the summit of a mountain in the distance.

The curl of smoke triggered the recall of other pillars, ones of whirling sand. The dream and the memory of the storm reminded Relliq of the legend of Belrum who started the School of Mages. Of how the wizard had walked out of the desert, then as an old man returned to it, never to be seen again.

"If Belrum is real," Relliq mused, "then maybe the lost city in the book also exists." A rumble of hunger erupted from his stomach. Swift movements rummaged through the saddlebags. Only a book fell out. There was no food left. "Since I can't leave, I might as well read." *It might keep my mind off my empty belly.*

> *"Book of old, holder of knowledge,*
> *Show me Belrum and the city of gold."*

Pages flipped as an invisible force moved through them. The book lay open to a sketch of the city beneath the lake. Relliq lay his finger on the center of the image. Once again the city rose from the crater. An unseen narrator translated the faded cryptic markings. "In a time before memory, the fires inside the mountain cooled. Those who wanted to study the Way built a great city inside the volcano's crater. Protected by magic, they summoned storms to fill the great bowl with water to protect their land from outsiders." A pause and a final fact was disclosed. "Once every 100 lifetimes the city re-appears."

A pen and ink drawing of a smoking mountain filled most of the next page. Smaller images, all drawn by the same hand, surrounded the base of the mountain. Relliq leaned in closer. Two of the pictures looked like the chamber he was in and showed its creation from liquid stone flowing from the mountain. Tight script beneath it referred to the tunnel as a lava tube.

Hope whispered the prayer that what looked like a lake in the drawing wasn't in actuality a lake of boiling rock like what oozed from the smoking mountains of the southern continent.

Curiosity entered its own comment whether somewhere in the cave, in an adjoining chamber (or chambers) he corrected, was another exit. One that would lead to the center of the mountain—and the sunken city.

Or his stomach added, to another traveler's shelter, one with food. The reminder of food came with a growl.

"Exploring it is." A ball of magefire to lead the way and he headed through the impromptu stable and into the cave itself. At each intersection, he marked his path with a glowing rune so he could find the way back. One chamber led into a second, and a third, each becoming wider and taller. The magelight showed something else. The walls and roof were rounded as in the drawings. It wasn't a cave, but a tunnel. No, he corrected, an escape tube for the molten rock. I'm in what was once a smoking mountain. Candlemarks later, hunger forced him back to the entrance.

Chapter Fifteen

Relliq traced the blue runes with a finger. He repeated the incantations and the preparations to use them until he was sure of their recall. Page after page, he repeated the process. However, Bashim's cryptic notes raised more questions than they answered.

"Come on," Relliq growled. "The answer has to be here. Bashim was a great mage ... and I have his notes." A candlemark later, a triumphant "Yes!" echoed around the chamber. Glowing on the page were instructions on binding a subject's mind.

Anger pulled a curse from Relliq's lips. The final rune, the key to the entire spell, flickered between a cold blue and an orange flame. Someone had placed a block on the notebook. Undeterred, he threw all his magic against the spell that stopped the wizard's mark from showing its true form.

Sparks flew from the page. In their wake a single word appeared–*blood*.

"Something is missing," he snarled. "That is only half the incantation." Head down, he flipped back to the first page and started over. The effort took more time than the other reviews as each page revealed a previously hidden rune. Line after line of cryptic symbols was interpreted. Not even the cool night air broke his concentration. By the first rays of the dawn, he closed the cover.

"I have the way of it now," he chortled. "The secret of binding another's will is now mine. All I need is someone in a position of power to take as my slave... and the blood to make it so." *The donor need not be willing.*

Satisfaction mingled with anticipation failed to overcome the exhaustion that pulled him down into the darkness.

* * *

Nickers echoed around the chamber. The stomp of an angry animal brought Relliq to full awareness. It is just one of the horses, he reassured himself. They stood with their heads down; nibbling on the last few bits of grain that had been found in the bottom of the saddlebag. "I will have to find some feed at the village," he muttered, "or the horses will never get me back to the temple." *Or anywhere else I want to go.*

A parched throat and the rumble of an empty stomach demanded attention. I can at least answer one need, he decided and reached for the water bag. Muscles stiffened from candlemarks hunched over the rock that served as a writing desk, then the awkward position he fell asleep in, screamed in agony. Deep breaths pushed back the pain until he could move. He walked over to the entryway and looked out.

Clear blue sky greeted him. Not a single column of whirling sand disrupted the horizon. His senses showed no remnants of the storm remained as far as his crystal could reach. I might as well start out now, he thought. The sun will soon be down. And with the cooler night air we can make better time.

The animals fidgeted. The packhorse bent its head and allowed the halter to be slipped into place. However, the other horse refused the bit. "Behave," Relliq ordered. "The book doesn't state donor blood has to be human." His voice sharpened. "I can always use a test subject." He jumped back as teeth flashed a finger length from his hand. Despite the horses' objections, the saddles were put into place and the girths tightened. Relliq carefully repacked the journals and tied the bags on the supply horse. Gathering up the reins, he led the two horses out of the cave. A final look at his place of refuge and he climbed into the saddle. Quick

151

flicks of the reins and the horse beneath him moved out. As it had before, the packhorse balked until the line played out, before slowly following.

Unlike the trip to the cave where the horses fought the bit and lead, now they walked without encouragement. The coming of full dark and they picked up their pace even more. Between the rocking motion and the lingering effects of fighting the storm, Relliq slipped into a light slumber.

The slowing of the horse's movement signalled an alert and Relliq opened his eyes. Instead of the endless vista of brown that accompanied him into sleep, the sky brightened with the first signs of dawning and revealed not the expected dunes, but a cluster of stone buildings. "I've arrived," escaped his cracked lips.

Moments later, he pulled up his mount when a young boy of about twelve turns blocked the way. "May I help you, stranger?"

"Yes. Take me to my quarters."

"Your quarters? And you are?"

Heat flushed up Relliq's neck. He straightened up and glared at the youth. "I am Relliq, special envoy from the Oracle of the Temple of Givneh."

Showing a poise greater than his age, the boy bowed. When he rose, he pointed towards the other side of town. "If you would follow me, sire."

With each building they passed, Relliq felt more eyes upon him. His back straight, he ignored the stares from the invisible watchers. *I am Relliq, a mage of the first level. Soon not just the residents of this two-horse town will bow to me, but all those with powers as well.*

The youth stopped in front of a two-room stone hut with what looked like a small addition. "This used to be the quarters for the village healer. Since he has returned to the temple, it is now yours."

"It is not acceptable," Relliq snapped. A low rumble issued from his stomach. "Go, boy, and bring me some food. I travelled far and long today and desire nourishment."

As he had earlier, the youth bowed. "As you wish. It is long past the breakfast hour. However, my mother might have something in the cupboard. I will see what I can find."

"And, while you are at it, summon the elders to attend me," Relliq added with a wave of dismissal.

The youth headed down the street at a slow jog.

"I might as well make myself comfortable while I wait," Relliq told the horses. "No sense waiting outside when a comfortable chair is a few steps away." His feet barely touched the ground before the animals walked the few feet to the patch of green that grew in the shadow of the building. Soon, both horses were contentedly munching the sparse sprigs of grass.

Two steps inside the door, Relliq halted. No comfortable chair greeted him. Only a rough-hewn wooden table and bench, and a rope bed devoid of sleeping furs filled the space. A thimble of salt had been carefully placed in the center of the table in the traditional signal of leave-taking that marked the building available for any who wished to occupy it. Legs made wobbly from time in the saddle carried him to the bench where he sprawled on the hard surface. While I wait for my dinner, I might as well visit Kia, he decided. It has been some time since we've been together.

Stripping off the headscarf and robe used for desert travel, he fished the crystal from his belt pouch.

"*From far and near, a vision clear.*
The image of the summoned one appear."

The heart of the crystal remained blank.

"That incantation should work," Relliq snarled. "My powers are now strong enough to pierce the wards around the isle." He tried again … then a third and fourth time. With each attempt anger added strength beyond his normal power. Yet, he did not see Kia in the crystal, nor sense her.

Maybe Kia has also grown in power, his heart whispered. That would make her an even better mate.

153

"She cannot be stronger than me. It is that damn archmage keeping her from me. Keeping me from what I want."

Anger quashed the competing thoughts as Relliq sought an acceptable excuse. "Wemsig is the problem," he growled. "It is so far from civilization even the power of magic is taxed."

Unable to sit, he stood and paced the floor. Each time he passed the empty door, rage built against the town, against the site of what was in essence exile from all he wanted. "Boils on everyone in the town," he snarled. Then in the same breath added, "No, that would not be enough for what they are putting me through. I will take their minds, then their coins, and then their lives." Passion warmed his face. "Then I shall take care of that archmage, and if she stands in my way, his silver-haired lady."

And Kia will be mine. With enough blood to boost my power, she will come to me willingly.

Plans formed and Relliq dragged the bench to the table. Pen and a sheaf of paper were pulled from one knapsack. Maybe I should use blood to write my plans, he thought. That will ensure their success. Just as quickly, he dismissed the idea. *The only blood to use is mine. And it is too good for such a simple use. I'll need it to cast the spell of sickness.*

Maybe, it doesn't have to be pure blood, curiosity cautioned. A drop or two in the ink would test the theory.

Careful so as not to spill it, he removed an inkwell from its wooden box and unwrapped it. Slowly, he pressed the pen into his thumb until a spot of blood formed. A squeeze and three drops floated on the ink. Dabbing the pen into the mixture, he scratched a few lines on the paper. *Come to me, little wizardling.*

The words glowed on the page.

"Yes," Relliq crowed. "Success ... and Kia... will soon be mine."

* * *

154

During the short walk to the barn, Brodie's fears grew. Each step he took felt like he went back in time until he was the scared boy who braced the older, experienced mercenary on that battlefield so many seasons ago. At the narrow door that led to the exercise ring, he stopped. Hands thrust deep into the pockets of the heavy coat, he relived the blow that disarmed him and set the direction for the rest of his life. The morning's chill didn't penetrate his skin, only his soul.

"This is ridiculous," he growled. "I am not that boy… and Dal is my friend. We have sparred many times over the turns." *And I've fought Murdo just as many times.* Still, the feeling persisted. In his heart he refused to acknowledge the real reason for anxiety. Today's session would not be only between him and the archmage. The session would begin with Dal working with Kia on a new control technique. *And I will be the target of both her magic and sword.*

"Good morning, Brodie."

Kia's voice broke into his reverie. He turned to see her hurrying down the street. Her coat flapped with her movement giving glimpses of the sword hanging from her hip.

"Sorry, Kia. I didn't see you."

"You were deep in thought."

Unwilling to discuss it, he just shrugged. "Ready for your lesson?"

"Yes, and no."

The raised eyebrow to encourage her also served to distract her from asking any more questions.

"Dal says I'm ready for the next phase in the control of my magic…"

"But, you're not sure." Brodie finished. A smile he really didn't feel flickered into being then vanished just as quickly. "Don't worry, Kia. Dal might be the archmage, however he wouldn't knowingly put you in harm's way. Besides, you have me to protect you."

Her sharp bark of a laugh repaid him for the comment and lightened his mood.

155

He pushed open the door and gestured her in. Stepping inside, he stripped off his coat and tossed it into a corner.

Kia considered doing the same. Instead she reached up and hung her coat on a peg alongside the door. Unbuckling the scabbard from her waist, she pulled out the sword and hung the sheath on a peg alongside the coat.

A sound shifted her attention to the hall that led to the main stable and Dal emerged from the shadows. Kia shuddered at the force of the archmage's stare. It went layer by layer, as if he saw through the skin to her essence. Still she held her head high, and her grip tight on the sword. Whatever he perceived must have satisfied him for he nodded approval.

"We don't need to consecrate the space," he said. "The spells won't be that strong. There is one thing, though. I'd like a little more light." He raised his hands and Kia felt the gathering of magic. Beams of sunlight flooded the room and banished the lingering shadows. Dal walked to the middle of the exercise ring. His sword left its scabbard with a sibilant hiss.

At his wave Kia moved to his side. She saw that TânOer's sheath lay atop Brodie's jacket. Light glinted off the naked blade in his hand. "Ready?" she called.

A deep breath to center herself and she started the spell.

"Without cloud, without thunder,
Skies now be ripped asunder.
Lightning be…"

The last line remained unvoiced. The power grew, building on its own unresolved energy. Kia's jaw tensed with the effort of maintaining control. A single word escaped … *"summoned."*

All the power released. A bolt of lightning flew from her sword—and its target was Brodie. "No," she cried. Her frightened gaze sought him out, expecting to see a charred, or at least a smoking body.

Relief gushed out from between her tight lips. The remnants of the spell glittered around TânOer's blade. Brodie stood unharmed in the middle of the exercise ring. His broad smile showed not relief, but a satisfied pleasure.

How is Brodie fine? Kia wondered. He is no mage.

Dal's warm hand on her shoulder stopped the reflection. "Congratulations, Kia. That was an excellent first try."

Kia hung her head. "I lost control," came out in a moan. "I could have killed Brodie."

A finger tipped up her chin, facing her to meet Dal's understanding gaze. "Believe me, Kia, daughter of Forsom, sister of Brantly, you did well." His tone softened. "Brodie was in no danger. I placed a protective shield around him and reinforced the inherent ability of TânOer's steel to block spells. So what you perceive as danger wasn't."

Silence greeted the statement. The cold chill of fear dissolved in the heat of anger. She glared at Brodie. "You could have told me."

The shrug and impish smile he returned cooled the heat that lingered in her heart. Despite her intention to stay angry, she couldn't hold the glare.

"All right," Dal said. "Back to work. Kia, try to call lightning and see how long you can hold off the final cue."

By the time Dal called a halt, the bright yellow beams of mid-day filled the exercise space, banishing the last of the morning's coolness. "I think that is enough practice for you, Kia." He ran fingers through sweat-dampened curls and Kia realized the archmage also had expended significant energy during the training session.

"Kia, Lady Ellspeth and I would like you and Brodie to join us for a meal. It was supposed to be a nooning, however, whatever Murdo is preparing is not quite ready." His smile told that he knew more than he let on about the 'whatever.' "Brodie and I have a few moves we've been wanting to work on." He shrugged. "Now's as good a time as any. Kia, you are welcome to stay and watch if you wish."

Kia searched Brodie's face, trying to discern his wishes. Although his face remained expressionless, eagerness radiated from him.

It has been a while since you spent some time with Brodie, desire whispered. There are no students here, only the archmage.

"I'll stay," Kia answered in response to Dal's raised eyebrow. Steps slow from both the physical and mental effort she had expended took her to the nearest wall and she leaned against it.

Bowing to Kia, Brodie murmured, "I hope it won't affront your sensibilities, but this room is warm." A single tug and his shirt joined the coat on the floor. He tipped the blade in salute, first to Dal and then Kia. Three strides and he stood in the middle of the room. His muscles rippled from the weight of the blade as he twirled it through a series of one-handed figure eights.

Waves of energy raced up Kia's back. She searched for the reason. None of the other men of her acquaintance had ever affected her this way. Between caregiving the ill at the temple and sails across Botunn Loghes, it was not as if she had not seen a man's naked chest.

She turned and realized that while she had watched Brodie, Dal had removed his vest, hung it on a peg and rolled up his sleeves. His sword glinted in the light as the archmage moved in a series of graceful moves. "Let us begin."

Brodie rushed. His sword struck Dal's block. Back and forth, the two men moved across the dirt floor. The sound of metal against metal mingled with the grunt of the fighters. With each attack and counter, the blows came quicker and harder. Brodie used his heavier weight to force Dal back, who then used his greater depth of experience to counter. Three steps took Brodie out of the mage's reach. Chests heaving, the pair sucked down long gasps of air. The tips of their swords rested lightly on the sand.

The tingle she had come to associate with her watcher tickled Kia's senses. Before she could say anything, "Come to me, little wizardling," hissed in her ears.

Tell Dal, fear urged.

Before she could react, the sparring resumed.

I can't, she wanted to moan. My call could break their concentration and Dal, or worse, Brodie could get hurt. I can't interrupt them.

"There is one thing I can do," she whispered. "Protect myself." A flick of her fingers and a dome of golden ribbons formed around her. A second gesture brought purple lines into existence. Her low command of "weave," sent the shimmering threads weaving in and out of the ribbons until they created a solid wall.

The shield shattered into tiny sparkles that flared into nothingness.

Surprise mingled with her fear. *How could he break through my spell? Ellspeth taught me the incantation and she is almost as powerful as the archmage.*

The presence returned, stronger than she had ever felt it. "Come to me, little wizardling. Join me or die."

Shock added to the exhaustion left over from her previous workings. Legs wobbled and refused to bear weight. Unable to move, she slid down the wall.

"Kia!" Brodie yelled.

Strength from the arms around her and from other sources as well flooded into her. "I've got you," he whispered.

She looked up into his tortured eyes.

"Dal, what's wrong with her? She's turned white." Brodie's voice thickened. "Is it her magic?"

"No," Kia stammered. "My watcher... he's back."

"Dal, enough is enough," Brodie growled.

"I agree," the archmage answered, his tone forbidding. Kia looked from one man to the other. The archmage's expression was as fierce as his tone. "Rest easy, Kia. My wife will be here in a few moments and we'll track down your watcher. And, if it's Relliq, as archmage I swear for his transgressions his powers will be bound."

The crash of a door announced Ellspeth's arrival. "I'm here."

"I didn't mean to cause such problems," Kia grunted. "It was just that he took me by surprise." She lifted a hand to Ellspeth. "I used the protection spell you taught me. Whoever the watcher is not only pierced the shield, he shattered it."

"Don't worry, my child," the other woman said. "You did well." Her gaze rose to her husband's. "He must have found something to boost his powers ..." Her voice trailed off.

Kia caught a look between the pair. "Please, tell me."

"Not now," Ellspeth said, her tone brooked no objection. 'I was on my way here because Murdo said the meal is ready. Kia, if you feel strong enough I think we'll all benefit from some food." A smile brightened her face. "Maybe Brodie can lend you an arm? After all, he's already holding you."

"I don't want to be a bother."

"You aren't," Brodie answered the comment not just with his voice. His arms tightened and he rose, gently setting her on her feet.

After a moment, Kia pushed away. "I'm fine now."

Brodie crooked an elbow. "In that case, m'lady. I'm famished. If the lord and his lady would lead the way, we can take care of that."

Chapter Sixteen

A sense of desperation covered the isle and its inhabitants, especially the archmage and Brodie. Depression at the ease of which the stalker had broken her spell still weighed down Kia's soul. Frustration drove her to study harder and train more aggressively with both sword and magic. Not even the passing of three sevenday had restored her spirit. Each night sleep eluded her. The closer the two moons came to conjunction, the stronger the sensation of being watched grew until not even the weight of the sword in her hand comforted.

Each morning, her training involved increasingly powerful magics until even Dal and Brodie were covered with sweat from blunting the force of her attacks. Then the two men continued on with their own session until they could no longer hold their swords up. Everyone would retire to their quarters, force down a few bites of food, then collapse until the morning summons to return to the stable for another lesson.

Exhaustion left over from the morning's training turned every step an effort. Despite the short distance of the walk from the stable to the stone cottage that served as Dal and Ellspeth's private quarters, Kia felt she would not have made it if it wasn't for Brodie's stolid support and strong arm around her waist. At his knock the door opened. Inside was more than just the archmage and his lady, their first two apprentices were hunched over papers spread out on the sideboard. What surprised her most was the isle's sergeant-at-arms, and master cook, Murdo, towered over the two younger men adding his own comments. This would be a war council.

Brodie's gentle push moved Kia over the threshold. She didn't resist when Ellspeth pointed to the nearest chair. Leaning on Brodie, Kia staggered to the seat. Steam wafted from the covered dishes in the center of the table. The enticing scent reminded her of where she was—and—who she was with. "Sorry, mistress, I don't think I will be much of a guest tonight."

Ellspeth laid one hand over Kia's. "No worries, my dear. I don't expect you to feast, but would appreciate you at least trying a little. After all, Murdo did work very hard preparing the repast." A smile flickered then vanished in a serious look. "There will be more to do this day. It isn't much, but please take this meager gift in appreciation of helping us identify our bad apple." The warmth Kia now associated with a healing spell flowed from the other woman's hands. Ellspeth's strength called out to Kia's magic, which responded in kind. Within a few heartbeats, her body once again felt vibrant, all yearning of sleep discarded.

"Thank you. I think I can eat now," Kia said.

Whether it was the restoration of the energy she had expended during that morning's training or finally recovering from the shock of the intrusion, Kia found her appetite returning with each bite. Looking around the table, she saw that the others were also doing justice to Murdo's creations.

Empty plates and a cup of steaming caffa in front of everyone marked the end of the meal. Dal took a sip and when he set the cup down Kia sensed a change in the room as he shifted from cordial host to a mercenary commander readying for battle. "Everyone, the plans you have all been making in your meetings with Ellspeth and myself are ready to be put into effect. We finally have news to act upon." His shrug conveyed a variety of emotions. "I hope I wasn't too distracted during dinner, but I've been trying to make sense of some disturbing messages that I'm afraid will involve us all, especially you Kia and Brodie." A deep breath and he continued. "The Oracle has reached out to me asking for help. Several villages have been struck by a mysterious illness, as have a number of senior members of the temple. He wanted any information we might have."

"My brother?" The gasped words escaped Kia's closed throat.

"Brantly is fine," Dal answered. "Since most of the students we sent there have come down with the same strange illness as the villagers he thought there might be a magical component." He briefly described the symptoms, and in a flat tone recounted the tallies of those sickened, those recovered—and those who succumbed.

Kia let the figures sink in. Her heart stopped when she realized that the oldest and the youngest had the largest numbers of those sick. "There is magic involved," she gasped. "Those with the greatest potential—or training—are hit the worst." An unthinkable thought rose. She tried to come up with something to dispute it, to no avail. "I don't know how I know, but I am sure my watcher is the cause."

"I agree," Ellspeth and Dal said in unison.

Ellspeth reached back and snatched a parchment from the sideboard. A flick of the fingers untied the ribbon and two sheets unrolled. "Ever since you came to my office, something stuck in my mind so I started researching." She smoothed out what appeared to be an ancestry chart and laid a finger on a middle box. Kia didn't have time to wonder about the strange look that passed between Ellspeth and her former apprentice, Nobyn, before the older woman continued. "Relliq is a direct ancestor of a rogue mage named Bashim." Her tone dropped. "Bashim placed curses on villages who he felt slighted him … killed both mages and non-mages alike."

Kia waited in silence. Something told her the archmage's lady had more information to share.

"Kia, don't feel bad about Relliq breaching your defensive spells," Ellspeth encouraged. "Brantly said an inventory of the temple archives showed several volumes disappeared just about the same time as Relliq was sent to serve as healer at a village deep in the desert. One of the missing books was Bashim's private diary." Ellspeth's silver hair swung with the angry movement of her head.

"Bashim used blood to boost his powers. Only the power of the circlet and Dal's amulet enabled us to defeat him. Brantly and I both feel that Relliq figured out his ancestor's secret."

"If Relliq is Kia's stalker," Brodie growled, "why was he let out of the temple?"

The sadness in Dal's eyes spoke of losses beyond what Kia could conceive. "Relliq attended services and lessons, gave no indication of any issues," the archmage explained. "In fact, he appeared to all intents and purposes as a model student."

"But he wasn't," Brodie pressed. "So what are we going to do?"

"First off," Dal answered, "we need to organize a healing campaign. Even though they won't be here in person, Voan and Jasmin along with the journeymen we sent to study with them in the Southern Sea will lend their strength to our spells."

He paused as if choosing his words. His gaze raked those at the table as if judging their skill. No, Brodie realized, Dal the mercenary lieutenant is evaluating his troops to determine who will not return. Resolve grew in his heart that non-tal or not, the next time he and Relliq met, the mage would die. *Even if I am carried home on my shield, Relliq will not leave the field of battle alive.*

"There aren't that many mages with enough training to both heal and hold the protective spells. With the sickness so far-flung, we will be spread thin. Barris will go work with his mother in Montrat. Nobyn will take two of the most senior students and go to the Temple of the Oracle to reinforce Brantly. Ellspeth and I will go to the towns at the foot of the Mtwan Mountains."

"By yourself?" Nobyn's question beat Brodie's by less than a heartbeat.

A smile flickered in the archmage's eyes. "No, Ellspeth and I won't be alone. Tairneach and several of the fàlaire will be coming with us." Now the smile reached his lips and he projected reassurance at his former apprentice. "Between their earth magic, my amulet, and Ellspeth's circlet we will be fine. In fact, each party will have at least two fàlaire to use as pack animals or extra mounts—and to boost all of your native powers."

Where before the search felt like his skin was being pierced, now an arctic cold enveloped him. Brodie gritted his teeth against the depth of the archmage's scan. No he corrected, not Dal's, but his wife's. As quickly as the cold struck, it vanished.

A look passed between the two leaders of the mages. With a minute nod from his wife, Dal gave one last set of instructions. "Brodie, Kia, I am assigning you the hardest task of all. I need you to head to Stratven. *Northern Pearl* is in port and Denai says the illness is raging there."

Brodie caught Kia's flash of fear. Before he could send her an encouraging thought, the archmage continued. "Kia, you may not have studied long on the isle, but your control is sure. Ellspeth and I have faith in you."

Ellspeth's smile echoed the sentiment. "You will have a secure base to work from. At least if you don't mind being on the water. My mother ordered all the apprentices from the guild hall aboard ship and all vessels to anchor beyond the harbor sentinels." She shook her head as if visualizing the stern guild master surrounded by a hoard of children. "Besides those bound to the House of Cszabo my mother is also sheltering children whose parents have been stricken, as well as the families of several crews who are at sea." Her pause told more than her tone. "And King Fraunces' two oldest children."

Brodie wondered at the sanity of the action, then decided without knowledge that the illness was a curse, putting distance between the contagion and those most vulnerable made logical sense.

"Kia, Brodie, you will not journey alone. Elendl and my mother will meet you on the cliff trail and accompany you to Stratven. Their power as well as Denai's will boost Kia's."

"Nobyn, Barris, Brodie, if the three of you would meet me in the council chambers in two candlemarks we can pull any additional maps you need from the archives. Tairneach summoned his strongest and bravest stallions as extra mounts and they should arrive by sunset. You can set out tonight or wait till morn."

Brodie mentally figured out the most strategic way to accomplish all the tasks necessary for an extended trip as the candlemark allotted for preparations would pass quickly. Retrieving leather satchels that would work as either a knapsack for a man on foot or hang from a packsaddle from the storage sheds was first on the list. Since Kia remained behind with Ellspeth for last-minute instructions on the clearing spells to remove the curse from ship or building, Brodie dropped three empty packs on Kia's doorstep. Energy raced through his veins urging him to a run. Knowledge that he would need all his strength in the coming days kept his return to his quarters at a quick walk.

The restraint vanished the moment he stepped over the threshold of his cottage, and he turned into a whirlwind of motion. His favorite weapons were laid out. Travel clothes folded and were stuffed into a satchel. "I won't be sleeping much tonight," he told the four walls. Practiced movements had the sleeping furs rolled in a ground cloth. Leather straps secured the bedroll so it could be tied behind a saddle. "Might as well take everything to the barn before the final briefing." Holding his bundles by their straps, he headed to the barn.

Saddles straddled the top rail. Knapsacks bulging with food for the trail hung from the paddock posts. All that remained was the travellers. The whiff of oats from behind announced Wirake's arrival. An identification reinforced when the fàlaire nudged Brodie.

"No, you greedy glut," Brodie said in a mock-growl. "I don't have any treats for you."

A whinny and the fàlaire tried to stick his nose in the coat Brodie draped over a fence post.

"All right, all right," Brodie snarled. He dipped a hand into his pants pocket and pulled out an orange root, dangling it by its green leaves. "You can have this, if you promise to behave."

A snuffle which clearly said, I don't agree to anything, and a snap of teeth pulled the root from Brodie's fingers.

"That's all the treat you get. Now eat your hay." A toss of mane and tail and the fàlaire pranced over to the pile of fresh fodder someone had forked down from the loft.

The low sun on the horizon told the time had come to go to the council tower.

Directions and maps were distributed. If anything, Brodie swore the tension in the archmage had deepened. After Dal laid a light hand on their shoulders, Nobyn and Barris walked out. Dal's signal to stay added to Brodie's own nerves.

Dal just wants a private word, reality suggested.

It is nothing untoward, hope answered.

Brodie waited for the archmage to broach whatever bothered the older man, and once again felt the archmage's piercing scan. The cold lightened, replaced by energy as tightly harnessed as Brodie's own.

Who needs my help? Brodie wanted to ask. The archmage or my friend?

Why can't it be both? His heart answered.

The tightening of Dal's muscles provided no clarity, nor did his low tone. "Brodie, you know both the sailor and wizard code. The connection between our swords will make communication possible. Contact me, anytime. Even if I can't come in person, I can send energy to TânOer." The strength of the other man's grip on his shoulder told Brodie the restrained emotions in the archmage. "I know what I am asking of you."

Forcing his tone level, Brodie answered the unspoken question. "I will watch over Eilidh and your daughters as if they were my own." In his heart he added, And Kia as well.

* * *

Sprites created by moonlight danced across the meadow. A subdued group stood at the foot of the rainbow bridge. "Master? A blessing for our travels?" Barris and Nobyn asked in simultaneous ritual. Dew from the cooling

167

air soaked through the fabric of Brodie's pants, as alongside his friends, he dropped to one knee before Dal.

A sense of sorrow washed over Brodie. He pinpointed the source to Dal ... and Ellspeth? Dal raised a hand in benediction. Although it was the archmage who offered the prayer, Brodie felt Ellspeth adding her own silent one to her husband's.

"May the blessing of light be on you,
Light without and light within.
The blessing of earth be upon you,
Soft under your feet as you pass along the roads.
Troubles rest lightly on your shoulders,
So your souls may be out from under it quickly.
Blessings be yours for the length of your days."

Magic sparkled in the air. It dissipated the gloom, leaving behind a sense of hope.

Ellspeth took Brodie and Kia by the hand, the warmth of her emotion transmitting through her touch. "Safe journey. Give my love to my mother when you see her."

Soon the farewells, whether a hug or the forearm clasp of brothers, were over and everyone sat in the saddle. Yet no one flicked a rein.

A collective sigh rose as if accepting the inevitable. Tairneach's bugle echoed in the stillness. Dal raised a hand in farewell and turned his mount towards their desired direction. One by one, the others waved and headed out on their individual tasks. Soon only two remained. Brodie wanted to take Kia in his arms, to tell her everything would be all right. But he remained silent.

Her tone soft, Kia said "It's all right. I'm ready to go."

* * *

The sensation of someone calling him broke through Relliq's concentration. He started to reach out to form a connection.

Don't, preservation cried.

168

His mental block back in place, he parsed the contact. Unlike the earlier ones since his arrival at Wemsig, this one did not contain a request for information. Instead it was a summons to return. And it did not come from the Oracle, but the archmage himself.

Reality insisted that if the order was ignored, someone would come looking. This time there would be no offer of clemency. *My powers will be bound.*

"Only if they find me," Relliq muttered. "But where to go?"

A knock on the door sounded into the stillness of the room.

Slow, so as not to make a sound, he pulled a short sword from the bag and held it alongside his leg. Quiet steps took him to the door.

"Yes?"

"Your dinner, master." Recognition of the high-pitched voice eased some of the tension from Relliq's shoulders. With the command to return just now received, it was too soon for anyone from the Isle of Mages to have reached Wemsig. Opening the door a crack reinforced his thought. Only the youth who ran the errands stood outside. Enticing scents wafted from the covered dish that loaded the tray in his arms.

Sending the boy to care for the horses, Relliq turned to his food—and the problem at hand. Those in Wemsig either did his bidding or were sick. There were not enough of the one to satisfy him and he ignored the other.

The archmage's stern voice echoed from a suppressed memory. *Magic solely for personal gain is not allowed.*

"Only if you get caught," Relliq hissed. "Bashim had the way of it. Control the non-tals. Destroy the competition."

Reality reared its contrariness. Before world control can be achieved, the mages must be killed. The sickness won't be enough. Something beyond normal magic is needed to counter the archmage's powers.

Swirling thoughts prevented neither study nor rest. The moon hovering above the horizon told how much time had passed. A stray moonbeam walked through the door and shimmered at Relliq's feet. Unable to refuse the invitation to escape the stuffy confines of the hut, he snatched a vest from the hook by the door and headed out into the night.

Unconscious control of his feet took him to the center of the village. The area was empty. No women pulled water from the well and the communal cookfire was nothing but a pile of glowing embers beneath a gray carpet of ash. He headed towards the benches which lined the square and let the full power of the moon guide his mind.

Deep in thought, he plotted his campaign against the temple and the wizards. Yet a final solution danced outside his grasp as an elusive sprite. A faint click came from the shadows between two buildings. Relliq cast his senses into the darkness. They encountered no sword-bearing assassin or mob of irate villagers. With a sigh, he dropped his head to his chest and pretended to sleep.

The noise repeated. This time he identified the sound as the scuff of leather on stone, but no woman carrying a jug to fill appeared, no youth stepped respectfully from the shadows waiting to be acknowledged. As if one fighting to stay awake, Relliq yawned and stretched. A shuffle took him to the ring of stones around the firepit. "Damn fire is out again," he grumbled. Poking in the firepit to cover his true action, he stretched out his fingers to gather in a handful of ash. Another curse and he returned to his seat. A sigh and he lowered his head to his chest and let out a low snore. Senses stretched to their full limits failed to show any movement. Clouds hiding the moon cast the entire square into darkness and not even magesight penetrated the stygian space. For long heartbeats, he waited for the intruder to reveal themselves.

A heavy weight knocked Relliq to the ground. Blood flowed from his forehead and dropped onto the ashes in his hand. Before the pain lessened, a tug on his collar pulled him to his knees. Cold steel pressed against his throat and a trickle of blood mingled with his sweat.

"I'll take your coins," a hot breath snarled in his ear.

Controlling his anger, Relliq forced out a stuttered, "I don't have any."

The pressure lessened, but the blade did not leave. A slight flick of the wrist would slit his throat.

Now you know why the archmage demanded everyone be proficient with weapons, reality hissed.

Pride answered with a counter. Magic conquers all.

Relliq shifted back from the knife at his throat enough to see his attacker. Before him stood a grubby, middle-aged man who looked like he hadn't shaved for a sevenday. And what he had thought was a knife was in reality a short sword. However, unlike the man, the weapon looked well cared for.

The footpad's lips twitched into a smile that was more the rictus of a death's head than mirthful. "I know you got coins and valuables. Now hand them over." The blade pressed again. "I won't repeat myself."

"Don't hurt me," Relliq whimpered. Fingers on one hand flicked in a spell of protection even as an incantation formed in his mind.

Ash of fire now turned cold,
Obey me with the word of old.
Let he before me become my slave,
Obey me now in night and ...

He clamped down on the urge to finish the spell, leaving it suspended. Only a single word and the full power of his magic would explode. The spell fought to be released, yet Relliq held it in firm control. He shrank into himself, presenting the image of someone thoroughly cowed. The sword wavered and moved another hair's breadth away. A shallow breath and he tossed the ash into the bandit's face with a yelled, "*Day.*"

All intelligence faded from the man's face. The sword fell from his hand.

Warmth flooded Relliq. *Now I have my first follower. And it isn't some feeble wanna be student.*

Now what to do with him, pride wondered.

A stoop to snatch up the dropped weapon and Relliq organized his thoughts. "Tell me, how many men look to you?"

"One hundred."

He has followers, and I don't, pride hissed.

But he is now under your control. Those who he leads will now follow you, reality countered.

Memory of the Oracle's attempts to contact him surfaced. Quick glances showed the houses remained darkened. The attack had been so quick and quiet it had not disturbed anyone's slumber. But, I had better get away before someone does awaken, Relliq thought.

"Follow me," he ordered the dull-eyed bandit. "And be quiet about it." Without looking back, he turned and headed down the street to the cottage he called his "hovel."

The former attacker silently followed a respectful three steps behind.

Relliq used the short walk to gather his thoughts. The realization that it would not be long before the oracle notified the archmage of his failure to return pushed away the warmth of his spell's success. Maybe this footpad would provide the solution of a new base of operations.

Once inside the door he ordered the other man into a corner. "You must obey me ... must answer me." Relliq gathered his magic and put steel in his tone. "Now tell me. Where do you gather? And are the villagers aware of you and it?"

The other man's brows furrowed. "No warrants bear my description or the name Cludwr." His voice faded.

"You will answer me." Relliq's voice brooked no refusal. "Where do you gather?"

The other man's shoulders slumped. "Caves near the smoking mountain. We have food cached and there is a freshet for water."

Fist raised in triumph, Relliq danced from foot to foot. *The mountain itself will help hide my location, and I can use the earth's magic to boost my own.* Reminder of the impending search returned his somber mood. "Cludwr, go saddle my horses. We'll leave shortly for your smoking mountain."

"Yes, master. Cludwr will obey."

The toneless answer warmed Relliq. It took less than a candlemark to gather up the journals and pack his few personal belongings. A call summoned the footpad, who silently carried the bags out to the waiting horses. A final look at the darkened hut and Relliq clambered into the saddle. A symbolic wipe of the village dirt from his boots, a hastily whispered cloaking spell over himself and the books, and he flicked the reins. *Finally, I'm leaving this hot hell hole.*

Chapter Seventeen

The dampness of the underground annoyed Relliq. But they could only have fires in certain spots where narrow crevices formed natural chimneys to remove the smoke. Even though more men had been conscripted and put under the thrall, despite the greater number of bodies occupying the space, the caves never seemed warm enough. To counter the chill, Relliq paced from one tunnel to another, learning and mapping the intricate maze. Tired, he sat down on an outcropping, snagged his crystal from a pocket, and summoned forth the image of Stratven to check on the status of the curse he had placed on the town. "No, no, no," he hissed. Not a single house showed evidence of the illness's black miasma.

Next the golden gates of the Temple of Givneh filled the heart of the stone. Where the day before the streets and the temple courtyard had been deserted, now everything looked normal. More curses flowed from his lips. "The mages are curing people too quickly." Instead of increasing, the number of those sickened kept dropping. He plotted the information on a mental map. Not only was the area covered by the curse shrinking, the mages were encircling Wemsig—and tightening the noose.

"It's a good thing I am not in the village," he muttered. "How to slow them down?"

An attack on Ysbail would remove two people from the curing. Barris would have to return to Montrat to care for his mother.

The spell cast, he watched in the crystal for the result.

Instead of the woman collapsing, she didn't respond at all.

"She is a non-tal, should have no defenses against a magical ailment."

Unless he thought, as a healer she has some natural immunity. So, who else's death would cause the mages pain?

One name rose to the front—Eilidh, the archmage's mother.

* * *

Kia squinted against the afternoon sun's glare to keep track of the rest of the group. Brodie, who had again shifted his saddle from one of the extra fàlaire back to Wirake, led the small caravan. A wagon length behind Brodie, Eilidh rode alongside her granddaughter.

The sun's slow drift below the horizon finally forced a slowdown from their frenetic pace. Darkness hid rocks. If any of the fàlaire stepped in one of the prairie hen burrows that were prevalent in this part of the plain, it could mean more than a broken leg. Legends told that the bones of an unknown number of riders lay hidden beneath the fetlock-high grass after being thrown from their mounts.

Brodie called out a low command. Quiet enough to not disturb any prairie hens in the area, it was still loud enough to be heard over the sound of hoof falls. No sooner had Wirake adjusted his pace from the dizzying run to a slower gallop than the dark shape of Eilidh's form wavered. Her low moan reached Kia.

"Brodie," Kia yelled. Her breath held, she breathed a prayer. "Oracle, keep Eilidh in the saddle until Brodie reaches her."

In front of her Wirake spun on his haunches. Dirt and clumps of grass flew. The fàlaire leaped. When his hooves touched down, he was nose to nose to Eilidh's mount. The fading rays of sunlight made it appear as if Brodie and Eilidh were one shape. Brodie's grunt as his shoulder took the brunt of the clanswoman's unconscious body rolled across the plains. Beneath him, Wirake jerked to a stop putting space between the two fàlaire so that Eilidh wouldn't fall beneath the deadly hooves. Brodie swung a leg over the saddle and stepped down. He knelt and in a single motion lay Eilidh on the ground. The clanswoman's body twitched in reaction to some unseen force. Her face was deathly white.

A sharp pain in Kia's chest forced a gush of air from her lungs. Fresh air triggered her healing instincts. She leaped from the saddle and ran to the stricken woman. Holding her hands above the clanswoman, she whispered a silent prayer and did a quick examination. "Eilidh is burning with a fever." Worry clutched at her chest. "It is like nothing I have ever seen."

Elendl leaned down and touched her grandmother's forehead. "Nor, I." The younger woman rocked back on her heels. Fear flickered in her eyes.

Kia fought to keep her own anxiety hidden. Healing—and magic—was still new to her. And the patient was not just the archmage's mother, but a friend. "Well, Elendl, let us see what we can do," Kia said.

Brodie stood. "While you ladies tend to Eilidh, I'll stand watch." After a quick scan of the area, he added. "Let me know if you need TânOer's power."

Smiling her thanks, Kia reached out and took Elendl's hand in one of hers. Cold fingers, to the point of icy, showed the depth of the young mage's emotions. "We can do this," she reassured the archmage's daughter. A fast search of her memory and she decided on a revealing spell. Giving Elendl the cue, she took a deep breath and whispered the words. Instead of the symbols indicating an illness or a damaged bone or organ, a black haze shimmered into existence. "Eilidh isn't sick. It's the curse."

From his spot a few feet away, Brodie released choice words Kia had only heard on the docks when a stevedore dropped a heavy box on his foot. His anger revealed to Kia the depth of his attachment to the archmage and his family.

I can't let Brodie's emotions control mine, Kia thought. A deep breath to achieve her center and she cast the spell. Alongside her, she heard Elendl's lighter tone echo the incantation.

"As the mind pictured,
So let it be.
Bring back Eilidh as she was,
Her body and mind again healthy."

"The mind has pictured,
So must it be.
Awake Eilidh.
Your health returned to thee."

Eilidh's twitching stopped, but the clanswoman's breathing remained shallow and her face remained the translucent paleness of a corpse.

"That was good, Elendl. We'll do it one more time." Satisfied, that the young mage was ready, Kia gathered her magic and repeated the incantation.

Unlike the other attempt, Eilidh's color returned. "Unnggghh." Her groan sent a shock through Kia's nerves. The other woman tried to get up, but her skin paled at the attempt and she slumped back.

"Easy, mistress," Kia ordered. "Rest."

"Rest, grandmother," Elendl encouraged.

With Elendl bracing Eilidh on one side, Kia shifted the older woman to a sitting position.

"This might help." Brodie handed Kia a mug. She nodded her thanks as the fragrance of wine wafted from the cup. She lifted the cup to Eilidh's lips. "Here, mistress, take a sip."

Quicker than could have been hoped for mere heartbeats earlier, Eilidh's strength returned.

Thank the Oracle, Kia thought. We broke the curse in time. Unbidden, the faces and names of those who had succumbed paraded through her mind. Fatigue that had vanished in the rush of action, returned with a vengeance. Darkness surrounded her and she fell backwards.

A strong hand stopped the movement. "I've got you," Brodie said in Kia's ear. He pushed a cup into her hand. "I don't know much about magic. However, I think everyone needs a few sips of restorative." His chuckle helped ease more of the tension. "It's a good thing that Murdo filled the skins with enough good wine to go around." He shifted to help Elendl wrap shaking fingers around a mug.

Although Brodie was only two steps away, Kia felt bereft of his presence.

"My father needs to know what happened," Elendl protested.

"Drink first," Brodie ordered. "As soon as Eilidh is strong enough to sit the saddle, we'll tell the archmage what happened."

"Then let's do so," Eilidh said. "I feel much better now. I think I'd like to reach the well and make camp before the moons are too high in the sky."

* * *

"No, no, no," Relliq snarled. He tilted the crystal as if doing so would change the image within the heart of the stone. Instead of a dying clanswoman, he saw Eilidh in the saddle. "The old woman is a non-tal. She couldn't break the curse. Someone else must have done it." A fleeting thought to send the dark shroud after Kia was ruthlessly quashed. "Killing the archmage's daughter will hurt him as much as killing his mother. The one onboard ship is vulnerable. She has almost no magic of her own." A smile twitched his lips. "I think I'll let her watch her grandmother die first. The archmage may not mourn the loss of his mother-in-law, but his lady will."

He leaned forward, catching the firelight in his crystal. It showed Denai standing on the bow of a ship anchored in a protected harbor. The spell echoed around the cave. Instead of either the archmage's daughter or his mother-in-law collapsing to the deck or falling overboard, the pair appeared unaffected.

Heat filled Relliq's face. "Something is wrong. They are non-tals. Yet my magic is blocked. Before I can control the world, I have to take out the mages. I need a weapon unknown to the archmage and his fawning students. And it has to be powerful enough to get around the protective spells on the temple and those the mages placed around their land."

Cludwr shambled into the doorway. The smell of his unwashed body preceded him. "Master, did you summon me?"

Relliq waved in dismissal. "Go away. I need to think."

"But, master," Cludwr persisted. "You said you needed something secret. There is one hidden deep in the mountain. Will it help?"

"What kind of treasure? Gold, jewels, coins?"

"I have to show you."

"Then lead on."

At the command, Cludwr turned and headed through the winding maze of tunnels and chambers of varying sizes. They went farther into the depths than Relliq had ever been. He stopped and held his torch out over a deep chasm. The light reflected off the steep sides. "We are here."

Magesight showed unrecognizable shapes below. Relliq's quiet call created a ball of fire that hovered over the crevice. In its glow, row after row of clay soldiers appeared to march out of the darkness. Ten rows of archers alternated with an equal number of spear carriers. Behind them, twenty rows of swordsmen bearing shields stood in silent attendance. Quick calculation provided an estimate that the chamber held over 2,000 individuals.

"And there are at least ten more chambers that I know of." Cludwr's voice echoed in the vaulted space. "Master, can this help you? Did I do good?"

Relliq fought the urge to smash the whine from the man's tone. "Yes, Cludwr, you did good. Now tell me, what else do you know about this army? Who made it? How do you bring them to life?"

Where before the other man's face beamed at the praise, now it was crestfallen. "Legend states they are defenders of a secret city." His voice dropped. "Sorry, master. I don't know the answers to what you ask."

The desire to bring the army to life called with an irresistible lure. There is no way down, reality argued. No steps are visible. Additional resources will be needed.

"I have the perfect weapon against the mages, and I can't use it," Relliq cursed. "Magic won't be effective against fired earth, and not even the archmage's prowess with a sword will save him." He smiled at the image of the sword in pieces at the archmage's feet and the statue's hands around the wizard's neck, squeezing the life out of him. His smile tightened his lips so much they hurt as he pictured a clay soldier forcing the archmage to his knees.

"And I will be there to watch." His pulse raced in anticipation. *The archmage will kneel before me. Then watch as my army of clay soldiers tears down the council chamber, stone by stone.*

The proper spell to turn the sculptures into living golems needs to be found, reality reminded.

Cursing at being blocked yet again, Relliq spun on his heel and headed back to the cave he used for his private quarters. A tug yanked one of the volumes he stole from the temple's archives from the shelf. Carefully, he laid it on the table and held his hands over it.

"What is now unseen, be revealed.
Pages flip to secret hidden.
Turn clay into creatures real.
Show me the knowledge forbidden."

A hint of movement flickered over the book, then vanished without a single page flipping.

One by one, Relliq searched the books to no avail. Throwing the last book onto the table, he stalked from the room.

Maybe there is a clue with the soldiers, hope encouraged.

The thought took hold and he made plans to reach the cavern floor. Frustration grew as only a few ropes were found among the bandits' stores. Snapped commands sent

Cludwr and several others to acquire ladders or the supplies and tools to make them.

In between bouts of stalking the caves and flipping through the pages of the journals, Relliq went to the cave entrance and scanned the desert. Each escape into daylight was shorter than the one before and ended with increasing rage as he had to retreat into the mountain to avoid the gossamer web of the archmage's search spell.

A page in one of the earliest journals mentioned a blood thrall. Relliq followed the crumb of a clue and found a scribbled mention in Bashim's hand about using blood to enspell coppers, and that all who touched coins so prepared became willing slaves. More candlemarks went into figuring out how to incorporate blood into the ritual to activate the clay soldiers.

"I can paint it on," he decided. "Now if Cludwr and his men would just get here with the ropes so I can get down to the cavern floor I can get started." Laying down on his bed, he sought the calm he'd need for the major working of magic.

Candlemarks later, hushed murmurs outside his room warned Relliq of the bandit's return. A look in the crystal showed the desert clear of the shimmer of magic or search parties. And that the twin moons, optimum for the use of magic, had begun their rise into the night sky.

"Finally, I can begin." Relliq snatched up the bag he had packed of items for the ritual and stepped through the door. Heat dampened his collar at the sight of the line of men awaiting instruction.

Cludwr bowed. The two men on each side just stood, slack-jawed. "Bow to the master, you dung-hill beetles," the bandit yelled. A cuff to the head of those next to him triggered the necessary obeisance not just from the pair, but all the waiting men.

Sometimes Cludwr has his uses, Relliq thought. Maybe I'll keep him around. "Well, Cludwr, report."

"Master, the rest of the men await you at the chamber. I fixed the ladders and the table as you requested."

"Then let us get to it." Without a look to see if the men obeyed, he headed deeper into the cave. By dint of cuff and yell, he arranged the men by height and age along the ledge that circled the chasm. Light from the torches in the men's hands made their faces appear to be faceless orbs floating in the darkness. Only Cludwr, who stood on the other side of the altar, had any form.

It took several tries, but Relliq finally got the small brushes and copper bowl placed to his satisfaction on the cloth-covered table that would serve as a makeshift altar. Stone shards whose edges had been chipped into razor sharpness lined one side of the table. "Begin the chant," he called to the silent men.

Hesitantly at first, the men obeyed. Their voices grew in volume until their echoes circled the cave wall.

"Moons are high, darkness leavin'
Soldiers come alive.
Mark of blood in moonbeams dancin'
Soldiers come alive.
Command, it shall be."

With each round of the chant, Relliq felt the magic grow. He gathered the streamers of sound and wove them into a single thread. A wave signalled for the next verse.

"By Shartle and Neba, their orbits aligned,
Soldiers come alive.
Clay creatures a target I assign,
Soldiers come alive.
Command, it shall be."

Where before the magic was a shimmer, now it solidified into a living, throbbing force. The power flowed into Relliq. A gasp escaped. *I've never felt anything like this before.* Exultation rose. *The archmage will fall.*

A deep breath and he picked up a rock shard from the altar. The chipped edge glittered in the torchlight. Whispered words consecrated the blade and in a single stroke, Relliq sliced his thumb. Blood flowed from the wound.

He smeared the blood across the forehead. *"Turn clay into creatures real."*

Then he drew a red line down and across both eyes. *"Soldiers come alive. As I command, so it shall be."*

What had been sightless eyes now shone with life.

Ignoring the pain in his thumb, he marked an "X" across where the heart should be.

"Move," Relliq screamed. "You must obey me."

For a long moment, he thought the spell didn't work. A finger twitched. Then with a screech, the fingers that had been curled into a fist straightened.

Reality dashed the exuberance of success. Each joint, from fingers and knees, shoulders to hips, would need to be marked to give the clay sculpture the ability to move and make the soldiers a fighting force.

"I need more blood," Relliq growled. "And it won't be mine. That is what the bandits are for." He made a mental note to order Cludwr to get more men willing to donate their life force. Either freely for gold or not, it didn't matter. "I will not be refused my birthright. But for now, one of these will have to do." *And he does not need to be a willing sacrifice, either.*

He raised his head and scanned the gathered men who stood in silence. Relliq's gaze pinned one who had grumbled at the change of leadership. "Let he who hears my voice come forward to honor his ruler. Descend from the heights. Join me at the altar of life."

Instead of the man obeying the order, he pushed a youth forward. The boy stumbled a few steps before gathering his balance and woodenly walking down the improvised stairs.

"Here, boy," Relliq snarled. He reached out, grabbed the boy's hand, and before the dazed youth could resist, yanked him over to the altar. Light flickered on the stone knife. The boy winced but didn't make a sound as the blade sliced his palm. Blood from the wound streamed onto the ground.

"Cludwr, you idiot. Hold the bowl under his hand. Don't waste the blood. If there isn't enough, I will use yours."

"Yes, master." The bandit snatched the bowl from the table. With each passing heartbeat, a thin stream of red liquid formed spirals against the copper.

"Has the boy given enough?"

Relliq started when Cludwr repeated the question. A half-finger length of blood swirled around the bottom of the bowl. The boy's low moan and pale face told of how much had been taken. It brought attention to his face—and recognition.

This is the boy who brought me to that hovel they called a hut. "This one is not yet finished serving his master," Relliq snarled. "Hold him up. He has much more to give." A target solidified in his mind. *Eilidh. The archmage's mother. And this time the golem will kill.*

Chapter Eighteen

Turbulent thoughts, colored by guilt and fear, meant a long night tossing and turning in the sleeping furs. Every time Kia fell asleep, she relived Eilidh's fall from the saddle. Only instead of Brodie catching the clanswoman, she fell beneath the fàlaire's steel-hard hooves. And the clanswoman's death screams always sounded like, "Come to me, little wizardling."

Finally, Kia gave up the battle. Eyes gritty from lack of sleep, she rose and found herself drawn to where the fàlaire rested. Wirake snuffled a welcome. A quick pet for his reward and she lay down alongside Rielle using the fàlaire's neck as a pillow. Soon the animal's heartbeat lulled her into the comforting darkness of the Cyrcle of One. The dreams changed. Tall-waving grass gave way to a mountain lake and fear was replaced by a sense of welcoming. The next time she woke, only a sliver of the second moon remained over the horizon. Movement beyond the glowing circle of the protective wards spiked her pulse until Brodie, his arms full of branches, walked from the grayness that heralded the dawn. He dropped the wood and took the few steps over to her. "Good morn, Kia."

"Couldn't sleep," she explained.

"I thought you would be over here." Brodie reached up and patted Wirake's neck. "Fàlaire are good company. They can spin a fine tale. I always liked Wirake's stories of the black mare that swam the ocean with the shipfish and the one of the brown stallion that sprouted wings to fly with the great hunting birds." The sympathy in his tone called out to Kia's pain when he added, "I also found the fàlaire to be good listeners, especially with their special friends." He nodded to the pile of ashes left over from the previous night's fire. "I'll cook breakfast if you start the fire."

The sense of calm that came with Brodie's presence enabled Kia to answer. Her voice stronger, she said, "Deal." Stacking several pieces of the wood into a pyramid, she held a hand over the cold ashes and whispered the incantation. A spark flared into being in the heart of the dry wood.

"Nicely done," Eilidh said.

Kia spun at the voice. "Mistress, you shouldn't be up. You should be resting."

"It is all right, my dear." The clanswoman took a few steps closer to the fire and held her hands out over the warming flames. "I feel much better now. We can leave as soon as everyone breaks their fast."

* * *

A sevenday at the camp beneath the short trees of the mage's oasis and a routine had been established. Brodie gathered dry grass for kindling and wood for a fire. Eilidh supervised Kia and Elendl as they cooked porridge sweetened with mountain honey or made pan-bread. After everyone broke their fast, the fàlaire were watered and brushed. The mages established protective circles around the camp. While Eilidh guided Elendl and Kia in the removal of the curse from the target village of the day, Brodie maintained a vigil, watching the tall grass outside the chalk marks and beyond that, the expanse of sand that encircled the oasis.

Nightfall brought with it conversations through the crystals with the other healing teams. Each night the news remained the same. More people were being cured of the curse than were coming down with it. And with each town being cleared, the mages were closer to locating Relliq. Several times their senses had touched his, but the contacts had not lasted long enough to locate him.

186

As he had since their arrival, Brodie stood sentry duty from dusk to dawn. This night, however, rather than sitting on his saddle sharpening his weapons, something beyond his ken kept him pacing within the protective wards. Even Wirake and the other fàlaire stallions felt something. They stationed themselves as additional guards around the camp, standing at the slightest breeze.

A click, as if stone on stone, sounded in the darkness beyond the firelight.

Brodie scanned the camp. All the fàlaire stood in the same position. None had moved and dislodged a stone. And the only noise the prairie hens that frequented the space ever made was the soft flutter of wings.

Another click, louder this time and closer, reached the camp. Brodie focused on the source. Shifting grass showed something approaching. Yet there was no "hallo," no customary trader's call of greeting. Brodie moved to within a finger length of the chalk circle marking the boundary of the magical wards. A tug and TânOer's blade left the scabbard with a sibilant hiss.

Low voiced orders followed. "Kia, wake the others. Saddle your mares and Wirake. Tie the food bags to the saddles and be ready to ride."

Silence greeted his order. For a moment, he thought Kia would refuse. Her quick steps to the clanswoman and the young mage resulted in quiet murmurs. Brodie sensed rather than heard the preparations being made to leave the camp. His gaze remained focused outward and he stirred the fire. Sparks and flames rose skyward.

A figure shambled into the firelight. A stop as if to orient itself, and it lumbered towards the center of the camp. Its destination was clear—Eilidh. The creature which could now be seen as a stone man headed straight for the clanswoman who stood between Kia and Elendl. Flames from the now-roaring fire revealed impassive clay features and what appeared to be a sword scabbard.

"Halt and be recognized." Brodie held his breath to see if his yell brought a reaction.

The creature lumbered forward. It stopped at the protective wards and stood with arms raised.

"Ancestors, let the wards hold."

Magic can't stop magic, fear put in. And magic had to be used to make a clay statue move.

But Elendl is the archmage's daughter, hope added. Her magic should be stronger than the one who brought the statue to life.

Brodie kept his gaze on the creature. It hammered at the invisible wall with his fist. Deafening peals reverberated with each blow. The wall shimmered into visibility. A heartbeat later it exploded into splinters.

A stream of fire flashed past Brodie's ear. He didn't know if it came from Kia or Elendl—and didn't dare turn around to see. The fire splayed over the intruder without doing any damage, just covering it in a layer of gray ash. With the magical protections defeated, the walking statue advanced.

"Kia, get the others in the saddle." To gain time for the women to obey, he waved his arms. "Hey, you ... over here."

Like before, the strange intruder ignored Brodie's attempt to distract it and remained fixated on the elder clanswoman.

Brodie raced behind the creature and swung with all his strength. Light flashed on TânOer's blade. A loud peal rang out as metal hit stone, but only a small chip flew off. "Unggh," escaped in a groan. His entire right side was numbed. TânOer slipped from his fingers and dropped to the ground. Even as he bent to reach for the weapon, a back-handed blow from the creature sent Brodie sprawling in the grass.

Heavy hoof falls signalled Wirake's approach. Brodie stooped and snatched his sword from the ground and shoved it into its scabbard. As the fàlaire passed, Brodie used the animal's momentum to swing one handed into the saddle. "Wirake, take it down."

At the command, the fàlaire spun. Three long strides and with the unique ability of its magical breed leaped. As it passed a meagre handspan above the statue's head, Wirake kicked back.

The contact between Wirake's steel hard hooves and the hard clay shook Brodie. However, it accomplished one thing. The force knocked the soldier forward onto its face. Using its fingers to pull it along, it scrabbled towards Eilidh.

Wirake's bugle overrode Brodie's yelled, "Eilidh, ride." Wrapping his arms around Wirake's neck, he added, "Back to the others." In heartbeats, the fàlaire reached the long stride his kind was known for, leaving the crawling intruder far behind in the dust. Trusting his mount, Brodie closed his eyes against the blur of the ground.

After what seemed like an eternity, the fàlaire slowed.

"Brodie, over here."

Opening his eyes, he saw Kia waving from behind a pile of rocks. Standing in the stirrups, he stared at their back trail—and the spot that moved inexorably towards them. "Kia, Elendl, this involves magic. It is beyond my experience as a soldier. Any ideas on how to stop that thing?"

Kia looked at the other women and at Eilidh's nod answered. "We'll contact the archmage. Either he or Ellspeth will know what to do."

Satisfied that end of affairs was under control, Brodie returned to his watch. Murmurs, then raised voices, told him the archmage had been reached.

"Brodie, my son has some ideas," Eilidh said. "Keep watch and tell us what works."

What the clanswoman left unsaid chilled Brodie. *And what doesn't.*

Kia's voice raised in a chant.

"Without cloud, without thunder,
Lightning be summoned.
Fly to the target I see,
And rip it asunder."

A crack of lightning split the sky. The figure staggered and fell down. As Brodie watched, it pushed itself onto its knees, then back to its feet.

"It barely slowed it down," Brodie hissed.

"Then we'll try something else," Eilidh encouraged. She gave Elendl the clue, who started the casting. Kia joined in and added her power to the spell.

"Water full, water empty,
Cloud release on the prairie."

Brodie held his breath and sent a silent prayer skyward.

The creature slowed.

"It's working," Brodie said. "We need more."

Behind him, Kia's voice echoed off the rocks as she added more power to the spell.

The rain turned into a thick blanket of water that encircled the creature. Elendl's lighter tone grew louder as she drew on her youth to throw more power into the working and the column of water thickened.

"Stop, you devil," Brodie chanted. Again and again, he repeated it even as he feared the sight of an arm breaking free of the water.

Inch by inch, the tornadic shower kept pace with the now struggling statue. Lightning bolt after lightning bolt struck the crawling figure. Finally, all movement stopped.

Brodie's breath released in a gush. "We're safe."

For now, contrariness added.

Throughout the moonless night, hope and reality warred within his thoughts. Not even the mid-night watch he spent with Kia helped ease his mind. With the dawning and magesight no longer needed, he sent her back to catch a few candlemarks rest. However, she must have had her own unease because she returned to the rock and every few moments twitched beneath the light blanket.

Brodie reached out a hand.

Don't, his mercenary senses ordered. Focus on the task.

A sigh and he resisted the urge to pull her into an embrace. *Kia is not mine.* His throat closed on the unsaid. *And never will be.*

The tug and pull continued until the sun directly overhead blinded and waves of heat rose from the sands. Brodie shielded his eyes with a hand and yet again scanned the backtrail. Beside him, Kia shifted on the sleeping furs that provided what comfort could be had against the hard rock that served as their lookout point. He repressed a sigh. The vigil could have been almost enjoyable if it hadn't been for the threat of another attack. And this time, he thought, rain might not be weapon enough to stop it.

A distant dust column caught his attention. Even before he could see anything besides the gray cloud Brodie knew who approached his hideaway. The sound of thunder betrayed Tairneach's heavy-footed run. And where the head stallion went, so did the archmage. Finally, Brodie thought, reinforcements. Kia's presence had made it difficult to keep his focus outward during the stints of sentry duty. But, he admitted, he wouldn't have traded the candlemarks spent with her for any amount of gold. Finally, four fàlaire, two with riders and two with neither saddle nor rider, appeared as more than black specks.

Kia's released breath mirrored his own. She called back to Eilidh and her granddaughter. "The archmage and Ellspeth are here."

Half a candlemark later, Tairneach slid to a halt at the entrance to the narrow cleft in the rock.

Brodie stood and gestured into the shadows. "Welcome, Dal, Ellspeth. Your mother and daughter are down there." He nodded at the archmage's back trail where the dust was settling. "Did you stop by our visitor?"

Light glinted on Dal's dark locks when he shook his head. "Elle and I figured we'd come here first. She can take over guard duty while you and I check out the intruder."

Ellspeth's mount edged past Tairneach and stopped below the sentry point. "Kia, why don't you ride back to the others with me?"

"Very well, mistress."

191

Even though she had only moved a few feet, Brodie felt the absence of Kia's presence. *At least I can now concentrate on what needs to be done.* He wrenched his attention from the implications of his thoughts to focus on the more immediate issue. "Dal, I'll stay here and keep watch while you and Ellspeth get settled."

A wave signalled the other man's agreement. Tairneach walked away with Ellspeth's mare on his tail. Soon, high squeals mingled with happy murmurs reached Brodie. Sadness clutched at his heart as he pictured the family reunion going on behind him. To help squelch the emotion, he clambered down to the ground and leaned against the rock in the small patch of shade provided by a protruding ledge.

Dal's soft tone came from behind and dispersed the last of the musings. "Brodie, my mother told me how you coordinated the defense against the golem. Thank you for keeping Eilidh and Elendl safe."

Another scan of the heat waves rising from the sand and Brodie took the canteen the other man offered. A long swig and he recapped the container. "Golem?"

A smile twitched at Dal's lips, then just as quickly vanished. "That is a name from legend of a statue or some other man-made creature that a wizard has brought to life." The archmage ran his fingers through his dark curls. "Since we don't really know who or what your intruder was, that seemed as good a name as any." Hoof falls announced the arrival of Tairneach and Wirake. Dal pinned a glare on the waiting fàlaire. "Please, Taer, keep the thunder to a low roar. I want Brodie to give me his impressions before we arrive at the oasis camp."

Dusk greeted their arrival at the oasis that had served as staging point for Kia's and Elendl's healing missions. They slowed as they passed through the last remnants of the previous night's wards. Brodie pointed to what appeared to be a small hill. "It's over there."

"I'll take the lead," Dal said. A flick of the reins and Tairneach, his entire frame tense, moved out.

Brodie reined in Wirake a wagon length away from what now appeared as a six-foot long pile of clay. An unease, as if someone watched him, refused to leave. This must be how Kia feels when her stalker is out and about, Brodie thought. Sword in hand, he approached the figure on foot. He glanced to his right where Dal kept pace. A clenched jaw showed that the archmage also felt the tension.

Dal made three slow circuits around the golem, then knelt down at its head. "Look there, the discoloration on the eyes and hands." Anger flooded his face. "Relliq must have used blood to animate the statue."

Brodie's growl matched the archmage's tone. "And I bet the blood wasn't his."

"How Relliq brought the golem to life explains why the rain stopped it," Dal added. "Water washed off the blood."

A thought rose. Although he feared the answer, Brodie voiced the question. "What happens if he mixes the blood with paint or seals the golem with wax?"

Silence was the archmage's response.

* * *

The image of the archmage kneeling, arms bound behind his back, danced in Relliq's mind. *But how to accomplish it?*

Kill him ... slit his throat, rose to mind.

Anger colored the next thought. Make him watch his wife die. Then kill him.

"I have to find him first," came out in a growl. Frustration added to the rage. No matter the spell or the amount of blood used, the crystal remained blank. It revealed neither the archmage's location nor actions. Plans to lure his enemy out with the death of his mother failed to yield any results. "What happened to her?" Relliq's yell bounced off the cave walls. Scrying showed no sign of the woman, nor of the creature he had sent to kill her. All contact with the golem ended when it crossed the wards around the camp. "Damn whoever created the oasis, their children, and their children's children. Whatever magic they used to create the well must also block it to scrying."

A cough from the hallway outside his quarters shifted his attention from the books that littered the table. Relliq stalked to the entrance and pushed aside the curtain that provided the only privacy in the mountain lair.

The trio of bandits bowed. Excitement radiated from their taut frames. Relliq basked in their obedience. "Well, why do you disturb my meditation?"

The tallest of them stepped forward. "Master, we have searched as you ordered."

Relliq caught the pong of Cludwr's mud-encrusted clothes. "And what have you found."

"We were exploring as you ordered. We followed a cold breeze several candlemarks into the heart of the mountain. When we got low on torches, we sat down to rest a few moments before heading back."

The man's slowness infuriated Relliq, but he resisted the urge to cuff the bandit. *At least until his usefulness is finished.*

Cludwr is good at acquiring supplies and doing other boring chores, countered reality. And is especially effective in bringing in new recruits.

Both for strong backs and—blood, Relliq silently added. He glared at those before him. "Hurry up, Cludwr. My time is important."

A duck, as if the bandit expected to be hit, followed the order. "Sorry, master. While I rested, I reached out and my hand went through the wall."

Relliq's hand whipped out and caught the bandit on his jaw. "Explain ... and be quick about it."

Cludwr backed away. "I stretched and my hand, instead of touching hard rock felt a cold breeze. We searched and discovered the rock was not solid. A thin veneer curved away from the middle of the wall for several feet and behind it was a hidden tunnel."

Interest swept away the irritation that hovered. "And where did it go?"

"A short ways down, it split into three. We followed one passageway until it opened onto a ledge above a golden city."

How can these clods have found Diomharid?

The sight of the three men's hopeful look brought Relliq back to the here and now. "Get more torches and show me."

"But, master, we are tired. We walked all day, without food," one moaned.

Cludwr bowed. "Please, sire, can't we rest until the dawning. It is only a few candlemarks away."

For long moments, Relliq glared at the men. Reality warned that rested servants were better than exhausted ones. They would be able to travel faster.

And I could use the time to plan my attack on the city. "Very well. Go eat, rest. Return one candlemark after dawn with torches, water, and food to last two days."

As soon as the men left, he arranged several sheets of paper and writing tools on the table. *How to conquer the city? I need something to control the people. But how?*

Memory of how his ancestor, Bashim, enslaved the elders of a village surfaced and Relliq reached out and pulled a small book from the stack on the shelves. Page after page, he searched until he found the reference. "Enspelled coins won't work," he growled. "I'd have to be in the city to distribute them." *And if they are as high-minded as the archmage, gold or silver won't tempt them.*

The continual drip of water in the corner, a sound that always irritated him and sometimes chased him from the room, seemed to whisper, "Rain."

"Rain, that is what I need," he muttered. "The spell to summon water from the sky isn't that difficult."

But not an ordinary shower, his magic whispered. Enspell it with the same power you imbued into the coins to take over the will of the bandits and those who lived in the miserable town the Oracle sent you to. The silvers only got you one town. Rain will gain you a city.

The argument went back and forth, whether to use a tried-and-true method, or to risk everything on an untested one. A cold drop of water landed on Relliq's collar and ran down his neck. Reflexively, he pulled the hood of his robe over his head, then shivered as the damp cloth touched his skin. *And for those who were not outside in the storm, touching the clothes of those who were or stepping into a puddle will also trigger the thrall.*

All during the night, he worked on the intricate incantation. He needed something more than fog but less than a downpour. After all, he thought, it would not do to force people indoors before they pledge obedience to me. By the time, a servant returned with a bowl of cooked porridge "to break your fast," he said, piles of crumped paper lay on the floor at Relliq's feet. *But I have the workings set in my mind.*

After three spoonfuls of the now lukewarm porridge, he couldn't stand the excitement any longer. "Cludwr!"

At the summons, the bandit appeared. "Ready to go, master. Supplies are packed and ready."

"Then let's do so."

This time the trip to the hidden entrance took less than half the time of the bandit's original journey. The light from Relliq's torch cast an eerie reflection in the narrow space beneath the concealing fake wall. The floor's slight downward slant provided a natural direction to follow. Through chamber after chamber he walked ever deeper. In some, spires as tall as a man rose from the floor to trip the unwary. A sense of unease caused by the weight of tons of earth on top of him grew stronger the further he traveled. Each time a drop of cold water fell from the ceiling onto his neck, or some other spot of bare skin, he jumped. His head ached from repeated whacks against one of the many plinths that hung down from the ceiling. Curses on Cludwr's ancestry followed each encounter.

Relliq stood at the junction of three passageways, wondering where the other two led.

Cludwr gestured from the leftmost tunnel. "This way, master."

"Where do the other two go?"

Sadness, that of failure, filled the bandit's face. "I don't know. We didn't explore them all. We just followed this one until we saw the city. Then we returned to report to you."

He looked so crestfallen, instead of berating the man, Relliq bit off the sharp retort. "You did right to do so. There is magic involved." A curt wave started the others moving. Excitement flooding his veins, Relliq followed.

Time lost all meaning in the eternal shadows within the mountain. Apart from the hiss of the torch, the only other sound was the occasional splat as water dropped to the floor. Relliq found himself tiptoeing in the silent underworld, hesitant to disrupt whatever might sleep in darkness beyond the limited glow of the torches held by Cludwr and the other two bandits.

A partially collapsed wall forced him to climb on hands and knees over the rubble. Using the opportunity to stop and catch his breath, he sat on the edge of the debris. A compulsion to close his eyes tugged at Relliq. Sleep was the last thing he needed, yet his eyelids grew heavy. When they closed for the third time, an alarm rang in his mind. This must be one of the traps set to guard the city! *I must be close.* "Soon," he chortled, "I will walk triumphantly into my new headquarters."

Chapter Nineteen

The journey through the narrow winding tunnels seemed interminable. Nothing existed beyond the glow of the torches. Not even magesight penetrated the darkness enough to reveal traps for the unwary. Relliq's head throbbed from bumping against low-hanging ceilings. The burn from clothing rubbing against skinned knees made every step torture. Whether from the weight of the mountain above them, or the fear a misstep would send the inattentive into a pit, the bandits closed ranks. With two in front of him and one behind, he couldn't escape the pungent smell of unwashed bodies and damp clothes.

"Not far now, master," Cludwr whispered from his position in the lead.

"That's what you said a candlemark ago," Relliq growled.

"I promise, sire," the bandit said. "The entrance is just beyond the next bend in the passage. A few more steps and you'll be able to see the light."

Too tired to answer, Relliq waved the men to continue.

In less time than predicted, the faint glimmer of distant light appeared. Instead of relief, the feeling of dread increased with each step. They closed the distance and magesight soon revealed a round circle backlit by sunlight. Only a step later something else became visible. Threads of protective wards interwove to form a shimmering wall—a barrier that blocked his way. Frustration heated his neck. *I am so close. I will not be denied.*

He moved forward until the blue symbols of individual runes could be distinguished. He recognized some, but others were so old their meaning was lost in the mists of time. Once again Relliq cursed the archmage and those who had ruled the Isle of Mages.

"I go where I wish," he snarled. But muscles refused the command to move.

"Did you say something, master?"

Relliq wasn't sure which of the bandits spoke. Although he suspected it was the man behind him. The voice echoed making identification impossible. "Nothing for you to concern yourself with." Satisfaction at the silence that greeted the order warmed him enough it chased away some of the underground's chill.

But the main problem remained. *How to get past the wards?*

A group of symbols flickered drawing his gaze. One by one, he slowly decoded the symbols enough to pierce together their message.

A wall remains unbroken,
Magic remains constrained.
To enter the city of legend,
No trace of pride or greed can remain.

Those without powers,
Our city will welcome thee.
But if a mage to enter,
A humble man he must be.

I will not humble myself, Relliq vowed.

You knelt before the archmage to achieve your goal, memory whispered.

The cold reminded him of where he was, while the scuff of leather against stone as one of the bandits shifted from foot to foot told of impatience. One idea after another of how to get past the wards were reviewed and discarded. Whispered dispersal spells were followed by stern commands to allow passage. To no avail. The internal argument finally ended. *A humble man is on his knees.*

Curses on the archmage allowed some of the anger to fade. A deep breath to center himself and Relliq imagined his magic as a large ball. Then the ball shrank, collapsed into itself until the glowing sphere covered the head of a pin. He encircled it with layer after layer of rock until none of the magic's glow could be seen.

But, I do not have to allow these clods to see me on my knees. "I'm ready. Go on," he told the other men. "Wait for me at the entrance."

Cludwr and the others walked on through, unaware of the warning.

Satisfied his men were out of sight, Relliq dropped to his knees. The immediate area fixed in his mind, he closed his eyes and crawled.

Fingers numbed from the cold stone competed with the throb of knees. Pain flared in his mind, then just as quickly vanished.

Relliq opened his eyes, not to the darkness of the tunnel, but to the circle of an exit.

Triumph flooded his veins—and his soul. There in front of him lay a city. Sunlight turned the walls the same golden color as the large gates that provided access to the interior of the city.

"Did we do good, master?"

Relliq turned to the speaker. This time it was Cludwr. However, the other two men had the same expectant look on their faces.

"Yes, my faithful ones. You acted wisely and correctly." At their confused look, he added. "Yes, you did good."

* * *

The view from the high ledge revealed more. Plots of what appeared to be carefully tended gardens formed a colorful patchwork against the dull gray stone. However, his gaze kept shifting between the river of water that circled the city and the stone tower in the exact center of the smaller buildings built out of the same lavender-hued rock. *I have it,* Relliq thought. *Magic is imbued in the city and the nexus is the tower.*

200

Desire raced his pulse. "This will be the site of my school, the true school of wizardry."

What of the isle? curiosity pressed.

A look at the steep rockfaces surrounding the city and an answer appeared. Use it as a summer house. *Now how to achieve the goals?*

He pulled the crystal from his pocket and inch by inch he analyzed the city's defenses. Scans of cliffs surrounding the valley revealed both natural and man-made fortifications. A dozen dark circles at ground-level indicated tunnel entrances suitable for staging troops. The water acted as a moat, forcing any invaders into a narrow kill zone. Residents could use rocks or arrows to defend themselves while their unwelcome visitors had limited access to the city.

He turned his attention to the city itself, but except for the tower and the structures immediately around it, the crystal showed neither mage nor tradesman. The size of the area should accommodate many more buildings than were revealed. "It doesn't matter if I cannot scry within the city," Relliq muttered. "I can still see enough from up here to direct my troops." Five of the clay soldiers will be an optimal strike force. With fifty of Cludwr's men to support them.

After all, confidence added, the residents will be under my control. I won't need a large army outside. I will have one already inside, awaiting instructions.

Light glinting off the moat brought another issue to mind. The clay soldiers would need to be protected in case they fall into the water. Lack of air wouldn't stop them, they could keep moving. But they will need to be sealed to stop the blood from being washed off.

Ignoring the shuffling of his men, Relliq watched the setting sun turn the entire city gold until the night's chill pulled him from his plans.

"Cludwr light the torches. We're returning to camp. Tomorrow, you visit one of the villages. I need a dozen volunteers so I can bring my clay army to life." Heat dampened his collar at the vision. "Soon, the gates will come off their hinges, and I will walk triumphantly into my new headquarters."

* * *

The evening meal over, Kia sat on her saddle beside the fire. Low murmurs and an occasional giggle came from the shadows on the other side of the fire where Dal sat with his kin. Sorrow at the reminder of her own missing family clutched at her. I can visit Brantly via crystal, she decided. The moon beginning to show above the distant horizon told the time as sixth hour. Just as quickly as she had decided to contact her brother, she quashed the idea. *The Oracle will be at service. I'll try again later.* To push away the loneliness, she looked for Brodie, but only his empty saddle greeted her gaze. *I can't even take comfort from his presence.* He had volunteered for another stint of sentry duty so that Dal could spend more time with his wife, daughter, and mother.

Her clenched fingers hidden beneath the sleeping fur wrapped around her shoulders did nothing to remove the chill from her skin—or her soul. No matter how hard she stared at the flames, she kept seeing a city of gold and hearing, "Come to me, little wizardling."

"Kia, you look pensive." Dal's voice came from behind her. Though soft, it still interrupted her reverie and she looked up to see the archmage and his lady standing there. "Can we help?"

"I don't want to be a bother, but I've been having a dream."

Ellspeth's quick, "Nightmares?" beat Dal's softer, "Tell me." At his encouraging nod, Kia said, "I see a golden city in a lake." The words she wanted to say refused to come. At Ellspeth's sympathetic look, she took a breath. "I keep hearing my stalker and it is harder to resist the call to join him."

Ellspeth knelt down and put an arm around Kia. "We already know who your stalker is." Her voice held an assurance Kia wasn't sure if was meant for herself or the archmage's lady. "Don't worry, Kia. Every mage is watching for Relliq. Sooner or later, he will pop his head up out of whatever hole he's hiding in long enough for one of us to locate him. In the meantime, tell us about the city."

"Every time I see the city it feels like your call to come to the council fire. Only it is not an urgent summoning, more like a welcome" She stopped but continued on at Dal's wave. "There isn't much to it. Just a strong sense that if I wish to come, I would be welcomed."

Dal scanned the camp then squatted down. "Long before I became archmage, one of my early instructors at the School of Mages had a favorite tale of how the school began. He said that in times long past, all magic was centered in a city protected by golden gates and guarded by a lake. An ancient mage named Belrum walked out of the desert, made his way to the isle, and created the rainbow bridge. He stayed many seasons until he had gathered all those with talent and taught them all he knew. They became the first group of instructors at the School of Mages."

Kia watched the flames. In their dancing movement, she saw the man she now knew was Belrum look back at his city. She followed his trek out of the desert and heard the incantation that created the rainbow bridge. Tears filled her eyes at the sadness she felt as she saw him give the master spells to the first leader of the council of mages, for she knew Belrum's next journey would be through the veil to the world of his ancestors.

"What happened to Belrum?" The words slipped out even though she knew the answer.

Dal sat for long moments, watching the fire. "After he gave the master spells to the one chosen to be the first archmage, Belrum crossed the rainbow bridge, supposedly to return home."

With a surety that she didn't know where it came from, Kia answered her own question. "Belrum was never seen nor heard from again."

* * *

Shartle rose above the horizon. Its twin moon was a second ball of light a finger length higher in the sky. Soon, Kia knew, there would be a rare confluence of the two moons and the sun. She dreaded the darkness caused by the eclipse. Just the power of a single full moon increased her stalker's powers. His magic would be magnified even more when the moons and sun aligned. To pull herself away from the thought, to prevent creating an opening for him, she focused on the task at hand. "I can handle sentry duty for a few candlemarks," she said in a mantra to reassure herself. "Help is just a gallop away if I need it." *Besides, Brodie could use the sleep.* Straightening her legs to give them a stretch, she pulled them back and tucked them under the sleeping furs she had brought to ward off the desert's chill.

A desert hen popped out of its burrow, looked around, then flitted off into the night sky towards the waterhole. Kia laughed to slow her racing pulse. She cast out her senses to track the bird. Whether it was the moon boosting her powers or from the archmage's lady, something impinged on her senses. Tilting her crystal to catch the moonlight, she searched for what triggered her attention. No image appeared in her crystal, just the impression of intense concentration.

"There is someone—or something—coming," Kia called. Her voice echoed down the crevice. No answer came back, but she heard Dal's reassurances in her head. A tug pulled the sword from its sheath. The weight of the blade in her hand comforted. *Even if it won't stop the golem, I can slow it down until the archmage gets here.*

But her fears remained unfounded. While the sense of someone approaching the sentinel rock grew, nothing untoward appeared. And unlike the night the golem attacked, there was no sense of dread.

The thunder of hooves announced Dal and Brodie's arrival. Instead of dismounting, the pair just stood in the stirrups and stepped onto the rock. Reassurance at their presence flooded through Kia. *I don't have to face the golem alone.* What little calm she had faded when Tairneach's bugle sounded into the night.

Dal and Brodie stood silent, watching the stallion. The fàlaire's ears were forward, every muscle in his body projected alertness. Kia wondered what the animal sensed for the fàlaire had their own kind of earth magic and as head stallion of the vale, Tairneach had even more abilities than his kin. Before she could pursue the thought, an answering call returned. With Wirake at his side, Tairneach trotted a few feet, then waited.

Tension, stronger than anything she had ever felt encompassed Kia. Although Brodie appeared unchanged, Dal's silhouette shifted. His dark form morphed into the transparency of crystal. Flashes of lambent energy flickered within his frame.

"Hello at the fire. May I approach?"

The nearness of the voice startled. Involuntarily, Kia tightened her grip on the sword's hilt.

"You won't need that, Kia," Dal said. "Our visitor poses no threat."

A glance over showed that the archmage had not only returned to his own form, but had taken his own advice. His long sword was back in its sheath. And the wizard himself presented nothing more than a mild curiosity. He jumped to the ground, landing lightly on his feet with Brodie close behind.

Dal called out the traditional welcome. "Approach in friendship."

Magefire blossomed in the darkness. Its glow revealed a tall, thin man, Kia judged to be about 70 turns. He rode a fàlaire that could have been Tairneach's twin. The fàlaire trotted up to the head stallion of the vale. Knickers between the pair sounded more like a couple of old women catching up on the local gossip than fighting words.

When the pair stopped, the two vale fàlaire turned to form an honor guard and escort the newcomer to the sentry rock. He climbed down out of the saddle with a nimbleness belying his apparent age.

"Lord Dal, I bring you and yours greetings from the homeland of Belrum. I am MarBelrum, head of our ruling council. My people have urgent need of your help."

Although she had expected more hesitance from Dal, he clasped the visitor's forearm in greeting. "I appreciate your meeting me on the ground as equals. Our camp is a ways down the crevice. If your need is that dire, the fàlaire can get us there faster than on foot."

MarBelrum looked at his mount whose whuff seemed to say, "Then back into the saddle it is."

"Kia?" Brodie's soft tone came from behind Kia. "Wirake says you can ride back to the camp with me. If you'd like to."

The expression on his face hinted at what he hoped her response was. Since it was so close to her own, she fought to keep her own feelings hidden. "It is easier than walking."

Wirake knelt to make it easier for Brodie to lift her into the saddle and climb up behind her.

The ride back to the fire was too short for Kia. Brodie must have felt it too, for he waited until after both Dal and MarBelrum had dismounted to swing his leg over the back of the saddle and step down. Even then he stood and watched the crackling flames for several moments. A sigh and he reached up. "If m'lady doesn't mind this humble non-tal giving her a hand?"

How to answer, Kia wondered. One side of her wanted to stay where she was and ride forever with his arms around her. Another recognized that she couldn't. *Someday I will have to do something about the talent versus non-tal issue.* "I would be honored for your assistance."

At her words, he placed his hands around her waist and lifted her from the saddle. He stepped back with a bow in apology of the familiarity. "M'lady, after you."

Kia stood beside Brodie while Dal performed quick introductions. She shook her head at his gesture for her to join him.

"Come, Kia," Ellspeth said. "You are the next senior mage here. Sit next to me."

Unable to resist the second invitation, Kia left the security of Brodie's side and sat down next to Ellspeth. Her nerves vibrated. *This will be my first time at a meeting of senior mages ... and I serve as one of the council.*

"I am sorry we don't have the luxury for a more leisurely getting acquainted," MarBelrum said. He pulled a small bag from his pocket and withdrew what appeared to be a twig with a single leaf attached. "This will prove my need and identity."

Dal didn't say anything, just took the offering, cradling it as if it were a valuable gem. Without a word, he passed it to Ellspeth. Her look communicated something, but Kia wasn't sure what. "Kia, you are one of us, joined on the kapuna tree." With that the older woman passed over Belrum's offering.

Although she had only seen a sketch of the kapuna tree, Kia knew instantly that it was the source of the leaf. Potent emotions surged forward the moment the leaf touched her hand. In her mind she saw a small jungle clearing, and in its center, an ancient tree. Long tendrils hung finger-like from the branches that formed a high canopy. Heart-shaped leaves covered each narrow strand. Bright red veins pulsed in the leaf in a rhythm that mirrored a pulse. In most of the leaves, veins, the brown-red color of dried blood, made the tree look like the grisly aftermath of battle.

One of the old books at the Council Isle had talked about how the tree held a record of all those ever born with magical powers. Tilting the leaf to catch the light of the fire revealed a faint symbol—a mage identification. MarBelrum offered indisputable proof of his association. She looked up to feel the other mage's appraising scan. It didn't stop at the scuffed leather of her travel clothes but felt like it pierced to her soul. As quickly as it started, the scrutiny stopped to be replaced by a sense of welcome.

"That leaf is not from the kapuna tree in the Aberden Archipelago." Dal's tone brooked no disagreement.

"You are correct." A smile tweaked MarBelrum's face, but in pleasure or worry, Kia couldn't tell. "Because of Diomharid's separation from the rest of the world, when Belrum returned from his sojourn, he brought back with him a cutting from the southern isle. Although the roots of both trees are the same ... and all of us joined through them, the leaves for those from Diomharid with power are on our tree. Not the ancient one."

Silence filled the campfire and looking from face to face Kia saw each come to the acknowledgment of the truth of what he said.

Dal handed back the leaf and gestured for MarBelrum to continue. "How may my wife and I, and the rest of the Isle mages assist?"

"Lord Dal, Lady Ellspeth, one called Relliq is attacking my home. We could have handled the attack on our gates, however, we are also being attacked from within. Men, women, and even children have taken up weapons against their kin and neighbors. We have already had to restrain many." MarBelrum's hands clenched as if an unhappy memory surfaced. He shook his head and raised a hand to Dal. "Can you help me save the city? Our magic hasn't done anything."

Dal's deep, "Do you know how Relliq controls your people?" beat Brodie's growl by a heartbeat.

Kia's mind flickered back to the time Relliq had tried to place her under a geas. Shivers racked her body at the remembered whisper of, "Come to me, little wizardling. Come to me ... or die." Her gaze shifted to Brodie. If he recalled Relliq's attempt to lure him to the woods and his death, Kia thought Brodie hid it well. His touch on her shoulder was light.

Sadness flickered in MarBelrum's eyes. "Those afflicted had the misfortune to be outdoors when it rained. Since rain usually only falls on the fields where we have crops growing, it was so unusual to see it in the city that many of our residents left their quarters to dance in the shower. Now they obey Relliq." His tone hardened and Kia felt her fists clenching. "He calls himself the Master."

Kia shrank back from Dal's rage. She tried to shrivel into herself, to imagine herself part of the stone. Her gaze shifted, seeking out Brodie. But found no respite from the heat emanating from Dal. Brodie's face mirrored Dal's.

Why is Brodie so upset, Kia wondered. He is not a mage. In her heart she knew the answer. *Brodie is an honorable man and would not tolerate harm to innocents.*

Chapter Twenty

The war council the night before ended with Dal ordering everyone to their sleeping furs. Then, Brodie mused, Dal, MarBelrum, and I sat up until the dawning planning the attack. A few hours rest, a quick meal, and they followed MarBelrum down the crevice towards Diomharid ... and Relliq.

Not even the battle energy building in Brodie's veins eased the heaviness in his soul. The upcoming fight would not be like those of his mercenary days or his time in the king's guard. There would be no opposing forces comprised on trained professionals. Now, the enemy would be the men and women of Diomharid, intellectuals dedicated to the betterment of man. Or, he added, the residents of the desert villages Relliq conquered. Men and women who wanted nothing more than to earn their livelihood and raise their families.

How can I wield my sword against innocents ... against children?

Even as he asked the question, he knew the answer. *I can't.*

He prayed the mages would be able to break Relliq's control over the inhabitants of Diomharid.

Candlemark after candlemark the fàlaire travelled a winding narrow path between steep cliffs or beneath hanging ledges that hid the sun. At times the riders dismounted and walked through tunnels where spires hung down from the ceilings as a trap for the unwary. When the tunnel ceiling lowered and seemed to touch Wirake's saddle or the walls closed until hide scraped rock, Brodie swore the fàlaire shrank into itself until the large animal easily fit in the tight space.

Whenever the trail allowed it, the war council continued on horseback. "Without any real hope," Brodie wanted to growl. He had to keep his frustration in check. Every time he allowed it to build, he felt a responding chord in Kia. "She needs to keep her focus on her magic. Not on me." A deep breath to regain his center and even though he knew she couldn't hear his mental reassurances sent them anyway.

Every contact with her deepened the darkness of his soul until it matched their stygian surroundings. I've seen too many men bid final farewell to loved ones on the eve of battle, he cursed. His heart ached to slip off with Kia. And just as fervently, knew it could never be. *Kia deserves more than a non-tal.* He justified his refusal of the desire he felt. Kia is destined, if not to be a member of the council of wizards, to be a senior leader at the temple. Or, he realized, the next Oracle of Givneh when her brother steps down.

Another voice added its support of desire. Kia also deserves the comfort given any friend.

Wirake's low snuffle warned of an impediment in their path. The fàlaire's keen sight had once again seen an obstacle before human eyes did saving Brodie from yet another head knock.

"We're almost there." MarBelrum's voice rolled down the tunnel. "You'll see daylight around the next bend."

Three steps later, the chamber opened up, and just as MarBelrum promised at its end was a circle of light. Brodie followed the others with slow steps, as if by not reaching the exit he could delay the upcoming fight. By the time he reached it, the rest of the party already stood on a ledge midway up the rock face. After candlemarks in the darkness or near-darkness, it took a few moments for his eyes to adjust to the afternoon sun. A scan took in the scene below. They looked out upon a round valley surrounded by steep cliffs. Shadowed circles, some at ground level, others half-way up the rock face, showed the entrances to more tunnels. Golden gates and the sound of combat told the tale. They stood above Diomharid.

Deep breaths pushed back Brodie's fears. From here on in the man had to give way to the warrior.

* * *

Kia put her back against the rock face to quiet the shakes in her legs. *I never realized how much I hate heights.* She blocked the real source of her fears. Unlike Dal, and she admitted Brodie, she was not a warrior. Her skill with a sword was newly acquired. *They have battle experience. This is my first.*

"Come to me, little wizardling. Come to me or die."

The whisper in her head broke the burgeoning mental paralysis. "You will not win, Relliq," she hissed. *I too am a mage.* She fingered the warm metal of the amulet hanging around her neck. *And, I have the faith of the Oracle.*

With Brodie to secure her, she leaned out only far enough to see the path MarBelrum pointed out that led to a side entrance of the city, then returned to the safety of the rock. As soon as he released his grip on her belt, she shoved her hands in her pockets to keep from taking him in her arms. And to prevent the others from seeing how badly her hands shook.

The sound of stone on metal pulled her focus from the heights to the floor below. Five golem hammered on the gates to Diomharid.

"Thank the ancestors," MarBelrum breathed. "The city has not yet fallen." He pointed out several groups arranged in lines behind the golem. "That group over there is from Diomharid. If you break their thrall they will join us." His finger shifted to another, larger group. "Those are innocents from the desert villages. You can use the differences in clothing as a means to distinguish between them." Then he indicated the defenders gathered on the walls, and where the hidden entrance was.

212

"We don't have long before the gates go down or the sun does." Brodie's tone held an edge that Kia had never heard before.

Waves of sadness and pride were replaced with reassurances and comfort. Kia searched to pinpoint the source and centered on Dal as he hugged first his mother, then his daughter. He pulled Ellspeth into an embrace. She didn't say a word, just leaned her head against her husband's chest and closed her eyes.

Dal and Ellspeth's bond will not break just because one falls in battle and crosses through the veil. Will I ever find a love like that? Kia wondered. Unbidden her gaze centered on Brodie. The muscle that throbbed in his taut jaw told of strong emotions.

What is he thinking? Is it about me?

* * *

Although the low murmurs were only reassurances of love and his faith in them, it was still hard for Brodie to listen to the archmage's parting from his family. It only reinforced to him that he had no kin. Which was why he had been part of Ruaridh's mercenary troop that attacked the archmage. *Dal spared my life that day. For that and for all that came after, I owe him.*

When Dal held out his arms and Ellspeth moved into them, Brodie turned his back to give the couple what little privacy he could.

Now is the time to speak to Kia, his heart encouraged. *Tell her your true feelings. Give her the amulet you made. It will serve as a promise token and she will be yours. There might not be another chance.*

No! Reality overrode desire. He searched for Kia to get one last look and found her standing as far from the others as the ledge allowed.

Before he could move, MarBelrum walked over and touched Kia's arm and whispered something in her ear. Her contemplative look made Brodie wonder what the older mage had said. She nodded and worked her way over.

Brodie readied himself to resist the urge to embrace her. But she solved the problem when she stopped an arm's length away.

"Kia ..." Although he could project his voice to be heard above the clamor of battle, his voice failed. He tried again. "There is no time to say what I wish."

She laid a finger on his lips. "Shhh."

Her fingers were cold as he kissed them. "Kia, I want you to promise me something. Keep yourself safe this day. And, in time, find yourself someone to make you happy."

"I have found someone," she whispered. Reaching up, she tugged his head down and kissed him.

Unable to resist both his urges and hers, he pulled her close. Although she tensed at first, her pliant body melded against his. "Kia," he breathed.

Kia's skin tingled from the surge of energy where Brodie held her. Previously unknown emotions blazed into existence. Her powers flared stronger than she had ever felt them before. *No one ever told me a non-tall could boost my power.*

It is a magic older than time, her heart answered. One that recognizes neither riches nor rank.

A soft cough behind them signalled the time to part had come.

Brodie stepped away. The thrall that held Kia in its sway shattered, leaving nothing in its wake but loss and sorrow. Even worse was the change in him. With each heartbeat, she could see him lock his emotions away until nothing was left but the cold of a glacial lake.

Magic shimmered in the air. The archmage's final scan on his troops left behind reassurance as to their ability and the righteousness of their actions. A low, "See you at Diomharid," and he turned and headed down the trail after MarBelrum. In her mind Kia swore she heard an unsaid thought that could only have been meant for Ellspeth. "If need be, I will wait for you on the other side."

For heartbeats, Kia stood and watched Brodie make his way down the path to where the battle with Relliq's forces would take place. A final look at the scene below and she moved to stand beside Ellspeth and Elendl. Ellspeth took each of their hands. "Kia, Elendl, you can do this. Your powers are strong and your control sure."

"What if the rain isn't enough to break the spell?"

Kia sighed. Elendl had asked the question she had been too frightened to.

"In addition to your powers, which are not negligible," Dal's mother interjected. "You will also be the focus for the other Isle mages as well as those of Diomharid itself."

Ellspeth fingered her silver necklace. "And we have the power of the circlet to boost them even more." Bidding the others into a circle, she helped Eilidh down onto her saddle, then gestured Kia to sit beside the clanswoman. Everyone settled, she folded her legs in a graceful descent to the ground. A deep breath and she took their hands.

Like the others, Kia tried to calm her spirit. The serenity she knew she needed failed to come.

I can't let the archmage and Ellspeth down. The lingering heat from Brodie's embrace turned her thoughts to him. She grabbed his image, not as she had last seen him laden with weapons, but relaxed as they rode the beach.

The sense of being watched flickered around the edge of her being. Squashing a momentary fear that Relliq had launched a pre-emptory attack, she opened her eyes. No danger lurked. Only Eilidh's knowing look greeted her search. Although the older woman didn't say a word, Kia knew her message. Strong emotions can block powers or enhance them, especially fear, hate ... and love.

Brodie and the archmage need my help. I will not fail them. A deep breath swept away the last of the fear. Detail by detail, Kia rebuilt up the image of Brodie in her mind. Her powers centered and she reached out to the mages assigned her. As each one sent along their energy, she heard a ringing chord. As if grasping the traces of a team of horses, she gathered first Barris' spell, then his mother's brighter one, in her hands.

At Ellspeth's quiet order, Kia wove the other's spells into a thick rope. One end connected her to Eilidh and the other to Elendl. A glowing circle formed around the women. Even Eilidh, despite not being an active mage, held a flaming element.

Elendl's gasp dimmed her rope. Kia fought to keep hers intact where the two connected. At her mother's murmured mantra, Elendl regained control. Magic flowed into the circle from without and within.

Her target firmly in mind, Kia let the power build, awaiting Ellspeth's final word of command.

"Now," Ellspeth whispered.

A final prayer to her ancestors for strength and to the Oracle to guide her aim, Kia called forth lightning. Soon the rolls of thunder mingled with the cries of men. But of panic or pain, she couldn't tell. *Please ancestors beyond the veil, guard and protect Brodie. Don't let it be him falling to the sword.*

Chapter Twenty-One

Measured steps took Brodie down the steep trail from the ledge. Kia's gaze burning into his back threatened his resolve. He quashed the urge to look behind him. This was a new feeling for him. He had been in battle before, but never had as much to lose. It was, he admitted, because he had never had anyone he had ever wanted to live for. His fingers brushed the hilt of TânOer and the cold steel took command until the last remnant of Kia's passion shrank to a glowing coal that Brodie locked away in the deepest recesses of his heart. No spark of his love—or memory of hers—remained. Calm entered his soul and his mind. Ready for battle his senses turned outward, alert for any sign of the invading force.

Behind him, the fàlaire stallions walked single file. Although their magic muffled the sound of their movement so it didn't carry beyond the small caravan, the rhythmic click of the fàlaires' iron-hard hooves on the even harder stone slowed Brodie's pulse until the two beat in time.

A brief clasp of the forearms, a murmured "Victory to you and all in your shadow," and MarBelrum headed to the city to lead the defenders of Diomharid. Brodie waited for Dal's command to move forward. However, no order was whispered, no signal given. The mage stood silent, a granite statue garbed in dull gray leather. His gaze centered on a spot on the cliff face. A sigh and his lips moved in a soundless spell. Although he couldn't feel the gathered magic, Brodie knew the archmage protected his family and Kia.

Dal gestured at their back trail. No circle marked the tunnel's entrance. In fact, no evidence of the ledge or its precious occupants remained. "Kia and the others will be safe. Neither mage nor man will reach them. And if they do, they will regret the day their ancestors led them there." A smile twitched the older man's lips. "My mother held the clanhold against all comers, including Bashim's monks. And she will do the same for his descendent. Though her hair may be gray, her arm is strong." The smile broadened. "And my mate has taught more than one man the folly of underestimating the power of a woman. She is almost as skilled with sword and spell as I am."

He pointed to a spot just off the bottom of the trail. "We will wait there for MarBelrum's signal. It's protected from the lightning and rain, yet we'll be close to the gates." His tone darkened. "They must not be breached. Relliq cannot be allowed to enter the city."

After a final look at where the women prepared the storm that everyone prayed would break the back of the enemy and free those under Relliq's thrall, Dal headed down the trail at a quick pace. Wirake's whinny told of the stallion's own worry for Kia.

A quick pat on his neck and a, "She'll be fine, boy," and Brodie took his own look at the hidden ledge. He locked away the last of his emotions. "This time, Relliq is mine."

Long strides quickly took him down the mountain. The fàlaire followed behind in a single line. Brodie knew that the concealment mesmer the archmage had thrown over them to hide them from any sentries or watchers Relliq might have posted also stifled the sound of the travel. Not a single hoof fall reached his ears. Yet, no matter how softly he tried to tread he swore his footfalls echoed out over the valley.

By the time they reached the desired hiding space and pushed back into the concealing shadows, Brodie wished the battle would already start. The scent of leather and horse filled Brodie's nose. For long moments, he stood, senses extended, listening for any alarm to be raised. His entire body pulsed with barely restrained energy.

Dark clouds formed overhead, their color that of a winter storm. The women are ready, Brodie thought. He couldn't see exactly where the bolts struck, but knew they landed close to the golem and the few men from Relliq's forces that had gathered around the clay warriors. Deafening booms rolled across the wide expanse of grass until the reports merged into a solid low rumble. It became impossible to tell which peals of thunder came from Kia and those with her or which were the golem's continued attack on the gates.

Lightning struck a golem and a chunk of the statue flew off, sending the nearby men scurrying away. Two more spears followed on the heels of the first. A sharp crack told the mages had hit their target when an arm dropped to the ground with a thud.

One golem down. Brodie wanted to cheer, but he was experienced enough not to count the victory until the enemy was vanquished. There were still four golem at the gates.

And Relliq's army, his mercenary side added.

However, a cold resolve had the final word. And Relliq to kill.

The time between the loud booms shortened until it was a single, continuous roar. Brodie swore the earth shook beneath his feet.

A bolt of lightning severed a clay soldier's head from its body. The earthen ball rolled into the moat knocking down three bandits on the way. A tall bandit fell to the ground clutching his leg, while a shorter, more lanky one, slid into the water. An arm waved in a frantic cry for help, then sank silently beneath the surface. Piece by piece, the clay attackers were reduced to inanimate piles of rubble.

Now to soften up the army, Brodie thought.

A cold breeze blew down his back. Where before the storm was thunder and lightning, now the wind shifted and carried rain from the clouds in great steel-colored sheets. The pounding of water on earth competed with the rushing waves as the moat turned into a giant whirlpool sucking down any bandit unlucky enough to be standing close to the edge.

Although he and the fàlaire remained dry, the cries of Relliq's men rose at the sting of the water on bare skin. Brodie's lips tightened. *I hope Relliq is in the heart of the deluge.* The slight smile he permitted himself did not reflect the real pleasure he felt. His expression tightened. *Ancestors beyond the veil, guard those who defend this day and guide those who fall to their eternal clanhold. Let rain and spell break Relliq's geas on the innocents he holds captive.*

The battlefield erupted into chaos. Groups of men broke ranks in a disorganized retreat. Some raced for a tunnel entrance half-way across the vale. Others, those dressed in garb that identified them as villagers or MarBelrum's townsmen turned their weapons on the remaining invaders.

A flick of Dal's fingers sent Brodie to a spot at the archmage's left. He felt more than heard Tairneach and Wirake slide into position directly behind him and Dal. The rest of the fàlaire ranged themselves in a secondary line of defense. Neither their color which blended into the rock nor a nervous whinny betrayed their presence.

I might not have a troop of men at my command, Brodie thought. But I have the fàlaire. And the stallions are worth a company of men.

"Now!" At Dal's command, Brodie pulled TânOer from its sheath. Sword held high, he charged into the melee. Wirake kept pace with his rider. Rearing and kicking, the stallion created his own path of destruction.

A thick-necked man wearing the chain-mail of a mercenary blocked Brodie's path. Steel rang on steel as Relliq's guard tested Brodie's reactions. TânOer blocked the first blow. Grunting, the mercenary launched a flurry of strikes.

Brodie easily parried each blow. Now, he thought. Gold glinted off TânOer's blade as he attacked. Without armor, he was at a disadvantage and every time he gained ground, Relliq's soldier forced him back. Back and forth, the pair fought. First one man advanced, then retreated in the face of the other's renewed assault.

Brodie lunged. A spin of his wrist and TânOer caught the edge of the other man's blade to send it careening into the moat. The back side of the spin sliced across the man's chest, ending the fight. A few deep breaths to ease his heaving chest and he headed towards where the archmage fought his own battle. Between his and the archmage's skill with the sword and the fàlaires' teeth and hooves, foot by foot, the small force worked their way across the field of battle. With each yard of ground they gained, more and more of those besieging Diomharid threw down their weapons and ran.

High pitched creaks rang out over the din of battle. Brodie ducked a blow and spared a glance at the source of the sound. Diomharid's gates started to open and a man slipped out between the metal panels. With each inch the gates separated more and more people joined the battle until MarBelrum and those who followed him surged out in a human tide. The reinforcements came with a price. As soon as the flow stopped, the gates closed, cutting off all hope for retreat. . Those who defended the city had to succeed or die. Within heartbeats, the clang of sword play replaced that of the golem's hammering. The sound grew until it echoed around the valley. Where before he and Dal fought alone against a larger force, now small groups battled.

MarBelrum raced over to Dal and Brodie who spun to create a small space of calm around the two leaders. "No one will get past me and Wirake. Do what you need."

The mages nodded and after a glance at the battlefield, huddled into a quick conference. "My people are still under Relliq's control," MarBelrum yelled. "I left some men to keep guard over them, but I'm not sure how long the doors of the hall will hold."

"One battle at a time," Dal ordered. "We'll free the rest of your people later." He turned to Brodie. "Where is Relliq?"

* * *

The glare of hate, something beyond the normal focus of men fighting, drew Brodie's gaze to the opposite side of the battlefield. A hard look revealed a figure standing in a tunnel a shoulder's height up the cliff. The distance made determining features difficult, but the emotion could only come from one man—Relliq. Brodie's eyes narrowed. Determination radiated from his frame. "That one will not leave the field of battle alive."

Relliq threw a jaunty salute, jumped down to the valley floor, and shouting commands, ran amongst his forces.

Two men jumped in front of Brodie, blocking his view. By the time he disarmed them, Relliq had disappeared. Spinning Brodie searched for the opposing forces' leader. The glow of magefire provided a clue to his quarry and he ran towards it. However, instead of a single man challenging him, now groups of two or three men blocked his path. No sooner did he disarm or wound one group than another took their place. Curses learned in numerous troop bivouacs leaped to Brodie's lips. "It is as if they are being guided."

Even worse, while he fought with the bandits or townsmen, the mage would duck down and disappear, forcing Brodie to devote time fighting when he wanted to search for Relliq. It seemed each time he located the renegade, the same half-dozen mercenaries provided cover. "So, Relliq, has his own private guard," Brodie growled. "But I have the way of it now." Instead of looking for one man, he looked for six in a specific defense pattern. The larger group made it easier to locate his target.

Another bandit fell to TânOer. "Finally," Brodie breathed. His pulse leaped. No more combatants stood behind him and Relliq. The way to the mage was clear. It also revealed a problem. Relliq was raising his hands for a magical attack—and his target was Dal.

Brodie's throat hurt from the force of his yell. "Dal, behind you." In a single move, he snatched a dagger from his belt. Even though he knew it would not reach Relliq before he loosed the stream of fire, Brodie threw the blade. A prayer that it would distract Relliq and ruin the rogue's aim so that the lethal bolt would miss his friend, Brodie ran after his throw. If Relliq's first strike wasn't successful, he didn't mean to allow him a second.

Only two steps and a heavy blow knocked Brodie to his knees. Pain sliced across his shoulder. A roll and upward stab and his attacker, a skinny bandit, fell clutching his stomach. Blood streamed from beneath the man's hands.

With a grunt, Brodie got to his feet. Sword in hand, he charged towards the last place he had seen Relliq. Fire burst into life and raced down his arms. It danced around his fingers where they clutched TânOer's hilt. One-handed slaps ended the illusion and the flames vanished. "Relliq, I'm not falling for that trick again," Brodie bellowed.

An insane laugh drifted across the battlefield in answer.

Burning, not of a fire, but from a blade ripped down Brodie's back. He spun, TânOer raised in defense, to face the new attack. But instead of delivering a fatal blow, he checked his thrust at the terrified gaze of his attacker, a slender boy who didn't even reach up to Brodie's chin. The youth held a sword almost as long as he was tall. His awkward grip on the hilt showed an obvious lack of skill.

Ice chilled Brodie's heart. His worst fears had come to pass. Relliq now used children in battle. He turned innocents into human shields—and weapons.

A flick of Brodie's wrist spun TânOer and the boy's fragile protection flew off into the grass.

But what to do with him? I can't kill an innocent. Again, Brodie cursed Relliq and his ancestors. TânOer dropped to the grass. Before the boy could run away, Brodie grabbed the youth's collar and yanked his tunic

223

down over his shoulders, turning the garment into an improvised restraint.

"Go over to the wall, and sit there until a woman grants you freedom." Brodie hardened his tone. "Your master commands." Although he knew without powers Kia might not receive the message, he quickly built up an image of her in his mind, and focusing his thought through TânOer's magic, pictured the boy sitting at the wall. *This innocent awaits you. Break the thrall.*

One problem cared for, he scanned the battlefield for Relliq and the squad of mercenaries that protected him.

* * *

Kia sucked down a ragged breath at the sudden pain in her side. Her breath escaped in a gasp. What hold she had on her spell broke. In that instant the rain she directed onto Dionharid's attackers stopped. She arched her back in response to the fire of another wound. But no blood flowed, no weapon had ripped her skin. No one on the ledge even had a sword in their hand. Except for Eilidh whose hands were empty, the other women held nothing but a scrying crystal. So where did the pain come from. There was only one answer. "Brodie ... no," she moaned. An ice statue, she searched her crystal, praying to see his image. None appeared.

Resolve filled her soul. *I may be dammed for doing so, but I swear if Brodie falls, I will send those who killed him across the veil.*

"Lady Ellspeth ... mistress, Brodie needs me. I can't help from up here." Kia put all the love she had in her plea. "Please let me go down to the valley floor."

The older woman's pinched lips didn't provide any encouragement. She knew the real reason she wanted to go wouldn't sway the other woman, even if she could speak it. *There has to be some excuse Ellspeth will agree to.*

"I can't tell Relliq's bandits from the innocents and townsmen. My crystal doesn't show me what I need to control the rain. Please, Ellspeth, let me go down there."

This time, Kia's voice trailed off, leaving unsaid that she had to know how badly Brodie was hurt.

Ellspeth's face remained impassive.

Kia prayed the older woman would give her permission. While she waited the answer, she evaluated her options. To obey the archmage's lady or go to Brodie's defense.

Fear raised the first question. What if Ellspeth refuses? Disobedience could mean banishment from the Isle. No more students ... no more magic.

More positive thoughts countered the fear. *But I will have Brodie ... and a life at the temple. Brantly will not disown me for helping another.*

Eilidh laid a hand on Ellspeth's arm. "Elendl and I will be safe. Dal's mesmer protects us. The fighting is on the valley floor, and those running away look for an exit, not the solid wall we appear to be." Sadness filled her gaze, as if a painful memory flickered into existence, only to be banished. "Go to your mate. Let Kia go to Brodie." The far-away look of a vision also faded. "I don't know how badly he is hurt. Only that she is needed."

Neither breath nor the sound of battle broke the silence. Kia dared not acknowledge the possibilities of Ellspeth's refusal. Sparks danced behind her eyes from a breath held too long.

Ellspeth inclined her head to her mother-in-law, acknowledging the logic of the argument. "Very well. Kia and I will go add our powers to those of the healers of Diomharid."

An unspoken "Thank the Oracle," and Kia released her tension in a gush. She bowed her head, waiting to be admonished for interrupting her mistress, but Ellspeth was silent. Her expression turned stern. "Elendl, obey your grandmother. The mares will provide a line of defense. But both of you promise me. If the ledge is breached, get in the saddle and ride. The fàlaire will keep you safe."

"I promise," in Eilidh's strong tone, echoed by Elendl's lighter one, were followed by quick hugs.

"Kia, I know you're more used to walking than riding." Ellspeth pointed down the path. "The incline will make for a fast run." Her eyes sparkled. "Just don't bowl me over getting to that metalsmith of yours."

Chapter Twenty-Two

Kia strained to tell one figure from another in the mass of fighting men. Despite the urge to search for Brodie, she followed Ellspeth to the gates of Diomharid. The number of wounded laid out in long rows sliced at her soul. "No one deserves to be treated like this," she growled. "They were doing nothing but defending their home."

While Ellspeth conferred with MarBelrum, Kia scanned the faces of the wounded, afraid that she would find Brodie, but praying that she wouldn't. The archmage's lady returned with a basket of bandages and a young woman in tow. "Kia, this is Gwenivar. She could use some help." She pointed to an open area half-way down the wall where a handful of wounded had been placed. "Why don't you two start over there? It is away from the fighting, yet close enough for me to come if need be." In a sotto voice which didn't carry to Gwenivar, she added, "Kia, keep your sword close to hand."

A nod to acknowledge the older woman's order, Kia put an arm around Gwenivar's shoulders and guided her to the waiting patients. The closer they came, the slower Gwenivar walked. After one look at the girl's pale features, Kia locked away her own needs. "Well, Gwenivar, why don't you tell me the healing spell you use? I'll follow your lead."

Between Kia's encouraging words and quiet instructions, Gwenivar splinted an elderly man's broken arm and laid on a healing spell. A moan caught Kia's attention. She tapped Gwenivar on the shoulder and pointed. Handing the girl the basket, quick steps took them to the cause of the sound, a young boy barely fourteen-turns old. Pressure and a bandage failed to staunch the flow of blood from a deep wound. *He is no older than my students at the isle,* Kia thought. *He should be in class, not the battlefield.* Her mental tone hardened. *Relliq has much to answer for.*

"Sorry, mistress, nothing works." Sorrow crossed Gwenivar's face. "I am but recently come to my powers and don't know much magical healing."

"You are doing fine, Gwenivar. Just keep the pressure on the wound. Do you remember the incantation?"

The girl's nod reassured Kia that her new protégé would do well. "Then let us do it together." Kia started the spell and Gwenivar's lighter tone joined in.

"By magic and bandage,
We summon health for thee.
Blood no longer flow,
So let it be.

"Wounds be closed,
His body again healthy.
As the mind pictured,
Selah let it be."

Kia held her breath and prayed. Although she had healing experience from her work at the temple and in the surrounding city of Givneh, she was still new to her powers. And this youth needed help if he was to live. *More help than I can give.* Once again, the urge to summon Ellspeth, or Kia considered, the archmage, rose. And as she had before, she quashed it. There were many innocents in just as bad a shape. *Ellspeth and Dal are needed elsewhere.* Resolution held tight, she closed her eyes, took a breath to center her magic, and repeated the incantation. When she opened them, a pale pink had started to color the boy's cheeks. His lips were no longer blue.

Kia bowed her head. "Thank you, ancestors for your help this day."

A squeal of surprise—and pain—rang out.

The sound, one so different than the cries of pain that rose above the battlefield, pulled Kia's attention from her patient. A glance showed Gwenivar on her feet. A bandit stood behind her, an arm around her throat.

Hot breath wafted against the back of Kia's neck. A vice-like grip twisted her arm up behind her back, while a hand over her mouth stifled a scream and prevented a yell for help. Her arm being leveraged even higher forced her to her feet.

"Master, time to leave. I have your prize."

The rank smell that followed the words sent panic racing through Kia. The bandit that held her summoned the one man she dared not meet—Relliq. A sharp kick aimed at a knee failed to connect. Her struggles yielded nothing but sharp pains that ranged up her arms and across her shoulders. She had to free herself. Soon the loss of circulation would render her hands useless to hold a sword or make the ritual gestures necessary to protect Brodie. Stomps to the man's foot and kicks to his legs failed to gain her freedom, but his hand moved from her mouth. Grasping the chance, she sucked down a breath to scream, to be rewarded with a belt behind the ear. A fist to the stomach doubled her over. Instead of a yell for help, the air just rushed out.

The bandit is still behind me. So who hit me?

Tugs on her hair pulled her up straight. It took a heartbeat for her to realize the insane gaze she looked into was Relliq's. Breath that smelled of spices wafted into her nose when he leaned closer and whispered, "You should have come to me willingly." Light glinted off the ritual dagger he waved in front of her eyes. "Since the archmage wouldn't bless my knife, I did." He pressed it against Kia's throat. Warmth trickled down her neck. "I just need something special for the final consecration."

Her head tilted back, Kia couldn't see how deeply he had cut her. All she could do was pray he had only split the skin. Another rivulet of blood ran down her throat and puddled between her breasts.

"Have you decided to join me?"

The rasp of the knife when Relliq rubbed it along her jaw resounded in Kia's ears.

"Choose wisely, my darling Kiansel," Relliq hissed. "If I can't have you, no one will."

Beyond Relliq, a dark gray shadow burst through an open space amongst those still fighting and streaked toward her.

Hope flickered into being. If Wirake was close, then so was Brodie.

Fear blasted the hope. Except for Tairneach, most fàlaire would not harm a man.

However, hope countered, Wirake had fought on behalf of Brodie before.

Kia prayed the stallion's approach meant he would do so again.

The fàlaire's shoulder hit the man holding Gwenivar. The bandit landed four wagon lengths away with a loud crack. He lay with his neck twisted at an unnatural angle. With barely a slowing of his momentum, Wirake spun and returned. Rearing on his haunches, he struck down Cludwr with his front hooves.

Relliq's shove knocked Kia back against the fàlaire. Off balance, she fell beneath the stallion. His legs quivered with the effort to stop his downward motion so he wouldn't step on her. The waterlogged ground soaked through her pants and chilled her skin. Even worse were the heavy footsteps that filled her ears. *Where was Relliq? He is not to leave alive.* The flap of his black cape showed him halfway to a tunnel entrance. Kia struggled to get her feet beneath her and reached for her sword, only to find an empty sheath.

Strong arms lifted her up and she looked up into Brodie's worried gaze. Comfort such as she had never known warmed her. It grew when he pulled her close with an anxious, "Are you hurt?"

Her skin tingled when he ran his hands across her shoulders and down her arms. He leaned in close and looked at her throat. The scent of sweat and leather filled her nose. A sharp intake of breath accompanied Brodie's gentle touch of the cuts. "They're not deep. They look more serious than they are."

Is he trying to reassure himself or me? Kia wondered. She had no answer to the question, but relished the sound of his heartbeat as she leaned against his chest. Nothing existed except the man in her arms.

His deep sigh broke the thrall. His arms dropped and he stepped back.

Kia gasped at the shock. More than a physical separation, she swore his action broke a magical connection. Happiness that Brodie had latent powers fought with the fear that she was mistaken. She reached up to pull him back. "Stay. You've done enough this day." She gestured at his blood-stained tunic. "You're hurt."

Brodie lifted up his arm. "Most of it isn't mine. I've been wounded worse." He looked down at her and smiled. "You can bandage me later." His low, "An innocent needs you," reminded her of a duty unfulfilled as did his nod towards Gwenivar who remained on the ground. A sad smile flickered into being. "I will be back soon. The fighting is almost over. You can heal me then."

Kia followed his gaze and tried to evaluate the scene as he did. To her untrained eye and ear, the chaos had not lessened. The only difference was that more wounded lay at the gates.

His focus shifted back to her with an intensity that contrasted with the lightness of his earlier words. A damp spot chilled her chin where his blood-stained finger touched her jaw to tip her head up. His gaze bore a sadness that cut worse than Relliq's dagger. "There is one more thing I have to do."

Anger in his tone revealed not just his plans but the subject. "You won't be safe, Kia, until Relliq is captured."

Before the last of the connection between them vanished, she heard his unspoken ...or killed.

* * *

Cold, that of the great ice fields of the north enveloped Kia. Duty fought with desire. Reasons for Brodie to stay with her fought with the reality that his sense of duty mirrored hers. He could no longer leave Relliq loose than she could leave wounded untended to.

Wirake's scream of anger broke through the swirling maelstrom of her thoughts. The stallion spun and thundered off, throwing great clods of dirt into the air.

All the arguments she was going to make to change Brodie's mind remained unsaid. Whatever the reason Wirake ran off, it meant the end of her dreams. Futility lying heavy on her heart, Kia lowered the arms that had been raised in entreaty and allowed Brodie to guide her and Gwenivar to one of the wounded. Even as she worked, she alternated her attention between her patient and Brodie who stood guard over them.

The deep gash of a grey-bearded oldster gave way to an even deeper slash on a woman three decades his junior. Patient after patient was treated. Young followed old, women followed men, until the world reduced to the need to succor another and an exhaustion felt to the bones. With each one, Kia found it harder to fight the growing tension in Brodie ... and herself.

Wirake's bugle rang out in victory and echoed around the valley. He trotted into view, pushing a staggering Relliq in front of him.

Kia's breath quickened at the sight of the pale-faced mage. He was raising his hands, aiming a magical attack. A fiery spear flew through the air—at Brodie.

"No!" Her head throbbed with the force of her scream.

Kia's warning sounded in Brodie's ears. Trusting her instincts, he spun TânOer in a protective circle before him. Sparks bounced off the sword to burn themselves out before they reached the ground.

232

"I will not be denied," Relliq screamed. Again, his fingers flicked in a ritual gesture.

Brodie held TânOer at the ready. His muscles tensed to deflect the mage's attack. This time instead of a stream of fire, a flicker of a glow fizzled at the edge of his fingers.

Someone is blunting Relliq's powers, revenge cheered.

Who? Ellspeth or Kia? It didn't matter, Brodie decided. Only one thing did. *I can fight Relliq man to man.* Flicks of his wrist moved the weapon through a series of double loops. Sunlight glinted off the blade as he lifted it in salute. "Shall we begin?" he said softly.

For several heartbeats, Brodie feared the other man would not accept the challenge. *If Relliq doesn't voluntarily, I'll make him. Even if I have to strip him of every ounce of his pride, he will fight me.* However, before the first taunt was issued, Relliq charged, his sword pointed at Brodie's heart.

A spin of TânOer's blade tipped the other man's first pass aside. Brodie took advantage of Relliq's inability to stop his mad dash and smacked the man on the breeches with his sword.

On the next pass, Relliq approached more slowly. His sword wove a frenetic net before him. TânOer's enchanted steel met that of Relliq's blade. The clang of metal rang out, sounding like the battle of a hundred men rather than just two.

By the time Brodie parried yet another attack and stepped back, sweat streamed down the mage's face and chest. Yet only light moisture dampened Brodie's skin. As Relliq shook his head to clear the liquid running into his eyes, Brodie waited for his opponent to resume the battle.

Experience said to end the conflict before the mage regained his powers. What if whoever is holding Relliq's magic at bay loses their concentration?

However, other thoughts countered it.

Revenge had the final word. *This one needs a lesson.*

233

Like a ship cat toying with its prey, Brodie lured the mage back and forth across the small area that had become their private arena. Gasping, Relliq sucked in ragged breaths. His dark hair hung in wet strands around a face pale with exhaustion.

TânOer's edge caught the other man's blade and rolled around it in a disarming move. Relliq's cry of anger accompanied his weapon's flight. The blade landed at the feet of a woman dressed in the brown and tans of Diomharid. She scooped down and picked up the weapon, clutching it to her chest.

"Well, Relliq, now you understand why the archmage ordered weapons training even for those with powers. Now for the next lesson." Grinning, he slipped TânOer into its sheath. His arm snapped out and his clenched fist connected with his opponent's chin with a solid thunk.

* * *

The blow that knocked Relliq to the ground sounded like a thunderclap. If not for the cloudless skies overhead, Kia would have sworn lightning struck the fallen man. Three steps took her away from Gwenivar and provided a clear view of the two men.

Her stalker struggled to his knees. The two men's voices reached her. Brodie was inviting Relliq to fight him man to man, challenging him not to use magic.

You can't trust Relliq, reality hissed. That one will cheat, lie, and kill without a qualm.

Even as the thought formed, she saw his hands moving in a ritual gesture. Fire leaped from his fingers. Kia gulped. The target was Brodie.

Air hissed out when Brodie spun TânOer, blocking the threat. Anger replaced fear. Kia clenched her fingers so tight the skin turned translucent. One with powers was endangering her friend. No, she admitted, her future mate.

Kia opened her mouth to call the archmage only to close it. Distraction could kill. Since Dal could not get to Brodie, she prepared to supplement TânOer's magic with her own. Taking a stand, she gathered her powers.

"Why should I stoop to your level? You're just a worthless non-tal," Relliq sneered. "Not worthy of Kia. I am a mage. A descendent of the great Bashim." His arrogance radiated an aura of righteousness. His smile widened. "You're too late smith. Kia was mine. While you were under my thrall, she joined me in the woods."

The look Brodie turned on her tore at Kia's heart. Fear that Brodie would believe the lie changed into anger. *How to answer Brodie? To reassure him.* Although she didn't feel any joy, she forced a smile to show her mind was her own.

Her heart leaped at the wink he returned.

She opened her mouth to warn him about Relliq only to see the mage launch a roundhouse punch.

Brodie ducked beneath the swing. His fist connected with his opponent's chin with a solid thunk. Before Relliq could hit the ground, Brodie threw a second blow into Relliq's middle. His breath whooshed out in a ragged gurgle and he collapsed to the ground.

Brodie entwined his fingers in the belt around the mage's waist. A jerk pulled Relliq upright. Open-handed slaps forced the man's head to the left, and then the right until the mage's eyes rolled up in his head.

Kia held her breath. Brodie stood over his enemy, a granite statue garbed in leather. His heaving chest was the only sign of life.

Relliq is also my enemy. One part of her wanted to urge Brodie to kill Relliq. But that is not part of the Oracle's teachings, her conscience whispered. She waited, silent.

Seconds passed as an eerie silence covered the battlefield. His gaze met hers and the anger that had flooded his face disappeared as he quickly regained control.

The paralysis that held her prisoner released in a flash. Her legs took on a life of their own. All the exhaustion of the day vanished as she ran to him. His lips pressed against hers. He pulled back to let a breath of air between them before tightening his embrace.

Kia sighed, relishing not only the fact that he was alive …but with her.

Chapter Twenty-Three

A stupor, that of the grave, haunted Kia. She fought back a sob as she watched five more litters bearing a white-draped figure snake their way up the valley to the funeral chamber. The slowness by which she stood told the toll three days of healing had taken out of her reserves. In addition to healing those wounded by sword or pike, magics had to be worked over those from Diomharid who had been caught in the rain. While Relliq's capture released his control over most of those he had enslaved, others, notably the strongest mages, required the combined work of all the Council Isle mages to break the enchantment.

More difficult was helping the handful of those whose will had been taken by Relliq who suffered psychological trauma. "Finesse is sometimes harder than heavy-handedness." She was thankful though that they only needed a mild adjustment in their thinking to relieve the guilt of betraying their friends and family. Her thoughts returned to the cryptic comments made at the war council about Dal helping Murdo after the mercenary was under the thrall of Relliq's ancestor, Bashim.

However, it was the weight on her soul of those she had failed to save that bowed her head. Although the entire contingent of mages couldn't be spared for every funeral, each healer attended the brief ceremony when the bodies of their lost patients were consigned to the pool of molten rock that bubbled in the depths of the mountain. Although she had only made the walk twice, the sorrow at the twelve people who had crossed the veil that it represented added to the heaviness of her steps.

"Tomorrow will be time enough to mourn," she muttered. "Today there are more to save." Scans of the rows of wounded that filled the large square in the middle of Diomharid told of the work that still remained. The teens she directed bustled up and down the rows, working in pairs to offer water and hot meals to both worker and wounded. *All but Gwenivar*, she amended. *I sent her to get a few candlemarks rest.* She bit back a moan. *Soon Shartle and Neba would rise and with it the additional healings needed to ease the pain that nighttime brought. Elendl had the vigor of youth to keep her going*, Kia thought. *And Ellspeth has her own strong magic as well as that of the circlet. All I have is sheer will power.* Fingering the amulet her brother gave her, she again debated reaching out to him for help.

"I can't," she muttered. "Brantly is still dealing with the remnants of the wasting disease Relliq let loose. He can't send me any energy. It's up to me."

Shifting her back against the low wall that surrounded the moat, she laid her hands palms up on her knees and focused on the first splinter of the moon that rose over the mountain peak. Three deep breaths to center herself, and she willed herself into a light trance. Deeper and deeper she sank into velvet darkness.

For long moments she allowed the serenity of the universe to restore her flagging strength. The shimmer of a silver cord emerged from the blackness. A parallel line, its silver tinted with gold, coalesced into being. An iridescent point, where the two lines intersected, wavered from blue to violet, and back to blue again. Wonder replaced surprise and with the ungainliness of a newly acquired skill, Kia willed her ethereal self towards the pulsing light. Before she reached it, the point of light exploded leaving behind a single image in its passing—Brodie.

Kia gasped and searched her surroundings. Unerringly, her gaze shifted to where Brodie gently rocked a young child. The sword that hung across his back contrasted with the tenderness he showed the child. *I never knew Brodie was so good with children.* She also realized that he was always nearby. Close enough to be a protective sentry, yet far enough way to give her the distance she needed.

"Mistress?"

Kia frowned at the closeness of the voice. Opening her eyes, she realized that Gwenivar had approached without a sound.

"Mistress ..." Gwenivar's voice trailed off. After a deep breath, she restarted. "I heard the council decreed that at the confluence of Shartle and Neba, Relliq's powers will be bound." She looked at the sky.

Kia followed the direction of the younger woman's stare and saw Shartle had cleared the rim of the valley and in a few candlemarks the moon would appear to merge with its sister moon to form a single orb.

Gwenivar's pale face turned even whiter. "I am just come into my powers and not sure what I can contribute. Or sure I want to."

Kia put an arm around the shivering girl. "Don't worry, Gwenivar, not all those with powers will participate in the binding ritual. Elendl and I won't be. While Elendl carries a journeyman dagger, she is new to the rank." She tightened her embrace until Gwenivar stopped shaking. "Most of the mages of Diomharid won't be helping either. They are still recovering from battling either the thrall or the curse and need to save their magic." A smile she wasn't sure was meant to reassure Gwenivar or herself raised the corners of Kia's lips. "I don't think many beyond the archmage and his lady, and one or two of your council at the most will be called upon. And then mainly to hold the protective wards."

At Gwenivar's worried look, Kia added, "There will be no dearth of talent at the binding. Dal and Ellspeth have special tokens and magics. They told me that linking the master spells of the archmage to the power of the circlet and the magic of the city will be sufficient to bind Relliq's powers."

Gwenivar dropped her gaze to her feet. "Thank you, mistress. I didn't mean to be a burden. I just have so many questions regarding magic. The way you explain things make them so clear."

This time Kia's smile was heartfelt.

* * *

Brodie leaned against the wall in the tower room that served as the council chamber for Diomharid's mages. Narrow beams of light cast by the twin moons, Shartle and Neba, slid across the stone floor while the flickering candles in the sconces on the walls added a solemn air to the room. He pushed off and stood at a loose attention at the archmage's approach.

"You know you don't need to be here," Dal said.

Brodie searched for any hint of condescension in his friend's tone. "I know. As a non-tal I can't contribute anything, but ..."

Dal nodded to the chalk circles on the floor made in preparation of the upcoming ceremony. "I understand. You want to see with your own eyes that the threat to Kia is ended."

The sadness in his friend's eyes only added to Brodie's own. "What Relliq did is not your fault."

"I allowed him to leave my control. I sent him to the temple."

"You couldn't have known he'd find Bashim's journals," Brodie persisted. "You did what you thought was right."

For a few heartbeats, Brodie hoped he had gotten through to his friend. But the archmage's next words proved the lie. "I knew what kind of man he was. I should have bound his powers right then and there on the isle."

Although the hand he laid on Dal's shoulder was light, Brodie hoped it would convey the sympathy he felt. "Dal, you and I both know you could not. That your authority as archmage also comes with responsibility." He took a breath, choosing his next words carefully. "And that means guiding those with powers as best you can. It is not on your head that Relliq chose to emulate his ancestor." The additional reassurances remained unsaid at MarBelrum's approach.

The head mage of Diomharid looked as exhausted as the isle mages. "You know he is right, Archmage." MarBelrum looked at the orange globe that appeared to hover outside the window. What had started out as two moons now appeared as one. "Shartle and Neba are in confluence. If you're ready, I'll have the prisoner brought in."

Brodie saw Dal's resigned look and knew before his friend spoke the pronouncement. "It is past time to do what must be done."

A nod to Brodie, Dal moved to the center of the room and waved Ellspeth and MarBelrum into position on each side of him.

Brodie fought to keep the building tension from showing in his face. He saw the same reflected in the eyes of his friends and wondered how much worse the event was for them. *After all, they are the ones who have to pronounce sentence on one of their own.* Presenting a nonchalance he didn't feel, he put his back against the wall, pulled TânOer from its sheath and leaned it tip-first against the floor.

Heavy footfalls and loud curses of "Unhand me," told of Relliq's arrival outside the council room. Raising his voice, MarBelrum called out, "Bring in the one to be judged."

Relliq strode in and stood before the tribunal. Despite the iron chains around his wrists and the stone-faced guards that held his arms, Relliq's entire being bespoke arrogance.

Brodie clenched his fingers to resist the urge to swing TânOer. A quick whip and Relliq will be dead. *No! I am not the only one he wronged. Dal deserves his revenge too.*

"Relliq, you are accused of insurrection, fomenting revolt, and improper use of magics. What say you in your defense?" Although MarBelrum spoke in a level tone, Brodie sensed the leader's barely controlled anger.

A sneer twitched Relliq's lips. "I answer to no man, especially a weakling too afraid to use the tools given him."

Dal winced and bowed his head. When he raised it, his gaze showed no emotion, least of all mercy. "Relliq, I once gave you an option. And by doing so allowed your continued misuse of your powers. That will be corrected tonight. As archmage I find you guilty of using forbidden magic, of using your powers against those unable to defend themselves." His expression and tone matched that of the rock that formed the tower. "I find you guilty of causing the death of innocents."

"You can do nothing," Relliq yelled. "You were weak before, you still are. I am the only one with true power."

Brodie tensed to leap, but relaxed against the wall. *This is mage business, not mine. As long as Relliq gets his due, it matters not if another's weapon deals it out.* He did admit to himself that he would have preferred to beat the smirk off Relliq's face with his fist.

Dal shook his head, dismissing the rant as if Relliq was an errant child needing to be disciplined. "Relliq, for your actions against the residents of Diomharid, the desert villages, and the stalking of Kia, you have shown yourself incapable of following the Way. I have communicated with the Oracle of Givneh and he agrees. As leader of the Council of Mages, I pronounce sentence. Your powers will be bound, lost to your forever. You will remain here in Diomharid to serve at whatever menial tasks they assign you until the end of your days."

Brodie allowed the flicker of a smile to his lips. Although he would have preferred Relliq's death, turning the mage into a non-tal would be justice.

When there was no response, Dal added. "But I shall show you more mercy than you did to those you wronged. You shall not have the knowledge of what you have lost to torture you." A deep sigh and he moved to the center of the floor.

Spidery lines of red sprang into view at his sharp gesture. Brodie's lips tightened. *How can I see the archmage's wards?*

Hope offered a reason. Maybe associating with TânOer some of its enchantment rubbed off or some resident magic in Diomharid triggered dormant powers.

Although Brodie wanted to reach for that lifeline, he didn't. *It must be through my physical contact with the sword.*

The lines brightened as Dal paced the warded circle to the unguarded doorway. His swift movement unsheathed his long sword. It dipped toward one edge of the door, the blade's tip catching several of the red threads. Casting a spell of protection, he traced the door outline with his blade. As the point moved up one long side then across to the bottom to the opposite corner, the space filled with a solid curtain of shimmering threads. He repeated the action on the opposite corners and with a final incantation laid the sword across the threshold.

Green ribbons flowed from Ellspeth's fingers and played over Brodie's form. His skin tingled from the contact. "An added protection." Her warm smile contrasted with the seriousness of the night. "You are too valuable a weaponsmith to lose to some errant magic." A wink and she returned to stand at her husband's side.

Dal and MarBelrum's deep tones filled the room along with Ellspeth's lighter counterpoint.

"Knowledge acquired be permanently gone,
Powers be bound in night and morn,
Never to be released by man or creature born,
Selah let it be."

"Memory of what was given,
And now taken away,
Be riven from the mind forever from this day,
Selah let it be."

"Kia will a stranger be,
No hatred, love or lust,
Your memory and desire we now adjust,
Selah let it be."

The room vibrated as the wizards fed the spell with more and more of their energy. And with each heartbeat, the arrogance in Relliq's face lessened. Dal silently walked over to stand in front of the rogue. As Brodie watched a glowing circle of thorns shimmered into being around Relliq's head. The crown spun faster and faster until sparks formed a golden cascade that enveloped Relliq's body.

Dal's whispered, "Make it so," echoed in the room far beyond the volume of the actual words.

The air within the tower throbbed with the heartbeats of all those Relliq had wronged until it became a living thing. Thread by thread, the cocoon that imprisoned Relliq unraveled until he stood alone. He wavered, only the steel grip of the guards who stepped forward to hold his arms kept him from collapsing to the floor.

For long seconds, silence filled the room. No sound, either from without or within, broke the tension.

So, this is what it feels like to be a mage, Brodie thought. *This is Kia's future. No wonder she cannot love me.*

But she does, his heart argued. That kiss said more than words.

No, reality countered. That was just an aftermath of battle, of someone rejoicing in surviving the day.

His heart had the last word. *Kia is now safe from Relliq. Her invisible stalker will haunt her no more. She no longer needs protection so I can stay in Diomharid.*

* * *

Sparks from the bonfire in the center of Diomharid flickered against the sky. Too tired to go indoors, Kia sat on one of the benches opposite the council tower, letting the serenity of the night and the warmth of the fire leach away the tension of the day.

An ember drifted skyward, drawing her gaze with it until the spark flared out. However, darkness didn't return. Light shone from one of the upper-level windows of the council tower. Even as she watched, the glow increased until it competed with the moons as master of the night sky.

The binding is taking place. Shivers from something other than the night's chill racked Kia's frame. Sadness that

244

anyone would be deprived of their birthright filled her heart. Wrapping her arms around her waist, she purposely looked away from the window, only to have her gaze return to it.

The faces of those who died under her care paraded in her vision. That of a gray-bearded oldster who died, not from battle wounds but from giving all his energy into a healing spell to save a child, haunted Kia the most.

At least the babe survived, Kia thought. Unlike the others I failed and who passed beyond the veil.

The child should not have been put in danger, anger hissed. Relliq deserves what he is getting.

Other thoughts competed with the sentiment. He will never again feel the power of magic gathering. Or Kia almost added, the satisfaction when a sick or ill person returns to health.

Relliq never healed anybody, anger countered.

The light emanating from the council window dimmed to that of a single candle. Although no sound, either before or after the ceremony, betrayed the binding, Kia knew the mages had finished their work.

She closed her eyes against the pain and, like one of the shipfish that had accompanied the ship when she sailed on *Windmaster,* dove for refuge. However, where the finned travelers sought the ocean depths, Kia sought the sanctuary of the Cyrcle of One. Her soul hovered just outside the circle that bound all life together. The restlessness in her heart prevented full immersion in the trance and between one heartbeat and the next she returned to her body.

Movement in the tower entrance drew her attention. Two figures held up a third who stumbled every few steps. Another man walked a few feet behind. The hilt of a sword peeking above his shoulder proclaimed the escort's identity—Brodie.

Which means, the prisoner was Relliq.

A stick fell into the fire sending flames skyward. Its light cast not just on Relliq, but on Kia as well. *He could not fail to recognize me.* Her pulse raced, but from anger or fear?

Her breath held, she waited to hear the hoarse whisper of, "Come to me, little wizardling. Come to me or die."

But no threat was heard by either voice or mind. Even though Relliq looked straight at her, he merely gave a polite nod and walked past without any sign of recognition.

The mages did it. They bound Relliq's powers and his memory. Finally, I am safe.

And so is Brodie, her heart cheered.

Chapter Twenty-Four

Sleep refused to bring with it an escape from the memories of the battle and its aftermath. Every time Brodie's eyes closed, his mind relived the pain of being stabbed. And even worse, the frightened look of the child who held the sword. Finally, he left the room MarBelrum had assigned him and went out to the stable. Wirake's worried nicker and the nudge the stallion gave Brodie's shoulder eased some of the tension. Brushing the stable dirt off the fàlaire brought with it the calm he sought. By the time he finished grooming Kia's mare, he was relaxed enough to pull a blanket around his shoulders and stretch out in a pile of hay. The soft snuffles of the fàlaire and the familiar scent of fresh hay lured him into the netherworld of sleep.

Warmth from a ray of sunlight walked across Brodie's face. Unwilling to wake, he just lay in the straw, relishing the peace of the stable. Wirake's whinny and a stomped foot told of the fàlaire's impatience. A second stomp declared the stallion hungry.

"All right, all right," Brodie growled. "You'll get your grain in a bit." A leonine stretch and he opened his eyes. Through the open barn door he saw that the sun was well risen.

"I thought you would be out here," Dal said from a nearby stall. He walked over and patted Wirake's muzzle. "Fàlaire are good company." The sympathy in Dal's tone called out to the pain in Brodie's heart when he added, "And can ease a troubled soul."

Brodie stood and shook the loose strands of hay from his pants. "I'm glad you're here, Dal." For a second, he reconsidered the decision he had come to the night before. "I'm going to ask MarBelrum to let me stay at Diomharid." At Dal's raised eyebrow, he added, "No reflection on your and Lady Ellspeth's work last night, but if I stay it will allow me to keep an eye on Relliq."

The archmage's expression didn't change, but Brodie swore Dal's scan pierced through to his soul. "That is not the real reason."

I should have known the archmage would not accept my withdrawal from the Isle without questioning it, Brodie thought. *We've been friends for too long.* He tried to organize his thoughts without success. He didn't want to put into words the real reason for his staying with MarBelrum and his people.

Admit it to yourself, even if you won't to Dal, his heart ordered.

Although his throat tightened, Brodie forced out the truth. "If I can't be with Kia, I can't bear to be around her." His friend's nod pulled out more words. "My excuse for staying behind will be that my wounds will take some time to heal."

An understanding, but sad look filled the other man's face. As if at one time he too had loved someone so much it hurt to be with them. "Promise me you will spend the day reconsidering. Then if you still feel the same way, we can both talk to MarBelrum tonight after dinner."

Surprise at his friend's, no, Brodie corrected, the archmage's apparent acceptance made him wonder what the other man had on his mind. *It doesn't matter. I do owe him that much.* Although his plans hadn't changed, he bowed his head. "As you wish."

* * *

The day passed too slowly for Brodie. Despite the pain of being close to Kia, he maintained a nearby watch as she and Gwenivar went from house to house, seeing their patients. At each stop he prayed Kia wouldn't lose another patient. Finally, the sun set, and he couldn't delay any longer. Determined steps took him to the council tower. Several benches had been moved into a semi-circle allowing those seated to observe the goings on at the bonfire, but still have some privacy. Cushions provided comfort. Brodie wondered why he had been invited to the group. The archmage and his lady sat side by side. MarBelrum sat across from him. Gwenivar and one of the boys Brodie had helped carry from the field of battle stood in an attentive silence a few steps behind the Diomharid mage. Eilidh and her granddaughter filled another side of the circle. From those in attendance it looked like this was mage business. Yet he felt somehow it did concern him. But how?

His steps slowed when he reached the group. All the seats were full, except one. The one next to Kia. Alternatives to that empty spot were noted and just as quickly dismissed. Brodie clamped his lips against the curses that threatened to spill out. His decision to stay behind wavered when she smiled and patted the cushion next to her. His tension rose while Gwenivar passed around glasses of wine. A bow and she backed into the shadows, awaiting a summons from the mages.

MarBelrum raised his glass. "Lord Dal, Lady Ellspeth," He nodded to Elendl, Kia, and the elder clanswoman, "Isle mages, on behalf of all of us in Diomharid, I want to thank you and yours for saving our city." He paused and his gaze lingered on Gwenivar who talked to the boy next to her in whispers.

To Brodie's heightened senses, it seemed like the young couple was unusually nervous for their current task. No, he decided. Their attitude was expectant. But of what, he wondered. The pair had done nothing wrong. Their serving was worthy of a page in the king's court. Another thought rose. *MarBelrum is not going to hold a journeyman ceremony tonight, is he?*

"Lord Dal, although we can never repay what you have done for us, the council asks a boon. Would you as archmage," MarBelrum inclined his head to Ellspeth, "and you, Lady Ellspeth, as the head of the school of mages, consider fostering several of our young people. The apprentices are advanced enough to do a journeyman's work, but their instructors feel the students would benefit from a season or two in the outside world. They will be no burden." A smile twitched his lips. "They are merely restless."

"I thought the city was inaccessible for one hundered turns of the world around the sun." The words slipped out before Brodie could censor them.

Ellspeth gestured at the watching pair. "Any who came with us would never be able to return. That is more than a temporary fostering, at least for them."

"Legend does say the city only appears from the lake that often," the older mage acknowledged. "However, there are a few of us who know even more ancient ways out, an emergency back door you might say. Since you are aware of our existence, just contact us via crystal and a guide will be sent." His expression took on a more serious tone. "Normally we are self-sufficient, however if there is an illness and we need special herbs they can be obtained. Or conversely, if a local townsman required healing beyond that of their own, we can go assist. On rare occurrences we look outside the valley to increase our numbers with those of special skills."

He gestured at the bonfire awaiting the spark. "Take the night to think about it. Tomorrow at sunset, after a recognition of the lives of those who have crossed the veil, there will be food and music." Sadness flickered in his eyes. With a visible effort his expression lightened. "If you are willing to stay an additional day before returning to your homes, all of Diomharid would love for you to be our guests." Now a genuine smile raised his lips. "My crystal shows those in the outside world affected by Relliq's curse are recovering nicely. The summoning of the water to protect the city won't begin until twelfth hour so there will be time for you to join us for the commemoration and still be safe on the ledge to watch the waters rise."

Silver hair touched dark curls as Dal and Ellspeth leaned their heads together. Their murmurs were too low for Brodie to hear, but he knew what the answer would be. The contingent of mages at the isle would be growing. It's a good thing, he thought, that I made all those blades and hilts. Even if I am not there to offer them at the ceremony, there won't be a shortage of weapons for those who answer the next call to the council fire. *And I was there for the important ones—Denai, Elendl, and Kia.*

"We don't need to take the night," Ellspeth said. "We would be pleased to foster those you care to send to us, either now or in the future. Does Tairneach need to summon mounts for them?"

Happiness radiated from MarBelrum. "No, our head stallion is sending one of his herd along with each person going. Besides transport, that way our travellers will have a friend and confidant."

Dal gave a short laugh. "The fàlaire are good companions to their special friends." In a formal tone he added, "Both Ellspeth and I pledge to support your people both in their learning and in their lives."

His friend's oath raised memories Brodie kept sequestered in a distant part of his mind. For a split second, he became the youth whose village didn't want him, the new recruit whose leader abandoned him, and then later, the outsider whose friends all had powers. A hard wrench brought him back to the present—and the woman he was sitting next to. A sip of wine helped restore his balance and he returned his attention to the Diomharid mage.

Feedback from the look the older man turned on Elendl echoed through Brodie's nerves. Confusion as to how he was feeling the magical scan didn't have time to take root.

"Before I introduce you to those leaving, our council wants to offer you something in return." MarBelrum's expression softened. "We know you have been worried about Elendl, about the strength of her powers and what would happen if they escaped her control."

Kia leaned forward and laid a comforting hand on her young friend's knee. The movement sent the hint of lavender wafting in Brodie's direction. The scent triggered the memory of Kia's early training at the school of wizards and her doubts as to her powers. Satisfaction warmed his soul. *At least I was able to reassure Kia, not only of her abilities but to her worthiness to wield them.*

Brodie tensed. He couldn't help but wonder at the thoughts going through Dal and Ellspeth's mind. Any anger they felt at what could be considered a slight on their parenting must be well controlled. Or at least enough so that nothing showed in their faces.

"I mean nothing untoward," MarBelrum said. His clipped words were conciliatory rather than accusing. "Dal, the other council members and I feel Elendl will one day take your place as head of the isle council. Time here could serve as her journeyman training. We guarantee she will not lack for resources or support. We have even older books here than my ancestor brought to your library." In lower tones, the city's mage explained other advantages, most notably that the stronger wards around Diomharid and the mountain would ensure the safety of others.

Before Brodie's eyes, Elendl rapidly switched from adult to child, then back to adult.

Dal reached over and took his wife's hand. No words passed between them, although the buzzing in Brodie's head told of the pair's mind link. Ellspeth's gaze went from thoughtful to sad and when a sense of resignation washed over Brodie, he knew his friend envisioned the loss of her child.

Brodie pictured the two girls as he stood with them before the council fire. He had been too busy tracking Relliq and fighting to miss the sisters. But now there was nothing to prevent it. The sense of being totally alone that had permeated his youth returned and he fought to keep his emotions in check. While Dal and Ellspeth could stay in touch with Elendl via crystal, it wouldn't erase the fact, that with Denai serving as journeyman on *Northern Pearl* with her other grandmother, both of their daughters would be gone. At least Dal and Ellspeth will still be able to see and talk to Denai and Elendl, Brodie mused. I won't even have that with Kia. When the waters rise over Diomharid and the full protections are in place, magic on both sides of the link will be needed. *And I am a non-tal with no powers.*

Maybe it is better to have a clean break, hope put forth.

Even as the thought rose, Brodie knew. Nothing would ease the pain of separation. He surfaced from his own sense of grief at the loss of the young mage to hear her father tell her that the decision to return to the isle or to remain for a time here in Diomharid was hers to make. Pride mingled with sadness and he added, "If you wish to stay, know that we will miss you."

Elendl's soft, "I will stay," held both willingness and hesitation.

"MarBelrum?" With one word, the older clanswoman shifted attention to her. "If you and your people don't mind; I too would like to stay."

Dal's, "Mother?" was an echo to Ellspeth's, "Eilidh?"

No, Brodie thought. Now Dal will be losing both his daughter and his mother. How much more can he take? He used his matrimonial voyage to take his mother to her ancient clanhold for her to die, but the trip strengthened her enough that she not only returned home, she thrived.

Maybe that is what will happen if she stays in Diomharid, hope ventured.

The clap of MarBelrum's hands signalled his answer. "Lady Eilidh, we could not hope for such riches. You would be most welcome. If you would not be depriving Lord Dal of his mother."

Elendl's squeal sounded into the night. Laughter rounded the group when she adopted a sophisticated air. More chuckles came when she gave another squeal and hugged her grandmother. Dal's droll, "There are some who don't always act their age," lightened more of the tension.

Dal's sad smile pulled at Brodie. *Now is the time to bring up my own request. But how can I add to his troubles. I am the only weaponsmith on the isle.* Counter thoughts rose. There are other men who could make the journeymen blades. And there is still Kia. Staying at the school of mages would mean being around her—and the pain that comes with it.

Act now, logic demanded. Before your will weakens.

However, instead of voicing his own request, Brodie waited. Buzzing in his head, as if a thousand bees nested, made it impossible for him to speak. It must be mindspeech, he decided. Private communications between Dal and Ellspeth? Or Dal and Eilidh? But how? *I'm not even holding TânOer so there is no linkage through the blade's enchantment.* Although he couldn't answer the question as to who or how, all he knew was that he was aware of something that as a non-tal he shouldn't be.

MarBelrum didn't say anything, but the expectant look he turned on Kia stopped Brodie's reflection. There was only one reason he could think of for the Diomharid mage to evaluate Kia.

The icy grip of glaciers encircled his heart. *No, don't ask Kia. I can't stay here if she does.*

Once again, the sensation of being watched tickled Brodie's senses. All of those gathered seemed engrossed in Elendl and her grandmother. Except for MarBelrum, Brodie realized. The Diomharid mage had a strange look on his face.

The scan didn't come from his friends, Brodie realized, but MarBelrum? *Can he read minds like Dal can?* While he blanked his thoughts, Brodie couldn't quiet his desire, or stop the pain it brought with it. Seeing Kia's total concentration on the still smiling Elendl, he stood. Quiet steps took him into the shadows.

* * *

Happiness, excitement, and surprise at the announcements helped overcome some of the malaise that had afflicted Kia since the battle. She would miss Elendl, but even in the short time since their arrival at Diomharid, the young mage had blossomed and appeared to mature overnight.

A tingling sensation, not of needles, but of being the object of being under intense observation, had Kia catching her breath. *My stalker is back!*

No, it can't be, she reassured herself. Ellspeth and Dal took away Relliq's powers. And, last night he didn't even recognize me. *So, who is staring at me? Stripping away the trappings of life to reveal the real me?* Quick looks over her shoulder showed no one at the town bonfire paid any attention to her.

The rest of her thoughts were interrupted by Ellspeth's light touch. But it wasn't the archmage's lady who wanted the attention. She nodded towards MarBelrum.

"Lady Kiansel," said the Diomharid mage. After he was sure, he had Kia's focus, he smiled. "We don't increase our numbers often, but several handful of our townspeople died as a result of Relliq's attack. Among them were those who taught our younger apprentices. Our council has asked me whether or not you too would consider staying with us. At least for a short time. You would bring a new freshness to our classes. It has been many seasons since someone isle trained taught here."

Kia waved her hand in objection. "But I haven't been at the School of Mages that long. And I just received my journeyman's dagger."

The older man smile grew. "I told the others that you would say that. And this is my response." He inclined his head to Dal and Ellspeth. "The current leaders of the School of Mages felt you capable or they would not have blessed your status as journeyman. And it is not just your training there that we would welcome. Several of those with powers, as well as those without, have expressed an interest in learning the teachings of the Oracle and the temple." He gave a short laugh. "You can't tell me you have no knowledge or experience in that area. Brantly assured me you were his best instructor."

Dal's chuckle matched MarBelrum's. "Well, Kia, I guess you have no excuse not to consider the offer." His expression turned serious. "However, whether you stay here for a time or return with us on the morrow is your decision."

As if answering an inaudible summons, Gwenivar walked over and stood beside the Diomharid mage. "Kia,

Gwenivar will show you around the town tonight. As she would be one of your students if you stay, I wanted to give you the opportunity to get to know her before you make your decision. And, in hopes that you will stay with us, we adjusted the wards around the valley so that your brother's call, either through crystal or amulet, can reach you at any time. He assured me your contact if you care to make one would be no interruption."

"Please, mistress," Gwenivar begged. "Walk with me? The next group of musicians will start soon. I'm sure you'll enjoy their work." Excitement bubbled in her tone. "They're premiering a new composition tonight."

Her mind whirling with the reasons to accept the council of Diomharid's offer and the strident ones not to, Kia allowed herself to be pulled to her feet by Gwenivar. However, feet that had been tapping to the music just moments before refused to move. A lethargy, or was it fear, enveloped her. The hand she held out to Ellspeth quivered.

"Kia, go with Gwenivar," Ellspeth commanded in a gentle tone. "We can talk on the morrow." She waved a dismissal. "And why don't you take Elendl. Then Gwenivar can introduce both of you to her friends at one time."

Elendl gave a quick kiss to her grandmother, a wave to her parents, and slipped an arm through Kia's. "Come on, Kia. Don't tell me they don't dance at the temple."

Unable to disobey her mistress' command and fight Elendl's blandishments, Kia followed the floating mage light Gwenivar summoned. However, the one person she wanted to see, to talk over whether or not she should stay in Diomharid, was not there.

Where was Brodie? And why did he slip away?

Chapter Twenty-Five

Excitement from MarBelrum's offer to stay and study in Diomharid still pulsed through Kia, worsening the conflicts she felt. By instinct, she reached out to her brother. His rich, deep baritone came almost instantly into her mind. It felt as if Brantly was in the room with her. Surprise at the strength of the contact shocked her. That had never happened before, not even when she used the magic in the earth at the Isle of Mages to boost the crystal's strength. *This contact is even stronger than when I was in the temple, only a few rooms away from Brantly.*

It must be because of the magic inherent in Diomharid, she thought. I can't have developed that quickly. Putting the idea away for later evaluation, she explained the nature of her call. Mindful of his duties as the Oracle of Givneh she kept the questions brief and few.

Brantly already knew of the offer to stay in Diomharid and if he sensed ambivalence in her heart, he gave no sign of it. "You will make the right decision. If you decide to stay, you have my blessing." His benison warmed her. And as he broke the contact, his final words echoed in her head. "And I approve."

What did Brantly approve of?

Her heart supplied the answer—Brodie.

* * *

Still unsettled after her talk with Brantly, Kia sought out Ellspeth. "The archmage's lady will know what to do. She is not only worldly, she came into her powers late in life, just as I did."

Holding the blade of her journeyman's dagger between her palms, she gently blew on the stone in the hilt. Ellspeth's image didn't appear, however Kia had the sense of a bonfire awaiting a spark.

Quick steps took her to the center of town where a dozen youths stacked wood for the evening's celebration. Ellspeth sat on a bench at the base of the council tower. Her gaze was downcast, and she appeared to be talking to a small stone in her hand.

Ellspeth is speaking to someone in the outside world, Kia thought. Maybe one of the mages coordinating healing and restoration teams. It's not Nobyn or Barris, Kia decided. The other woman's attitude implied something personal. Probably Denai. An advantage of having powers, even if they are geared towards the sea, is that although while on your journeyman sail, you could still be in regular contact with your parents. "Ancestors beyond the veil, please let it be good news," Kia whispered. "That with Relliq's binding those he sickened are now recovering." The image of a toddler bathed in sweat with silent tears running down its red face surfaced.

That one lived, pride encouraged.

But how many more did not? Kia stopped a moan before it reached her friend. *How many more could I have saved if I had stayed in Givneh?* For long moments, she stood in the shadows, gathering up her courage. Finally, she couldn't delay any longer and moved into the light. "Mistress Ellspeth, I have a quandary."

Ellspeth patted the cushion next to her. "Please, my child, sit. I was just talking to Barris. He and his mother reported that almost everyone is recovering nicely. All should be up and about within a day or two at the most. Denai and my mother reported the same of those in Stratven or aboard ship." A smile twinkled in her eyes. "No more have passed beyond the veil."

The older woman took a breath as if organizing her thoughts. "Now as to your question, Kia, I think you are fully coming into your powers. A sacred place can do more than boost your natural abilities. Whatever blocked them

258

before was released when we worked to create the storms to aid our men, then your powers grew more when you healed the wounded after the battle."

Enlightenment pushed away curiosity at the phrase, "our men."

The more magic that has been worked in a given place, the greater the effect, logic supplied.

A smile twitched Kia's lips. "A self-fulfilling prophecy." Her voice dropped to a whisper. "Mistress, will I keep my abilities when I leave?"

Regret flickered in Ellspeth's eyes and Kia knew the answer before the archmage's lady spoke. "I can't answer that." Light glinted off the silver circlet around Ellspeth's neck when she raised a hand to it. "No matter where I am, the circlet multiplies my power beyond its normal limit." She pointed at the amulet that peeked from the neckline of Kia's blouse. "As your ancestress' amulet does yours."

Silence enveloped Kia as she thought about the senior mage's words.

"But you asked me about whether or not to stay a time in Diomharid." Ellspeth's smile encouraged and dispersed more of the cold around Kia's soul. Her head tilted in a manner Kia had come to know as contemplative. A sad sigh escaped. "MarBelrum didn't want to say anything last night and embarrass either you or Gwenivar. Or to influence your decision. However, I think you should know. He said your handling of Gwenivar impressed everyone on the council. Apparently, her instructors had pretty much given up on her ever gaining control of her magic." The pause told Kia her friend chose her words carefully. "The council was on the verge of deciding to bind Gwenivar's powers."

The horror of losing her magic, even worse of having it taken away, filled Kia. A deep breath failed to relieve the feeling of her body transforming into a statue of glacial ice. It was one thing to turn Relliq into a non-tal. She shivered at the word. He deserved it for those he murdered as surely as if he killed them with his own hand. But Gwenivar was

259

an innocent. "How can I stay here with people who would do that?" blurted out.

Comforting warmth spread from where Ellspeth's hand lay on Kia's arm. "It is because of you that option has been removed from consideration. Dal and I evaluated Gwenivar. She is much like Barris' mother, who has a natural tending toward healing. However, there are other aspects of Gwenivar's abilities that are just beginning to show. She is quick with the sword and enjoys the movement of the martial arts." Ellspeth's fingers tightened around Kia's. "Do not stay in Diomharid because of Gwenivar. If you return with us tonight to the Isle, so will she. Also, do not decide to stay with MarBelrum and his people because of Elendl. Stay because you want to. While you would be a friend and companion for my daughter during her time in Diomharid, personally, I think a time here would also be good for you."

Ellspeth removed her hand and leaned back. "I sense there is something else you want to talk about. But you have to speak it." The sharp edge she added to her words contrasted with the encouragement of the other woman's expression.

"What do I do about Brodie?" escaped in a moan. "I looked for him last night and again this morning, but he keeps avoiding me."

Once again, a hint of sadness flickered in Ellspeth's eyes. The emotion vanished and a smile brightened her face.

Anger flared. Why does my love life amuse Ellspeth?

Ellspeth's light tap on her hand turned Kia's attention back to her friend. The archmage's lady leaned close. Her voice dropped to a whisper. "I hate to see two friends in such distress. Brodie had planned to stay behind in Diomharid until their council asked you to stay. Now he's not only not staying but plans to leave the Isle of Mages. He told Dal he's going to find a mercenary troop to be weaponsmith for." Her gaze darkened. "And fight with."

"No!" The cry was torn from Kia's throat. "Brodie belongs at the isle. Why would he leave?" Even as the words passed her lips, she knew the answer. *Because of me.* Her thoughts swirled in a maelstrom of confusion, hurt, and anger. *Why would Brodie leave all he loves? Leave me?*

The cold realization of the truth stopped the whirl of her thoughts—and her heart. *He loves me.* Once again, the question of why Brodie would leave pushed itself forward.

Have you ever told him you loved him? Anger hissed. How can he know your feelings?

Kia had to admit she hadn't. Truth thundered in her mind. Brodie felt he was not worthy of being the mate to a mage. "Brodie runs because he is a non-tal," slipped out in a hiss.

Ellspeth fingered the circlet around her neck. "Dal decided our paths would be joined long before the prophecy decreed it. At the time I had no knowledge of magic and was well beyond the age when abilities first show themselves."

Her friend's words started to penetrate the confusion swirling in Kia's mind. "Mages can love those without the Talent?"

Now Ellspeth's face lit with remembered joy. "Love has a magic of its own. Dal told me about two very dear friends of his, Gabrielle and Olier. She was a member of the Council of Mages and a senior instructor at the school. The price for her magic was to lose her spell memory. Eventually she couldn't remember the runes long enough to complete an incantation."

Her breath quickening, Kia leaned forward. "And Olier was not a mage?"

"No. Although he lived on the isle side of the rainbow bridge after his handfasting to Gabrielle, Olier was a mill keep and a talented brewer of braga wine. After Gabrielle resigned her position, he took her to his forest home."

The maelstrom in her heart settled and Kia knew the one question she had to ask. "Mistress, what do I do? I want to stay in Diomharid. But I don't want Brodie to leave because of me."

Ellspeth remained silent, but Kia followed the other woman's gaze to where a lone figure stood in the open gates of the city. "I can't provide your answer," Ellspeth said, a hint of regret in her tone. "Both Dal and I agree Brodie has some talent. Maybe not those of the archmage, but his ability to use TânOer to block fire goes well beyond those of the sword's own enspellment. Dal says that not all metalsmiths can create the journeyman blades nor have such an affinity with metal."

Determination flooded Kia as she watched Brodie, head down, walk through the gates and disappear from sight. She rose and took a step before turning back. "Excuse me, mistress, I need to go." Her feet took control and she was running towards the last place she saw Brodie. *He will not avoid me again ... At least until we have a talk.*

* * *

Kia raced down the street, unconsciously dodging those in her path. The sound of each footfall echoed off the buildings. Even louder was the pounding of each heartbeat. Chest heaving from the exertion, she caught herself on the edge of the open gate. "Nooo ..." The space beyond was empty. *Where did Brodie go?*

Find him, her heart urged. But how? A scrying incantation should find him. *It has to.* She closed her eyes and detail by detail built up the image of Brodie in her mind.

"Stone of power, map to earth,
Show me the location of the one of worth."

No seeker orb came into being. Nor did Brodie's location appear. Kia's fingers knitted together into a translucent web. She pulled them apart to shove them into the pockets of her tunic. Instead of fabric, they grazed the smooth leather of the sheath hanging on her belt. To locate someone with magic, you either had to have their mental signature or something personal of theirs. *My journeyman dagger. It was made by Brodie.*

Brodie's image firmly fixed in her mind, she snatched the blade from its sheath and blew on the stone.

His image didn't appear, however Kia caught the whiff of oats mingled with the scent of tall grass.

Brodie is in Wirake's saddle. They're headed for the woods. Just beyond them is the tunnel to the outside world. Panic engulfed her. Once they passed the barriers of Diomharid's wards, he would be gone forever. Not even the head stallion of the vale herd would be able to catch his offspring if Wirake didn't want to be. At least not before he reached the outside world. Another hope surfaced to be immediately quashed. Not even Rielle could help. There was no guarantee that the attachment between the mare and the stallion would be enough for Rielle to entice Wirake to return to Diomharid against his rider's wishes.

Kia cast a desperate call into the ether. "Wirake, I'm coming. Wait for me. Don't let Brodie leave Diomharid."

All during the frantic run across the meadow, she sent call after call. "Brodie, wait for me." Each time, the pain in her chest made her stop, the need to continue was too great and she raced on.

Her breath coming in ragged gasps, she skidded to a stop. The cool shade of the treeline did little to ease the burn in her legs. Stooped over, her hands braced on her knees, her gaze raked the shadows. *Please, ancestors beyond the veil, let Brodie be there.*

A shadow detached itself from a clump of trees and stepped into the dappled sunlight. It resolved into a man dressed in well-worn travel clothes. What she thought was a tree branch was the hilt of a sword sticking up above his shoulder. Brodie sat light in the saddle, a bemused smile on his lips. "Wirake said he waited for someone. But not who."

The big gray snorted. You didn't need to know.

Brodie slapped the stallion on the neck who pranced a step.

Flicks of the fàlaire's ears and a swish of his tail gave the stallion's response. And you didn't ask. A flick of the reins and he settled. Well, talk to her.

263

Brodie inclined his head to Kia. "So, Lady Kia, what can this lowly non-tal do for you?"

Heat flooded Kia's face. "I will not allow you to denigrate yourself that way any longer," she snapped.

The flash of anger in Brodie's eyes cooled Kia's own, quicker than any retort he could have made. A deep breath to send a silent prayer to her ancestors beyond the veil and she cast her fate. "Please, Brodie, I need to talk to you."

Fear seized the heart in her chest. If Brodie left, she'd never catch him. *What can I say to make him stay? What words to persuade him of his value to Diomharid? To me?*

Her heart supplied the only answer she had. Still, she didn't say them. "I love you," remained unspoken.

Chapter Twenty Six

Only the chittering of the wood insects broke the silence. Kia dared not breathe as she waited for Brodie's response. A deep sigh and he stood in the stirrups, hesitated for a moment, then swung a leg over the back of the saddle and lithely stepped to the ground. "There's a bench not far down the treeline that MarBelrum said his people use for meditation."

Kia gestured for Brodie to lead on. "Sounds perfect."

All during the short walk, Kia's thoughts swirled. Up ahead, a beam of sunlight lingered on a bench created from the intertwining of several tree trunks. Their branches arched into a canopy of green. Light filtered through leaves sparkled on the dark bark in an illusion of the impending nighttime sky. No, she decided, it looked like the firelight on Ellspeth's circlet.

Now I know how to approach Brodie.

"Now, Lady Kia," Brodie said in a low tone that did not disturb the serenity of the woods, "my time is yours." He glanced at the lengthening shadows. "At least for a few candlemarks. MarBelrum said I need to be through the tunnels before the full moonrise. The council will use the extra energy of the confluence of Shartle and Neba to create the protective dome over the city and remove the wards so that the water will fill the valley."

To calm her racing nerves, Kia took a deep breath. "Ellspeth said you were leaving Diomharid and the Isle of Mages." She leaned in and laid a hand over Brodie's. His fingers felt like a fire against her ice-cold ones. "I hope you are not leaving because of me."

The flash of anger in his eyes told her the bolt had struck home. "Brodie, you are, or have been, many things. A talented horseman, an officer with Telarim the Red's troop, a trusted member of the king's own guard. Both the archmage and his lady call you friend." As she ticked off each item with a finger, she watched to see Brodie's reaction. When he remained silent, she fought down the rising panic. "Even my brother Brantly approves of you. As Oracle he looks for the good in everyone, however, as my brother, if he did not approve of you as a man he would not give us his blessing."

A deep breath and she allowed more passion into her tone. "A non-tal you are not." She held up a hand to halt his objection. "It takes a special talent to use TânOer to block fire, one that goes beyond the sword's own enspellment. I agree that you will never lead the Council of Mages. Your power is not that of the archmage, but your affinity with metal and ability to create the journeyman daggers means you have some measure of magic."

She pinned the stone-faced Brodie with a stern gaze. "Deny it."

Regret darkened his gaze. "I can't. But that doesn't change anything. I can't stay at Diomharid if you do."

"Don't you see? There is no reason for us not to be together."

The tightening of his lips showed his reaction.

In desperation, Kia tried one more approach. "Even if I am a mage and you had no magic at all, it wouldn't matter. Love has a magic of its own." Her voice caught and what she tried to hold back came out in a rush. "Unless you don't love me?"

All that could be said was. A single tear escaped to run down her cheek.

* * *

Pain, his own and that which emanated from Kia, ripped through Brodie. His fingers tightened into a fist until his fingers hurt from the force.

266

How could I fight my own feelings and hers?

You can't, his heart answered.

But I am a non-tal. Kia is a mage, she deserves better.

His heart countered. She wants you. She loves YOU. Being with you will make her happy.

Unbidden, the question rose. Don't you want her to be happy?

To that he had no answer. As he watched, a tear rolled down Kia's cheek.

His arms moved of their own accord and pulled her into his lap. With one finger, he lifted her chin to him. He wondered if his expression mirrored the expectant look on hers. It is time, he thought. Before he could find another objection, he lowered his head and pressed his lips to hers.

For long moments, he floated on waves of joy. Sharp pain in his chest returned him to his surroundings and he pulled back enough for a breath to pass between them.

Kia reached up and wrapped her arms around his neck. Fire spread from where she touched to flow down his spine. Her embrace tightened and she crushed him to her as if the action would keep them together. For a second Brodie tensed within the embrace, then melded his frame to hers. With a sigh, she rested the side of her face against his chest. Two hearts beat in symphony to a tune older than time. Contentment stronger than any he had ever felt filled him.

A tug pulled the leather thong he had kept hidden beneath his shirt over his head. He held the strap, and the pair of small interlocked pieces of silver metal that hung from it, in his hand for several breaths. *Ancestors of mine past the veil, grant me the future these tokens hold.*

His decision made, Brodie shifted Kia to the bench. "I started casting this the moment I finished your journeyman's dagger. It was to be a gift to you on your naming day." He opened his cupped hands and held the matching amulets so that the engravings sparkled in the light. "In my heart, I always hoped they would have another use."

His chest burned from his held breath as he watched for Kia's comprehension. *Would she understand their meaning? Two pendants. Two people. A representation of promises made and accepted at a handfasting.*

"Promise tokens," she murmured. Her finger traced the delicate engravings of a dagger and the symbol of the Oracle of Givneh. It lingered on the cloud-topped mountain in the background. "I understand why the Oracle and dagger, but why the mountain?"

How to answer, Brodie wondered. When I don't know myself. "I don't know. It just felt right. So I told myself because of my association with Dal and his mountain clan, it symbolized my people." To hide the wry smile that twitched his lips, Brodie bowed his head. "Even though they were not the village of my birth."

Kia's silence encouraged more. In response, he gestured back towards the city. "Now, I think somehow I had made a connection to Diomharid."

"All the more reason for you to stay in Diomharid ... with me."

Hope rose. Brodie let the desire show in his eyes. "Are you sure?"

Unable to fight the entreaty in his voice, Kia nodded and gave him a warm smile. Before he could move, she took the leather strap and draped the thong from which the tokens hung around his neck. "Now, Brodie, by the giving and receiving of a promise token, you are mine and I am yours. In this world and the one beyond."

Brodie captured her hand and kissed it. Releasing her, he removed the string from his neck. A deft rip separated the woven strands into individual strips. Now two leather necklaces dangled from his hand, each bearing a metal token. He knotted one strand and slipped it over his head. Her skin flamed beneath his fingers where he held the other strip around her neck and tied the ends into a knot.

Her fingers grazed the metal and Brodie felt her reaction to the potential stored within. "It's magic," she whispered.

"Yes," he sighed. His arms crushed Kia to his breast.

* * *

Only the coolness descending on the woods broke the tableau. Brodie scanned the heavens. The burnt orange glow around the mountain peak signalled the closeness of nightfall.

A whistle summoned Wirake. The fàlaire trotted up, stopped in front of Kia, and touched his nose to an outstretched leg in salute. He backed up and tilted his head in a clear message that it was about time Brodie wised up.

To Brodie, the stallion's snuffle sounded happy.

Cool breezes whispered from the trees. Shivers wracked Kia.

Brodie slipped off his jacket and draped it around her shoulders. "They will be lighting the bonfire soon. We should get back to Diomharid."

She pulled away. "But that is going the wrong way. We need to get through the tunnels before the valley is flooded."

He chuckled at her protest. "In due time, my love." He relished the sound of something he had never believed would be his. "What kind of man would I be to leave you out here, all alone in the dark and cold to walk back to the city when I have a perfectly good mount?"

At the comment, Wirake puffed out his chest and pranced a few steps. Kia's laugh at the animal's antic lightened Brodie's heart even more.

"The council won't be flooding the lake until tomorrow night so there is time. I had just wanted to make sure I didn't get turned around in the tunnels. And, it would be most unkind not to tell Ellspeth and Dal of our plans. We need to go back tonight, if only for that."

Kia's nod showed her agreement.

Brodie tried to think of a way to say what he needed to. He didn't want to ruin the mood. What needs to be done is best done quickly, common sense put in. A breath and for a heartbeat he allowed his tension free rein before returning to the calm of the night. "I will have to leave for a little while."

Kia clutched at him.

269

His lips grazed hers in reassurance. "MarBelrum showed me and Wirake one of the hidden passageways through the mesmers. We can leave and return any time we want. If you want to stay and start work with your students, you don't have to leave with me. I promise to return as soon as my tasks are done."

A pout flickered on Kia's lips then vanished. "And they are? Can I help?"

Brodie laid a finger on her lips. "I looked at the tools and shed that the city's blacksmiths have used. If I'm going to stay here for a while, I need some of the tools from my workshop to make the journeymen daggers for the Diomharid mages." He fought to keep the feeling of being an unbearded youth on the night before his first battle. "Kia, it is the custom of my people to post the bans ... to ask the parents before a handfasting. I need to stop by Givneh and see Brantly and your father."

Now it was Kia's chuckle that filled the air. "I'm sure they both already know."

"I still have to formally ask them," Brodie said. "And while Dal or MarBelrum would officiate at our handfasting, I think I'd like Brantly to do it. That way Dal could stand at my side."

Kia placed a light kiss on his cheek. "I'm sure my brother would be honored to do the ceremony, and I am too. Brodie, you don't have to go there in person. Why don't we contact them through my amulet? I think you've enough powers for that if I start the link."

The shiver that shook her frame had her back in his arms. Two steps and he placed her in front of the saddle. A quick swing of the leg and he was seated behind her. "We can contact Brantly on the way back to the city." He dropped the reins. "Wirake can always find his way to the stable. Now tell me what to do."

He listened as Kia quickly explained. All the time, he fought to slow his racing pulse and prayed that Kia couldn't hear its pounding.

She took the amulet from around her neck and slid it over the blade of her dagger. "Ready?"

270

A deep breath to clear his mind and Brodie placed his hands over hers. Lines of fire spun from the metal to form a web around him and Kia. Yet where the red line touched his skin there was no pain, no burning. Instead, the image of Brantly, in the white robes of an acolyte, appeared in Brodie's mind. The sense of another in the background, an older man, Brodie decided, came through the link.

He reached out with both voice and mind. "Oracle, I come before you to publish the bans. Do I have your blessing to marry Kia and would you honor us by officiating?"

The image smiled and the warmth of a benison washed over Brodie. He heard the answer in his mind as if the other man stood before him. "Yes to both questions. I won't keep either of you long as I sense you are almost back to the city. Now that it's been done once, we can stay in touch." As the vision faded, there was an additional comment Brodie wasn't sure he was supposed to hear. "Well done, little sister. I approve."

The shock of the mental link breaking felt like a dunk in a mountain lake after a spring thaw. Brodie gasped at the cold. It vanished as quickly as it came, shattered by the warmth of the Oracle's parting blessing.

Kia touched his cheek and the last of the chill disappeared. "The first time can be tiring," she explained. "And for your knowledge, Brodie, except for initiating the contact, you carried the link all by yourself." Moonlight showed the pleased smile on her face. She leaned into his chest. Her quiet sigh echoed his own contentment.

Brodie sought for the same serenity and let the rhythm of Wirake's slow walk ease the rest of the tumult in his soul. A triumphant chord sounded in his mind. *I may not be a mage, but it doesn't matter. Kiansel loves me.* His thoughts calmed until only one remained. *Love does have a magic of its own.*

The End

Review button by Michelle Lee of Stardust Creations:
https://michelleleedesigns.net/

Windmaster
Windmaster Legacy
Windmaster Legend

A published author, feature-story writer and correspondent, Henderson has also written fiction as long as she can remember. Her heritage reflects the contrasts of her Gemini sign. She is a descendent of a coal-miner's daughter and an aviation flight engineer. This dichotomy shows in her writing which crosses genres from historical westerns and romance to science fiction and fantasy.

Join her on travels through the stars, or among fantasy worlds of the imagination.

Website: https://helenhenderson-author.blogspot.com
Facebook:
https://www.facebook.com/HelenHenderson.author/
Twitter: https://twitter.com/history2write